STALKING POINT

DUNCAN KYLE was born in Bradford and worked as a journalist until the publication of his first novel, *A Cage of Ice*, set in the Arctic and published in 1970, gave him the time and opportunity to become a full-time novelist.

Duncan Kyle's home is now in Suffolk where he lives with his Scottish wife and their three children. He has now published twelve novels, the most recent of which is *The Honey Ant*.

DUNCAN KYLE

Stalking Point

FONTANA/Collins

First published by William Collins Sons & Co. Ltd 1981
First issued in Fontana Paperbacks 1983
Third impression March 1989

Copyright © 1981 Duncan Kyle

Made and printed in Great Britain by
William Collins Sons & Co. Ltd, Glasgow

FOR CAPTAIN LUC BOUDREAU
AND 4-FD

PROLOGUE

November, 1918

Bars on the high window turned the small room into a cell; in peacetime – when the building near Mezières in the Ardennes was a school – they had protected only a storeroom. The door was left unlocked. Officers were imprisoned within the honour code. Escape was not contemplated, either by the prisoner or his gaolers, though one form was encouraged in cases like Zoll's and had actually been offered immediately – that was at squadron, with Zoll confined to quarters after landing. With the time still well short of noon, he had sat on his hard bed in the room he had left only two hours earlier, then with hopes bright and excitement rising. Tears now streamed down his cheeks.

The door opened and the adjutant entered: Schwarz by name: small, rotund and jolly when he had welcomed Zoll to the mess a week earlier, but grim-faced now and ramrod-stiff. Against the wall stood the table on which Zoll kept his shaving things. Schwarz placed something else on it and turned to speak.

'Thirty minutes. You may wish to write. Have you paper?'

Zoll nodded, not yet comprehending.

'One letter. I suggest you do not delay.'

As Schwarz left, Zoll wiped his eyes with the back of his hand and saw the pistol Schwarz had put on the table. He picked it up and broke it open: a single round.

Everything seemed to contract within him. So *this* was all that remained: time to write a letter; time to blow his brains out. He closed the pistol with a click, pulled out the chair and reached for the writing case his mother had given him.

'Write often, my son.'

'Of course, Mutti. Every week.'

He'd written to her only yesterday, reporting the excitement of the first two patrols, the joy of Max von Kleist as leader, the beauty of the high heavens with the front far below. 'We seem,' he'd written, 'to have cleared the skies in this sector.'

Zoll dipped his pen in the ink vial. Minutes gone already. 'Darling Mutti, I have disgraced . . .' He paused, then forced himself on: '. . . myself and our family. It is better you should not know the details. When you receive this I shall be . . .' He stared at the paper, hand trembling, tears flooding his eyes so that the written words swam out of focus. He wiped the moisture away, and the pen shook as the words appeared. 'I shall be dead.' What else? Not explanation: that would read like an excuse and there was no excusing what he had done. He glanced at his watch. Fifteen minutes left: he must be quick. He wrote: 'It was a moment I do not understand, and that is all I can say. I am bitterly ashamed. Please tell Father how deeply I grieve that I have brought this disgrace to our name.' Then: 'Goodbye.' Then: 'Your loving son . . .'

He put the letter in an envelope, addressed it, rested it against his travelling clock, picked up the pistol and looked at it for a moment. Here, at the table? Or on the bed? Where *did* a man blow his brains out? There would be a mess; he must consider the servant who would have to clean. So, not the bed. Blood would soak . . . therefore the floor. It was linoleum, and a mop would soon remove . . . everything, every trace.

He took the pistol more firmly in his hand and slipped off the safety.

Now.

He was numb all through, drained by the effort of the

8

letter, by the realization. He told himself it would be all over in a moment.

As he began to rise, the belt carrier in his tunic caught on the cracked crosspiece of the chairback, lifting it off the floor. It had happened before. He put his left hand behind his back to shift the awkwardly-dangling chair and somehow, straightening, became further entangled. The pistol fired and the bullet embedded itself in the table.

He was still staring at it, aghast, when the door opened and Schwarz entered, pistol in hand, ready to administer the *coup de grâce*. Zoll turned, the chair still hanging absurdly from his tunic. He said dazedly, 'It just went off.'

Schwarz was icily contemptuous. 'Twice,' he said. 'Twice in a few hours.'

'Please – another bullet?'

'Bullets are precious. Not to be wasted.' Schwarz called out and Kleber entered. 'This officer is under close arrest,' Schwarz told him. 'Remain here with him.'

'Another chance,' Zoll begged. 'Please. It was an accident.'

Schwarz did not look at him. 'He will go before a field court as soon as one can be convened. Guard him. You will be relieved in due course.'

The previous evening Kleber and Zoll had drunk wine together, members of the same cheerful group in the mess. Now Kleber would not speak. He sat on the chair, cold eyes on Zoll, expression stiff with distaste.

Zoll begged again for a bullet and was ignored; Kleber only stared at him. He could read and understand the thoughts in Kleber's mind. *Max von Kleist is dead. You had your chance to make the only possible gesture of atonement, and you failed in that, too. The consequence is disgrace not only to yourself, not only to your family, but to the squadron and the service: to me, to all of us.*

Finally Zoll ceased to ask and lay on the bed. In the silence he could hear the guns.

* * *

It had taken two days to arrange the court martial. Now, as he stood waiting in the little storeroom, officers were assembling in the hall and he could hear the scrape of moving tables and chairs as the makeshift courtroom was shaped. Officers of his own formation had been with him, changing on some rota system; he had not been alone, day or night. He had wasted the single opportunity the code allowed. Now Kleber was with him again, still entirely silent, but his expression somehow different. Kleber looked drawn and disappointed, sad-eyed, curiously lost.

Zoll lit another cigarette, and flexed his shoulders to ease the ache of tension, then crossed to the window. Because it was set so high he had to stand on tiptoe to look out at the walled square that had once been a schoolyard and was now a parade ground. A horse-drawn cart stood at the gate and two soldiers unloaded a crate, carrying it to one side of the square, setting it down.

It was a long crate and he wondered what it contained: nothing very heavy, not the way they handled it. They lifted the lid but took nothing out, simply leaned the lid against the crate and walked away.

Zoll swallowed, suddenly comprehending. The thing was a coffin, body-length and body-deep, a field coffin: for *him*. He couldn't take his eyes off the yawning box. Military preparedness. Somebody had had to think about the need for a coffin, to fill in a requisition, to have it here and ready when Zoll was found guilty: and executed at once.

The door opened. A voice behind him asked formally 'Unterleutnant Zoll?'

'Yes, sir.' Zoll turned and came to attention.

'The court is ready. Follow me.'

He marched, rigid and determined. He had failed twice and damned well would not fail again! When they lifted him into that box, they would lift the body of a man who, if nothing else, had died bravely.

He marched head up, between the escorts, down the short stone-flagged corridor with its row of hooks for children's coats; he turned smartly right into the hall, halted with precision.

'. . . you are charged with cowardice in the face of the enemy.'

A hard, upright chair was placed and he sat to attention. In the moment's pause before the prosecuting officer rose, he heard quite distinctly the boom of a field gun not far away.

'. . . Unterleutnant Zoll was flying number three in a flight of three aeroplanes on a patrol over the front line. The flight was attacked by enemy fighters and . . .'

Zoll only half-listened, remembering. The patrol had been his third: a bright autumn morning, clear and cold, and before they took off Von Kleist clapped him on the shoulder encouragingly. 'We'll have to find some action for you this time, young man. Time you were blooded! Give you something to tell your father about.'

'Yes, sir.' Two patrols behind him, with Von Kleist forward and to his left, that pale blue scarf streaming: the scarf that covered the *Pour Le Mérite*. Von Kleist was a tremendous hero: thirty-two kills. What a man to follow! The whole war was a shambles now, and defeat in prospect, and they all knew it, but among the fliers morale remained high and Zoll was young enough to believe in miracles.

They'd been airborne for half an hour in a sky dotted with bright puffs of cumulus which today hung oddly low, at no more than five hundred metres. And that was where the Sopwiths had been lurking: crafty, experienced and up-sun, masked by light and vapour, roaring down through its concealment to the attack, emerging so close, so *shockingly* close . . .

An officer entered the hall, a full colonel of infantry, a man recognizably cast in the same mould as his father.

'Herr Oberst, please describe what you saw.'

11

'Certainly, President. The attack took place on the left of my sector. I observed it through field glasses. The three aircraft were flying in arrowhead formation and I was concerned for them because a few minutes earlier I had seen a group of enemy aircraft at somewhat greater height and circling.'

'You were already watching when the attack took place?'

'Yes.'

'Continue.'

'The enemy aircraft appeared suddenly, as I had feared. There was, of course, no means by which any warning could have been given . . .'

But *you* knew, Zoll thought. You saw them coming, you expected it. I *didn't*!

'. . . they began firing at once, at close range.'

Zoll had heard nothing, seen nothing, until the first small impacts, the punches through the wing fabric. He'd glanced back, seen in horror how close the Sopwith was, seen the muzzle flashes and panicked, thrusting the stick forward, snatching at the throttle, seeking safety beneath Von Kleist like a child ducking behind its mother's skirts.

'. . . the aeroplane at the rear of the formation dived at once beneath the leader's machine which was thus immediately opened to the attack and shot down.'

'May I be clear about this, Herr Oberst? The defendant broke formation as soon as the attack began, in such a way as to expose his leader, while himself seeking shelter?'

'That is correct.'

'Can any other interpretation be placed upon his action?'

'I can see none.'

'What happened next?'

'The leading aeroplane was on fire, spiralling down. The left-hand rear aeroplane, number two in the formation, turned to face the enemy and was shot down very quickly. A few seconds, no more.'

'And the remaining one – the defendant's machine?'

'Ran.'

He'd scarcely known what he was doing, just that Von Kleist was gone in a rapid, slicing sideslip of smoke and flame and that there was cloud above. He'd swung up at it with two Sopwiths chattering at his tail, almost insane with fear, reaching it as more bullets stitched his wing, then flying tight circles within the concealing vapour until his fuel tank was almost empty.

'You continued watching, Herr Oberst?'

'I did.'

'And?'

'The enemy waited, patrolling the cloud. Then they must have tired of it, or perhaps were short of fuel. After ten minutes or so they flew off.'

'The defendant?'

'I saw him again half an hour after the original engagement.'

'You timed it?'

'I logged it, sir.'

'You have the log?' It was produced. 'Thirty-two minutes. The remaining aircraft emerged from the cloud and began to lose height, presumably returning to base.'

'You have experience of fighter aircraft tactics, Herr Oberst?'

'Not as a flier, no. But I have observed a great many dog-fights in the last four years.'

'Have you seen events similar to this one?'

'No.'

'How do you interpret what you saw?'

'As an act of gross cowardice and dereliction of duty, sir.'

'You have no doubt about that?'

'There can be no doubt.'

Did the defending officer wish to question the witness? He glanced at Zoll. Zoll shook his head. The colonel's

13

evidence as to fact was wholly accurate, the opinion correct.

There was another witness, an artillery major who had also watched; his evidence confirmed the colonel's in every detail. Zoll concentrated on avoiding eyes, which was not difficult; the five members of the court clearly couldn't bring themselves to look at him. Zoll stared straight ahead, at a point high on the long windows behind the court, windows that overlooked the yard where the box waited.

Soon, now.

He had asked the defending officer not to speak in extenuation, but the man had refused. It was his duty to speak.

'I beg the court to take note of the fact that the defendant is a young and inexperienced pilot; that he was in action for the first time and that he was attacked from the rear by a superior force holding the advantages of surprise and position. His cowardice, if such it was, was a momentary thing, fear occasioned by a first surprise exposure to enemy fire. The defendant is deeply ashamed . . .'

And guilty, Zoll thought.

'. . . not only of his own action and the result of it, but of the dishonour he brings upon his family. His father, as the court may know, is an officer of distinction, several times decorated. I beg the court to deal mercifully with Unterleutnant Zoll.'

Zoll could imagine his father's face. Disbelief, then that pale fury, then . . . nothing. His father would not understand. Oberst Zoll had disapproved of his son's entering the air service: the son was to be a soldier, fighting, not playing with modern toys. Nothing good could come of it. Nothing had.

He was marched out, leaving the court to consider, even though there was nothing to *be* considered: it was a formality.

14

In the storeroom with the silent Kleber he had barely time to smoke half a cigarette before he was sent for.

'The court finds the defendant guilty of cowardice in the face of the enemy.'

The President addressed himself to Zoll. 'We have considered the able plea of your defending officer for any clemency the court can show. None can be extended. The charge allows only one sentence: that of death by firing squad . . .'

Schwarz, Zoll thought, had said they couldn't waste one more bullet. How many now – a dozen?

'Sentence to be carried out immediately upon confirmation by the responsible general officer at field headquarters.' The President dipped his pen and signed a paper.

Zoll said nothing. He rose, was marched out, returned to the storeroom. Kleber said, 'Have you a final request – brandy, a priest?'

'No.'

'Do you require a blindfold?'

'I do not.'

In the distance the rumble of guns continued, a sound abruptly overlaid by the roar of a motor-cycle engine just outside.

'Hear that?' Kleber said unkindly. 'A despatch-rider is taking the finding to field headquarters for confirmation. When it is signed he will return immediately.'

Zoll swallowed and looked away. In what time remained, self-control was the only thing of any importance and Kleber knew that. Yet his tone was provocative. Strange. And indeed there *was* something strange about Kleber now: the icy manner had thawed, but not to compassion, rather to a venom barely concealed.

He said, 'I have no wish to talk,' and glanced at Kleber with what hauteur he could muster. The growl of the motor-cycle disappeared into the distance. The guns rumbled on.

Kleber remained silent, but Zoll, his back turned, could sense the urge to speak. Finally it could not be contained and Kleber said, 'There is news.'

'Of no interest to me.'

'The armistice. All firing will cease at eleven.'

Zoll no longer had his watch, but a reflex brought his eyes to his wrist.

'It is fifteen minutes to ten,' Kleber said. 'In one hour and a quarter the war ends.'

And I won't see it, Zoll thought. He'd wondered why the court had sat so early in the morning, convened at eight o'clock. Now he knew. It was a determination to finish him while hostilities continued: *that* was the reason for the despatch-rider, for the immediate carrying out of the sentence. And, he thought, the reason for Kleber's attitude. Germany was defeated: Kleber hated the humiliation and was finding satisfaction in Zoll's own, far greater humiliation.

Well, Kleber would get no more. He said, 'Speak once more, Kleber, and two of us will die this morning.'

He smoked cigarette after cigarette. There was sweat on his forehead and under his arms but he felt cold and tight and controlled within. Would it hurt a little, a great deal, or not at all? He'd find out soon. How quick was death? That, too, he would discover soon. He stamped out his cigarette. There was a little pile of ends beside his foot. Five. How many minutes each? Ten, perhaps. Fifty minutes. Where was the despatch-rider? He listened hard. Silence in the room; gunfire in the distance, but no engine. His own heartbeat was almost drowning the guns, hammering in his ears, pulsing at his temple and his throat. He felt himself tremble and deliberately stiffened his body.

Another cigarette. When he'd finished it, still another. His mouth was dry and foul with tobacco. He was very thirsty but damned if he'd ask for water.

He smoked on. The guns stopped, though it was

16

moments before he understood that it had happened and the war was finished. He warned himself not to admit hope: there *was* no hope. He was under sentence of a field court martial: death by firing squad: immediate. Still, the question ground into his mind. Could sentence now be carried out?

It was after twelve before the motor-cycle returned and Zoll was taken before the court again. There was fury in the faces behind the table.

'I regret to inform you,' the President said bitterly, 'that in view of the cessation of hostilities, it has been decided that sentence of death cannot now be carried out. The general officer commanding has exercised his prerogative to reduce the sentence to imprisonment for life. You will be taken at once to the military prison . . .'

Zoll scarcely heard the rest. He was so braced for death that its removal left him nothing. He felt himself close to fainting but managed to collect himself and march out.

Later, in the train, he heard what had happened: his escort had the story from the despatch-rider. The general had been at the front early in the morning and a stray shell had burst beside his car, killing his aide and wounding his driver. The general had himself been gashed in the face by a fragment of shrapnel. The despatch-rider, listening at the open door as he waited, had heard the weary words: 'There has been enough killing now. I will not sanction more – not on this day.' By then the guns had stopped. It was all a fluke: the general late in his headquarters because he had stopped for bandaging and stitches at a casualty station.

Zoll heard it all with an impassivity largely composed of shock and tiredness. He didn't know, couldn't think, whether he was glad or sorry. A lifetime in prison faced him: was that really preferable to death?

It was not. Conditions in the goal were appalling. After 1918 the quality of prison life was not a matter of concern

17

to the regional administration, and he was confined in a crowded, ancient, damp fortress full of cockroaches and bedbugs, eating food fit only for swill and sharing his cell with a man of sixty or so, half-demented and sentenced for molesting a child.

He would have killed himself, but the prison authorities, careless of every other aspect of welfare, were obsessive about the prevention of suicide. Zoll had no shoelaces, no braces, no belt. Shaving was done with a safety razor and under supervision. For eating there was only a spoon, removed after each meal. He was allowed to write and receive one letter a month.

The letter was to his father. It said simply that there was an urgent family matter which required discussion. His father did not reply. A month later he wrote to his mother, begging her to persuade him to make one visit.

Oberst Zoll came. He had always been austere and remote; now, as he sat opposite his son, separated from him by the rusting wire of the screen in the visiting room, he regarded the young man with a cold and manifest contempt.

'Well?'

Zoll felt himself shiver. 'You are to have a grandchild.'

The colonel blinked once. 'Illegitimate?'

'No. We married in . . .'

He was cut off. 'The girl's address?'

Zoll gave it. His father took out a silver propelling pencil and wrote on the small, silver-mounted pad he always kept in his tunic pocket. Zoll saw with surprise that the tunic looked worn.

'When?'

'April.'

Oberst Zoll closed the notebook.

'You must help her. I can't.'

'Do not presume. I am aware of my duty. I have this to say: you will not communicate again with any member of the family. You are disowned. You have chosen to violate

18

every part of the code by which we have lived.' He rose and put pad and pencil away, buttoning the pocket. 'I do not understand why you are not dead. I wish you were. As far as I am concerned, you no longer exist.' He turned, waited while the warder opened the door, and strode out.

Zoll almost vomited. He sat for a few seconds, his forehead shiny with sweat, seeking to control his stomach, then the warder yelled 'Move!' and he was returned to his cell. Yet he could understand, even share, his father's attitude.

But now Anneliese would be cared for. His father had never shirked a responsibility in his life and would assume this one, distasteful as it would be. But God, *how* things had changed for them! The young officer, full of promise; the charming, pretty girl he'd met in church: Anneliese, daughter of a Lutheran pastor now dead, whose life was spent looking after an invalid and demanding shrew of a mother. She was a deeply dutiful daughter, carrying a harsh burden with a pliant, generous spirit. They were frantically in love, determined to marry, but marriage was forbidden for him as a junior officer. Permission to take a wife came only with time and seniority.

Still, they did contrive to marry. Even the service itself was an adventure: more than a little furtive and certainly in breach of regulations; a young pastor, more liberal than most, and persuaded by Anneliese, performed the ceremony very quietly. No parents were informed, because Zoll's father would have insisted on disclosure to the military authorities, and Anneliese's mother would have been hysterical, terrified of losing the daughter who ministered to her so devotedly. They were young and confident, though, and no problems seemed insuperable. When the war ended, as one day it must, they would find their way.

When she had written to say she was pregnant, he'd been surprised but delighted: their meetings had been few, brief and secret. He sent her what money was in his

19

cheque account and promised to arrange quickly to withdraw rather a larger sum, an inheritance from his grandmother, which was in a savings account at home in Hanover.

But there hadn't been time. In every sense those damned Sopwiths had moved too fast for him. Now Anneliese, who had burdens enough, was pregnant, the wife of a man disgraced and in prison, stigmatized for life. And the child, when it came, would carry the stigma, too. He prayed often that Anneliese would give birth to a girl; a boy in a home dominated by his father's unforgiving soul would be too strong a reminder to Oberst Zoll of the son he no longer acknowledged.

April came and went. He hoped for, but did not receive, news of Anneliese's confinement. His father certainly wouldn't let him know, but his mother might, or his sister. They didn't. Nor did Anneliese: which mystified him until he decided it must be a condition of his father's support for mother and child.

In 1921 a partial amnesty was declared for certain categories of prisoner and Zoll, to his astonishment, found himself outside the fortress gate with a few marks in his pocket given to him by a charity for discharged prisoners. He used it to travel by train to Hanover, where he extracted from his bank the money he had inherited, took a dingy room in a cheap lodging-house and, next morning, began covertly to watch his old home. There could be no question of approaching his father, but he hoped that some womanly softness of heart would allow his mother or his sister to tell him about the child.

He saw his father come out and walk away, and wondered if Oberst Zoll had a pension, an income of some kind. His father moved with purpose, but then he always did. At half past ten his sister emerged, a shopping basket on her arm. He'd tried to watch discreetly, but she made straight for him.

Zoll tried to smile, then saw her expression. She said bitterly, 'Go away, Ernst.'

'Tell me about the child.' She was like their father: forbidding, self-contained Gretel, even as a child, had had the manner of a sharp schoolmistress.

'He is no concern of yours.'

A *son*! 'He's all right? And Anneliese?'

'Go away.'

He said, 'I'll go. But I must *know*.'

She stared him down and, as his gaze wavered, said, 'Go round the corner. I'll follow.'

She joined him moments later. 'I will not be seen speaking to you, Ernst. Not because I fear my father, but because I am ashamed of *you*.'

'I've told you: I'll go. But I have responsibilities now.'

She shook her head. 'You have none.'

'I have a son and a wife.'

'She will not hear your name spoken.'

'I don't believe you.'

Gretel's blue eyes were very hostile. 'Perhaps you should be told what you have done. Mother's health is in ruins. Your wife and her mother and her child live in the house. Two invalids and a child must be supported on your father's pension which, I can tell you, is very small.'

'Take the money Grandmother left me.'

'Do you imagine we would *touch* it?'

'You must.'

'You're not only a coward, you're a fool. If you have money, use it to go to some other country.' She paused. '*If* you are certain you can live with yourself.'

He tried once more. 'At least let me help. I'll find work, send money . . .'

'No.'

'Then I'll speak to Anneliese. She'll see the sense –'

Gretel said coldly, 'Anneliese could have borne being the widow of a man who behaved with honour at the end. She *detests* being the wife of a – '

'She loves me!'

'She despises you.'

'I don't believe you! Gretel, *please*.'

She said, 'I will do this, and only this. On condition that you go, and stay, abroad, you may send me an address and I will inform you of those things you should know. There will not be many of them, but you will be told.'

She turned and walked away. He called after her, but she ignored him. Had she lied about Anneliese? No, Gretel never lied.

But, damn it, he had to be sure. He would wait here until the chance came to speak to his wife.

For two days, hanging about miserably in the rain, he waited. She never left the house. When, on the third morning, she finally came out alone, Zoll could instantly see the difference in her. The joy that had been in her face was there no more; nor was there life in her step. She looked drawn and slow, drab and serious. He crossed the road towards her.

'Anneliese.'

She stopped, expressionless, stared at him for a moment, and then, with deliberation, spat in his face.

He thought again about suicide. That was what Gretel wanted, and his father, and presumably Anneliese. But there were two views of suicide and he had thought a great deal about both. To some it was the only honourable course; to others it was the coward's way, and Zoll had resolved that never again would he be accused of cowardice in any form.

He thought about it for long hours, lying on his bed in his dingy lodgings, smoking endlessly. In the end he came to a decision: a fresh start would require courage; a new country would require it, too.

He went to Hamburg and began to inquire about ships and passports and emigration.

ONE

January, 1941

There was one ship burning below: also, to judge from the inky pall of smoke disfiguring the horizon, a tanker was on fire somewhere ahead. They had passed over the convoy half an hour ago, the main body of it anyway, stretched wide over the water, with two corvettes and a destroyer dashing hither and yon like sheepdogs. Nothing the aircraft could do – the Liberator was a transport, not a spotter, and in any case had no fuel to spare.

She droned on westward. Sure enough, a tanker was ablaze and they could see two lifeboats in the water and the spreading, burning oil. Plenty of fuel down there, all of it going to waste.

Ross wrapped his greatcoat tighter round himself and slumped in his hard, metal-and-canvas seat, wishing he were piloting instead of sitting; wishing too that he had some idea where he was going and why.

There was urgency involved, that much was certain. Yesterday morning he'd been whipped over from Belfast at five minutes' notice, given his orders and told where to board the Liberator; that was all he'd been given, apart from a packet of sandwiches and an apple.

'You'll receive further orders at Montreal,' he'd been told by the transport officer. Apart from that there'd been nothing: nothing, that is, except a puzzling verbal check that he was the same Alexander Ross who'd been a senior captain with Pacific Airlines.

'Yes,' he'd replied, and wanted to add that he was a senior captain turned into a dogsbody. He'd gone to

23

Britain after the invasion of Poland with the idea that his experience would be useful in the war; but that wasn't, apparently, the way things worked. All the thousands of flying hours seemed to indicate only that he was too old. Ross had spent a year and a quarter doing random Air Ministry work: he'd re-written American-designed manuals so British pilots could understand them better; and done some ferry work, coaxing damaged planes back to factories for major repair. He'd made himself useful without ever feeling he was doing a solid job. Ross smiled a little ruefully to himself. Throughout his adult life, living and working in America, he had always felt British. But in Britain, where he'd been born, paradoxically he felt very American indeed, blue passport or not.

Hours later, inbound at Montreal, Ross saw from the tiny side window a couple of Hudsons leaving on the long hop across the Atlantic and, as the Liberator taxied, two more waiting to begin their take-off runs. Lonely work, he thought, but at least they knew where they were going.

'Captain Ross,' he said reporting in the onward transportation office. 'You have orders for me?'

An envelope was handed to him, and he found he was due aboard another aircraft in twenty-five minutes, this time bound for Vancouver. Further orders there.

He groaned inwardly. The whole continent to cross. 'Can't you tell me more? What do I do in Vancouver?'

'Further orders waiting. It says that, doesn't it?'

The hours ground by. He was unshaven and cold, yet still sticky with sweat in places, grubby and uncomfortable. They stopped once to refuel, but there wasn't time for anything else, though a big vacuum bottle of hot coffee was loaded. Across the plains, up over the Rockies, grinding out the miles: by the time he reached Vancouver, Ross could hear his beard rasp against his coat every time he moved his head.

Now there were more orders. He was to change into

the civilian clothes he'd been ordered to bring, then report to the Boeing assembly plant.

'Boeing?' he said, surprised. 'In Vancouver?'

'That's right. Transport's outside waiting.'

Again there was nobody to answer questions. Later he found himself sitting in the belly of a Consolidated PBY taking off and heading south, over the border into the United States.

Once in the air, he unstrapped himself and moved through the crawl-space from the belly towards the pilots' seats, then lifted his weary body on to the step and bellowed into the pilot's ear, 'Where in hell are we going?'

The pilot turned his head and grinned. 'Under orders not to say, Captain Ross.'

'Whose orders?'

'That's another thing I'm not to say.'

'Got any cigarettes?'

'Here.'

He clambered back, bruising his knee in the crawl-space, swearing softly to himself. What in hell was this damned secrecy about? When he got there he'd know where he was, damn it! Yet this wasn't Europe, wasn't a war zone. This was the United States, very much at peace.

It was fifty-two hours, almost to the minute, after he'd taken off from Britain, that the Goony-bird began to let down. He'd identified the route by then: no mistaking the shape of San Francisco bay, the California coastline, the mountains. He was familiar with this country. They were headed for some part of the Los Angeles area, or maybe further south and San Diego.

Los Angeles it was. No, correction: he stared out of the little window. That was Long Beach.

The amphibian came in, bumped once quite hard, slowed and began to taxi. As it stopped the flight engineer came back from his cramped, cold position half way along the crawl-tunnel, lifted the hatch and put the stay in place, then the ladder.

'Okay, Captain Ross. We're here. If you like to climb down I'll hand you your bag.'

Ross climbed. A white pick-up, new and shiny, was pulling in beside the plane. Ross reached for his bag, ran his hand irritably over the stubble on his chin.

'I think that car's for you,' the flight engineer said.

He slung his bag into the back and got into the passenger seat. 'Okay,' he said tiredly, 'solve the mystery for me. Where am I going?'

'Won't be more than a moment, sir.'

'For God's *sake*!'

A radio crackled and the driver lifted a hand mike. A voice said, 'Got Captain Ross?'

'Yes, sir.'

Ross frowned. 'I know that voice,' he said. 'Who – '

'Right over there.'

Ross followed the driver's pointing finger. A big, two-storey white building, new-looking, lay directly ahead, on the other side of the airfield's perimeter track. A red windsock flew from a flagpole, red and white lettering.

It couldn't be!

But it was. Ross got out and saw the familiar bulky figure with the carroty hair come bustling out of the front entrance, hand outstretched. Ed Martingale. Ed had moved factories again: always bigger and better: more and more success: more and more radios for aircraft. How many times a millionaire now? Ross had known him a long time.

'Alec, how are you?'

'Tired,' Ross said. 'And irritable. And dirty. And wondering just what stupid games are being played here.'

'Not a game, Alec.'

'It isn't? I've been forty-eight hours swathed in secrecy. Is it just to meet *you*?'

'You could say that. Hey,' Martingale called to the driver, 'bring his bag inside. Leave it at reception.'

'I need sleep,' Ross said. 'But first, I want some kind of explanation.' He looked balefully at Martingale.

'Simple, Alec,' Martingale said. 'You're needed here.'

'You said that once before. The answer's still the same. I am *not* going to work for you. I have a boss already.'

'Not to work *for* me.' Martingale held the door open for him. 'Round to the right, there, then straight through.'

Ross entered a big, comfortable office, with an attractive dark girl, presumably Ed's secretary, in the middle of it, and then another office, twice the size, which must be Martingale's.

'Shower and shave first?' Martingale asked him. 'Or coffee and breakfast. Or the story.'

'The story,' Ross said, then changed his mind. He'd waited this long; half an hour more didn't matter. 'No,' he said, 'the story last.'

'Wise man. You always were, Alec. That's why you're here. You know something – till I found out where you were, I'd forgotten you were British. Still a citizen. What d'you want? Ham, eggs, breakfast rolls, toast, that kind of thing?'

'You can load the plate with a shovel,' Ross said. 'Over there British citizens get two eggs a week.'

Martingale's private bathroom had all the gadgets. The needle spray in the shower blasted hot water at him from every angle, up, down and sideways. There were hot towels and sharp razors, toothbrushes and toothpaste, shampoos and a hair-dryer. Ross looked at the hair-dryer and wondered who it was for.

He came out feeling half better, then ploughed his way in silence through a hefty breakfast, lit a cigarette, poured another cup of coffee, and said, 'Now tell me.'

Martingale said, 'Did you say you get two eggs a week over there?'

'That's right. So?'

'Well, I don't know about eggs, but maybe they go over in convoys, too. A lot of other things do, that's sure.'

'Come on, Ed. You can do it in two words. What is it?'

'Sub hunting,' Martingale said.

'Me?'

'That's right.'

'I know nothing about it, Ed. Is that why you got me brought over, because if it is . . .'

'New equipment,' Martingale said. 'We're building and installing, but we're at a very early development stage. I'll explain the technicalities later. The first thing, though, is the right manpower. Now: I have the best radio research team in the United States right here, at least *I* think so. We're working in new territory. We're trying to pack equipment into one airplane that six airplanes couldn't normally carry. I need the right man in charge of the flying.'

'Ed, I'm not a technician! There must be a thousand people here in California who can do the job as well as I can.'

'No.'

'Why not?'

'Because there's nobody I'm as sure of as I am of you.'

'That's insanity.'

'Okay, it's insanity. You know the way I work, Alec. Maybe it's insane and always has been. But it works.'

Ross nodded. Eleven years ago Martingale had started out with a wooden shack and an ambition to build aircraft radios. The theory then had been that flying was changing, that air-to-air and air-to-ground would get more and more important with every passing month and that every set had to be right up to date with new technology and new *psychology* as well. The set, Martingale always insisted, was only half the battle. The other half was operator confidence, operator comfort, above all reliability. Double and triple banked circuits, flashing lights, gadgets here and gadgets there. He'd built a fortune in a decade – and a reputation for the best radio equipment flying.

Ross said, 'I'm listening.'

'Okay. Just this and you can get some sleep. You think I've always wanted you working for me, and in a way you're right. You think this is some slimy subterfuge to make that happen. It isn't. We've got a six-month development programme here and I want the best man I know in charge of flying because that's the way to get ahead fastest. Well, you're the best I know. Also – no, listen – also, you won't be working for *me*. Not on my payroll, anyway. You'll continue to be paid by your own people, the British. You'll be working with me, not for me. And when the job's over, you go right back where you came from. That's a promise. Okay – is that out of the way?'

'I suppose so.' Ross lit another cigarette. 'What do I actually do?'

Martingale grinned. 'Long hours of precision flying. I want a man who can fly ten hours at a hundred and fifty feet if necessary, and then ten more at two-fifty next day. That's my point, Alec. I might be able to find another guy like that around somewhere, but I might not find him first time, or second time. Whereas you – you I *know*, and you can do it. That's why you're here.'

Ross yawned. 'And in any case,' he said, 'I haven't any option?'

'Not much.'

'Okay. Sold to the gentleman in the rumpled suit. Where do I sleep?'

'I have a bedroom right here. Soundproofed, too. How long do you need?'

'Four hours,' Ross said, 'going on twelve.'

'Four it is. We'll have dinner tonight. You can have the other eight hours afterwards.'

Ross went out like a light. When the alarm buzzed he showered again, turning the spray to cold to finish off, then put on a clean shirt and underwear and reached for his suit. It had been cleaned, his shoes polished. Martingale philosophy, he thought: the comfort of the operator. One recent Martingale radio he'd seen had had a built-in photoframe for a picture of wife or girl-friend, and a special slot to hold a Thermos.

He ate an enormous steak, with a bottle of first-class wine from the Napa Valley, a crisp, clean-tasting salad, followed by more coffee and a swift run-down from Martingale on the new principles of submarine hunting, the urgent need for a more scientific approach, and the terrifying rate of loss of merchant shipping on North Atlantic convoy routes. Recalling the two ships he'd seen, he took the point.

'Can it be done?'

'That's what we've got to find out. Now, Alec,' Martingale said, 'we're going to have two planes fitted out, both Cansos – that's the Canadian version of the PBY-5, the one you call the Catalina over in Britain. Three names, God knows why. You'll be in overall command of flying operations. We'll work first of all right here. But after a while, and I hope pretty damm soon, we're going to move the whole outfit up to Canada, to the Great Lakes. You'll be flying out of Kingston – the Royal Canadian Air Force has the field there. Like I said, there'll be two Cansos, and we need a master pilot for the other. Co-pilots and crew aren't a problem, but that master pilot is a recruiting job.'

'In what way?' Ross asked.

'It's simple enough. I wanted you, not Charlie Farnsbarn who might be okay and might not. You need another pilot and you need somebody you have faith in. There's not time for settling down. You need somebody you know already, somebody you've flown with, somebody you can rely on – and talk sense with right away.'

'So I do the recruiting?'

'That's right.'

'That's all very well, Ed, but people have jobs already.'

'Nothing,' Martingale said, 'that can't be fixed. Whoever you choose gets a contract. Choose somebody from Pacific, for instance, and we'll set it up so he goes back there with no loss of seniority, pension rights or anything else. He'll get his pay, allowances and every other damn thing.'

'I've the whole world to play with?'

'Near enough.'

'Start in the morning?'

'I can stand the delay. Just.'

'No restrictions at all?'

'Only this: the US Navy's in on it, so are the British once we're up in Canada. The guy has to pass muster. But provided he hasn't actually been in gaol – '

Ross slept, showered yet again, and went to work. He had a strong feeling of unreality, part of it from disorientation and the long flight, part caused by the abrupt transition from a Britain in winter and at war to the sunlight and plenty of Southern California, and part from the freedom he'd been given. It was hardly the first time he'd looked for a pilot for a special job, but he had never done so on the terms Martingale set out: find the man and we strong-arm him into the project! Nor did he doubt by now Martingale's ability to do it.

Ross pulled a yellow legal pad towards him, picked up a sharp new pencil and began to write down names, staring at each as he wrote it, conjuring up in his mind a picture of the man, of his record, his flying style. Once or twice he crossed a name off: a partygoer, a man with a difficult wife.

In an hour he had nine good names: all of them he'd be more than happy to fly with, in whose company he could live comfortably for the promised six months. He started with the name at the head of the list: the name that had gone down as his very first, automatic choice. He buzzed for the secretary Martingale had assigned to him and when she answered, said, 'Get me Jim Carpenter. He's a test flier with the Glen Curtiss Corporation.'

A minute later the phone rang.

'Jim?'

'Who is calling Mr Carpenter?'

'I'm an old friend, Alec Ross.'

'Gee, I'm sorry to have to tell you, Mr Ross. It'll be a shock. Mr Carpenter was killed . . .'

Ross felt his mind go blank.

'Killed?'

'It was a power-boat race, Mr Ross. He hit a log.'

He muttered something and hung up. Jim Carpenter *dead*: his preferred companion in an aircraft or anywhere else. He sat for several minutes, deep in mourning. Jim dead – and in a bloody boat race, of all things! It was like . . .

No, later, Ross told himself. Jim wasn't the first and wouldn't be the last. He brought his mind back to the list. Who next? He put a two beside Jocko McCartney, a three beside Ernie Miller.

'Get me John McCartney. Last I heard he was with Eastern. They'll know where he is.'

Eastern knew all right. Jocko McCartney had joined the RCAF and was now in Britain, full squadron leader. Well, he could get him back, probably, if necessary. Ross chewed his pencil, caught himself at it and stopped. No point in bringing Jocko back if somebody like Miller was close at hand and available: Miller was good, an old friend, too; easy to work with, intelligent and possessed of enormous stamina.

'See if you can find me a man called Ernie Miller. No, I don't know where. He's freelance, moves about. The aviation board ought to have his address. He was in San Francisco last time I heard from him.'

The board had Miller's number. Ross put the call through, his mind still on Jim Carpenter. Jim's death put an ominous cast over things, right from the start.

'Ernie? Alec Ross. I'm in Long Beach and I'd like to see you if you're fit and still flying. Can you get down here pretty soon? Say, today or tomorrow?'

* * *

The sputtering roars drew him to the window and he glimpsed something small, fat and unfamiliar doing a fast, tight roll before it vanished beyond his field of vision. He smiled but didn't make the connection. When he watched aerobatics nowadays, he felt he was watching his own youth. Ross had done plenty of that stuff: three years in an air circus in the early 'twenties, wing-walking, smoke canisters, ribbon pick-ups, the whole crazily-exciting thing.

'Mr Miller to see you, Captain Ross.'

He went out. 'Hello, Ernie. It's been a long time.'

'Too long. Hi, Alec.' Miller was waiting in the outer office, shortish and four-square, feet planted slightly apart, creased trousers and an old leather flying jacket and – Ross grinned – a flying helmet crumpled in his hand.

As they shook hands, Ross said, 'That was you, wasn't it, Ernie? Just now – howling by my window?'

Miller laughed. 'Well, you did ask if I was still flying.'

'And you really felt the need to demonstrate to *me*?'

'Still do.' Miller smiled. 'Hell, I'm forty-two, Alec. But I had a Board physical two weeks back and I'm in top-class shape. How about you?'

'I'm fine. Don't know if I'm *that* fine.'

'You used a word that interested me a lot.'

'Would the word be "job"?'

Miller nodded. 'What I thought was – at my age he'll be wondering. People start slipping. I haven't yet, but people do. So do you take my word for it, or do I have to show you?'

Ross clapped him on the shoulder. 'With you, I'll take the demonstration. I can do with a little fun.'

'Okay.' Miller handed him the helmet. 'Put this on. I have another.'

'How's Dot – beautiful as ever?'

'She said to give you a smacking kiss,' Miller said. 'You want it now?'

'Thanks, but I'll collect in person. She doing any flying?'

Miller shook his head. 'My fault probably. One day I'll swap the aerobat for something she can handle.'

'She was good.'

'Yeah. Hey, what do you mean – *was*?' Miller led the way out. In the aircraft park four hundred yards away, twenty or thirty assorted planes stood.

Ross said, 'Which?'

'Over there. She's black.' Miller pointed. To Ross the plane appeared to consist of a massive radial engine, a three-blade prop and a pair of very short, stubby wings.

He said, 'Who built *that*?'

'Chuck Stetter. Me. Little help here and there. Dot did the needlework.'

Death again, Ross thought. He said, 'Did you hear about Chuck?'

'Hear what?' Miller's head swung round.

'I'm sorry, Ernie, but Chuck bought it. Over the Channel. Dog-fight with some ME 109s. He was Eagle Squadron, you knew that?'

Miller said, 'Oh *Jesus*!' The corners of his mouth clamped down.

'He got a DFC,' Ross said. 'Three months ago, it was. I thought at the time: whoever got Chuck in a dog-fight could really fly a plane.'

Miller patted the black fabric sombrely. 'Unless they jumped him,' he said. 'What was he flying?'

'Hurricane.'

Miller swallowed audibly. 'Today,' he said, 'one last time, he's flying the Stetter-Miller special. Get in.'

He flung the little black biplane savagely round the sky. It was more than a demonstration, Ross thought; it was a tribute and a farewell. Three times the G-forces blacked Ross out briefly as Miller pushed the stressed aerobatic special to the limit, diving into loops, then rolling off the top. He put it through the whole repertoire. At forty-two

34

he could certainly still fly. Ross doubted whether he himself was still physically in shape for this kind of thing.

Miller brought her in like a zephyr, then turned his head as the engine died and yelled back: 'Did I pass?'

Ross nodded. He felt a tiny bit dizzy as he climbed down, but contrived not to show it.

'If I passed, do I get the job?'

'You want it?'

Miller said, 'I'm in between, Alec. I'm certainly interested.'

As they walked back towards Martingale's white-painted industrial palace, Ross said, 'There's only one hurdle, Ernie. In Britain we'd call this a hush-hush project.'

'So?'

'So you'll have to talk to Ed Martingale. And to the Navy. They're in on it, too.'

'My life's an open book. Ed knows that. Can you tell me about the job?'

'Not yet – when and if you've been cleared. You brought the papers with you?'

'You mean, I can prove I was born? Yeah, I got all the papers.'

'Right. We'll do it as fast as possible. One thing, Ernie, though. Will you be able to move house?'

'Where to?'

'Here, first. Then onward. Can't tell you where, but for about six months.'

'Why not? It's only a furnished let.'

'There's Dot,' Ross said, but he knew the answer.

'Whither I go, she goes. You know Dot.'

A year later it couldn't possibly have happened. By then there was a functioning security apparatus, vetting procedures, a centralized and established means of checking whether Man A was suitable for Job B. The armed forces already applied such checks to their own men.

But Miller wasn't one of their own men. Miller was

presented to Commanders Briggs and Lenahan, the liaison officers assigned to Martingale Corporation, as the personal choice of both Martingale himself and of Captain Ross, whose own credentials were already well established.

Miller had stayed overnight to await interview by the two Navy men in the morning. When he appeared before them, Briggs accepted the proffered papers, looked at the birth certificate and said in a tone of surprise, 'You were born in Paraguay?'

'That's right. My father was a trader there most of his life.'

'So you had the choice of citizenship?'

Miller said, 'Dual nationality till I was twenty-one, then I could either become an American citizen or a Paraguayan. I became an American. It didn't seem like a difficult choice, not to me.' He could feel himself sweating.

'But you stayed there?'

'Came up here in 'twenty-eight, after my father died. Matter of fact, I came up as *soon* as my father died.'

'And you could already fly?'

'Oh, sure. I was always flying crazy. Solo'd at eighteen. Wasn't difficult if you didn't care what you flew, and I didn't.'

'And you've been here ever since.'

'All in the records,' Miller said. But it wasn't. He often wondered exactly what *was* in the records. Not the truth, certainly.

Lenahan was going through the passport. 'Mexico and Canada. What were those trips?'

Miller said, 'I've always been a freelance flier. Alec Ross was, too, for a lot of years, but then he joined the airlines. I didn't, I'm up for hire. Sometimes I'd have to make a trip north or a trip south, that's all. Otherwise I wouldn't need a passport.'

He smiled, and fancied he could smell his own fear.

'You certainly have a lot of air time.'

'Nearly seventeen thousand hours.' Plus some, Miller thought. God, if they knew how he'd got those precious bits of paper! And if they knew the trouble he was in!

In 1926, in the Paraguayan capital, Asunción, Ernst Zoll had encountered an elderly American expatriate, one Dean Miller, who ran a small and doubtful import business, dealing mainly in typewriters and accounting machinery, much of it stolen in the United States and illegally exported. Zoll's excellent, if rather precisely-European English, learned as a child when his father had spent two years as assistant military attache in London, had particularly pleased Dean Miller. The old man liked to speak English to him and especially relished Zoll's vowel sounds. '*Carstle*' he would chortle, 'and *grarss* and *barth*? That the way they talk over there?' Old Man Miller was usually drunk in the evenings, but good enough company at other times and Zoll enjoyed listening to the old rogue's tales of deviousness and corruption. Many of the stories, though half-fiction, nevertheless amounted to a kind of instruction course on getting by in South America.

A year after they'd first met, he was staying at the old man's home whenever he was in Asunción, partly because he enjoyed listening, more because hotels were expensive. He noticed, on that evening, a photograph he hadn't seen before: Dean Miller with his arm round a young man's shoulders. 'Your son?'

'Was.' Tears appeared in the old man's eyes. 'They killed him – some Brazilians I was crazy enough to trade with. They'd things they wanted to sell me. Hot as hell the stuff was, a consignment of refrigerators taken from an American distributor in Parana. They wanted more than it was worth, sure enough, so I sent Mike down river to beat them down. Never saw him again. Then one of them came up to see me and I said I wasn't talking, not

37

here. My son was doing the talking on the other side of the border.'

Dean Miller paused. 'Know what he said? He gave a kind of little grin, and he said, "What son? You have no son." So then I knew.'

'That's all you ever heard?'

'All I needed to hear. Parana River goes down to the sea, don't it? Nope, I never heard nothing more. Not in fourteen years.'

Days had passed before the thought came, and after that several weeks before he got to Asunción again. Then, carefully, a question or two at a time, he learned more about the son. Mike Miller, born in Asunción, had dual nationality and opted at twenty-one to become a citizen of the United States.

'So he travelled on a US passport?'

'Sure. Had it with him. Bastards sold it, I'll just bet. US passport's a valuable thing to some people.'

Next evening, choosing his moment, with the old man full enough of wine to be sleepy, he asked more questions. Had Mike's disappearance been reported?

'Sure, but they weren't interested. I'd no proof of nuthin' and I couldn't hardly say why I thought he'd been killed. So they just thought it was a boy left home and his dad wanted him back, that's all.'

'No death certificate?'

'Nope. No nuthin'.'

Next morning he was lying in his bed, looking at the fly-specked ceiling, when the old man came in carrying a worn evelope tied round with string. 'Just recalled,' he said, 'what we was talking about last night. Seems to me you was maybe interested in these.' He tossed the envelope on the bed. 'Have a look – somebody someplace might find 'em real handy.'

All were there: registration of birth, correspondence regarding dual nationality, confirmation of the choice, citizenship papers. Everything. Including copies of photographs submitted with the passport application. Young Miller had been a boy then, and boys changed a lot as they became men and the photographs were merely of a roundish, unformed face. Height and weight were less than his own.

He'd lain there thinking: *no death ever recorded!*

Then he'd thought about America. In America, on good papers, he'd be more secure than he'd ever be anywhere else. The English he already spoke would mellow naturally and quickly into American sounds and usages. Could he get work? Certainly he could.

Later that day Dean Miller gave him a sideways look. 'Reckon there's anything of value there?'

'Could be, for the right man.'

The eventual price had been a criminal act: a Paraguayan city politician, who had offended against the regime and was hiding in danger of his life, was to be flown out of the country. The papers were safely in his pocket as he landed in Brazil. Six months later Zoll had his shiny new passport and a new identity and was heading north: young Miller, returning to his native land.

He reasoned that the simple fact that the passport had been issued was proof of no other application in the same name. What it did *not* mean was that no other application would be received in the future. The old man could be wrong; the son *might* simply have left home, be living in some other country, might one day remember he was American.

He'd always felt that was unlikely; but the possibility existed. Confronted with somebody who'd known Mike Miller, he'd be finished. Unlikely, yes – but it was an Achilles heel, however small . . .

'I see your name is really Michael,' Commander Lenahan was saying. 'Yet people seem to call you Ernie. How's that?'

39

He said, this time with perfect truth, 'I've been called Ernie most of my life. Stuck with it, I guess.'

'I know what you mean,' Lenahan said, smiling. 'I have a nickname myself, not that I'm going to talk about it!'

Now Miller knew he was *in*. A few moments later the two officers were thanking him for his co-operation and wishing him luck on Project Cull.

He went at once to Ross's office. 'What's Cull?'

'Sit down. If you know the name they passed you.' Ross picked up the phone and told Martingale: 'You have two master pilots now, Ed. Do you want to explain, or shall I try?' Then he hung up. 'My job. Okay, Ernie, this thing is highly technical and you're not and I'm not.'

'I understand, Alec.'

Ross gave a rueful little grin. 'Anything you don't follow, you'll have to ask Ed. We're going to be chasing imaginary submarines. Now come with me.'

They rode across the airfield in one of Martingale's white pick-ups with the red windsock emblazoned on the side. Ross halted beside a hangar where the familiar shape of a Canso stood in the shaded interior. 'Had anything to do with these ships?'

'No. Just seen them go by.'

'Tons of lift, that's the important thing. You'll get flying instruction over at Consolidated, so don't worry about it. Meantime . . .'

'What's *that*?' Miller pointed.

'What's it look like?' A huge metal ring was fixed to the amphibian, encircling it from just forward of the nose almost to the point where the fuselage lifted towards the tail assembly.

Miller pursed his lips. 'Search me. Maybe a mine-detector?'

'You're warm. But it's on a big scale.'

'It'll pick up a sub?'

'Whoa,' Ross said. 'Let's not get too far ahead of ourselves. You know the general principle, as forever advanced by Ed Martingale. Science produces the knowledge; technology tries to keep up with it. Usually from a million miles behind.'

'So?'

'So what we're really talking about is the earth's magnetic field. It's fairly regular, as you probably know. You can map it with a magnetometer, right?'

'Yes.'

'Put a large body of ferrous metal down anywhere and you get variations in the magnetic field. Well, it seems that's true of the ocean, too. And subs are built of steel.'

Miller looked doubtfully at the big amphibian. 'Sounds fine. Does it work?'

'Not really, and not yet. But we hope it will. At the moment we're within very narrow limits. We have to try to widen them, produce search patterns.'

'Alec, I've seen a magnetometer. It's enormous. You can't get one of those things in a plane.'

'Martingale has, that's the point. He's got it scaled down as far as he can get it. In the process it's lost both power and sensitivity, but it functions. So, in accordance with Ed's theories, the process will be to fine-tune the equipment, then fine-tune the operator to it. We'll have his boys on the sets while we fly the planes: pilots and operators as a team. On this equipment the magnetic variations aren't going to be easy to plot, but Ed's men are going to work on that and you and I will learn to track. Okay?'

'Funny,' Miller said. 'I was expecting some form of radar.'

'It'll be part of the package: radar's going in too. But there's a problem there. The radar pulse goes out, you wait, back it comes. Time gives distance. You can tell something's there because the pulses bounce back. Trouble is, at the moment, we don't know which direction they're coming from. One of these days they'll get it hooked in with a cathode ray tube – it's been done

41

experimentally, I gather – and then you'll get bearings. But we don't get that yet.'

'Ed's working on it?'

'Well, yes. So are other people. For the moment the idea is to get everything in combination, make a systematic thing of it. Say you're at two thousand feet with a thirty-mile horizon. Anything on the surface will send radar pulses back, but you still don't know where the object is, only that it's there. Maybe the sub's on the surface, charging batteries. The crew, or part of it, is upstairs enjoying the fresh air. They hear an aircraft and crash dive, so radar stops registering.'

'And you bring in the magnetometer?'

'If you can find out where to look. Once the sub's deep you can forget it anyway. So Martingale reasons that if two aircraft fly parallel, thirty miles or so apart, and they *both* get a bleep on radar, then it's probably in between them. They can compare signal strength by radio and so on. And there'll be two magnetometers for the second phase, the hunt.'

Miller said, 'Remember Ed when he was a skinny kid with red hair and – '

'And a master's in physics, determined to make a fortune! Yes, I remember. The point about Ed is he *thinks* and the thinking's good here. But whether it will work in practice is another thing. The state of the art is Stone Age.'

Miller was looking doubtfully at the Canso and at the big gleaming aluminium ring that encircled it. 'What about that thing? I imagine the handling question's been solved, and I guess it's okay on land. But what happens if you have to bring a ship like that down on water? Everything else is way up high: wings and engines, I mean; but if that ring touches on landing, either the mountings will shear or the hull gets holes in it, or the whole ship stubs its toe and the tail comes over.'

Ross said, 'I've flown bumps and circles with a pilot

from Consolidated. On smooth water it's fine. You have to be bloody careful but it works. For the moment, though, we use them as land-planes. The water landing problem's another thing that's being worked on. They're thinking about ways to jettison the whole ring assembly, but it could be dangerous. That ring will have pretty complex aerodynamics of its own. I just hope I don't have to fly the trial.'

Miller took the little black biplane back to San Francisco with his head in a whirl, and not just from the technicalities he'd had to absorb. A large part of it was a sudden access of hope. Two words had been spoken: the first was *secret*, the second *Canada*.

On this secret project in Canada he'd be out of reach, for six whole months, of the bastard who now had him gripped in pincers.

That ought to give him plenty of time to work out how to disappear permanently. Christ, but what a fool he'd been to write that letter!

TWO

The man who held the pincers, and to whom Miller's letter had been delivered, was a minor functionary at the office of the German Consul-General in San Francisco. Baldur von Galen was twenty-four years old, fair-haired, partially crippled, and deeply bitter at his situation.

Shortly after the invasion of Poland, Von Galen had completed his training as a bomber pilot in Heinkels. He had been a member of a thirty-strong class, and to celebrate their graduation they had held a party. Leaving it late at night, and awash with champagne, Von Galen and two other newly commissioned *Luftwaffe* officers were returning to their quarters, arms linked and voices raised in song, when a motor-cycle, coming too fast round a corner, skidded into them. One was killed, one unscathed; the bone in Von Galen's right thigh was fractured in three places and in addition his head struck the road so hard as to cause a small fracture of his skull.

There was no question of his flying again. He now walked with a limp, and the skull fracture gave him a degree of tunnel vision which he tried hard to conceal, but which the thorough examinations of *Luftwaffe* doctors inevitably discovered.

Like many young men with powerful family connections, Von Galen had believed that influence could help. His maternal uncle, Ernst Wilhelm Bohle, was Minister of State at the Reich Foreign Office, and it was to him that the young man appealed. Surely there were ways to get round the regulations? There were not. Bohle, trying to intercede, found not for the first time that the armed forces actively resisted interference from the Party.

Bohle couldn't help. Von Galen didn't believe him – and nagged. His mother nagged too, and between them they pestered Bohle to the point where, out of sheer irritation, he acted to get Von Galen not just out of his hair, but out of the way. Without any choice in the matter, Von Galen found himself appointed an officer of the *Auslandsorganisazion* and sent to man its office seven thousand miles away in San Francisco.

And in that city he was busily making a nuisance of himself, hoping either that the United States would declare him *persona non grata*, or that the Consul would become so infuriated as to send him home. To that end Von Galen had been using his car, an eight-cylinder, black Horch coupé, as a battering-ram.

Patrolman McInerny saw the black blur, blunt-bonneted and supercharged, tearing along Market Street at half past six on a Sunday morning, and set off in pursuit. The Horch shot two red lights, swung up the steep hill towards the Coit Tower, big exhaust booming, then spin-turned on screeching tyres to come bounding down again, treating the hill like a series of ski jumps, wheels off the ground at every intersection.

The patrol car hung on grimly, just in sight all the time. Finally, in Sixth Street, the Horch was there at the kerb, by the newspaper building.

McInerny climbed out of his car, slammed the door and went purposefully over to the Horch. The driver sat relaxed behind the wheel, airily lighting a cigarette.

'Driver's licence, please.'

The man didn't even look at him.

'I said – '

Now a languid hand took something from a jacket pocket and held it out, and the driver said, in slightly accented English, 'Examine it, and – what's that American expression? – vamoose!'

'I don't need to.'

The driver smiled.

'I know what it is, it's a diplomatic passport. And you are Mr Galen.'

'*Von* Galen.'

It was McInerny's turn to smile. 'Sir, we have a request from the German Consul to impound this car on sight, and to return you at once to the Consulate. The Police Department has agreed to co-operate. Better get into the patrol car, sir.'

Von Galen stared at him angrily, but decided not to argue. He would save his wrath for Wiedemann, the Consul, who though his nominal superior, would soon know better than to interfere with the nephew of the Minister of State.

When he was driven back to the office, however, Wiedemann had a surprise for him. A few days earlier there had been a leading article in the *San Francisco Chronicle,* which, without naming Von Galen, had condemned the activities of a 'young German diplomat who, under the protection of diplomatic immunity, chooses to use our streets as a racetrack. He ill-serves the interests of his country.' Wiedemann had sent it to Bohle and Bohle had now replied. He handed the signal to Von Galen:

Inform my nephew that any further breach of proper diplomatic conduct will result in his transfer, not back to the Reich, as he may imagine, but to the coldest, dullest, most uncomfortable backwater I can find for him, and that he will remain there for as long as I care to keep him there.

'I imagine,' Wiedemann said, 'that he means Manchuria, perhaps, or Korea.'

'Why,' Von Galen demanded furiously, 'won't they just let me *fight*?'

'Because you're not fit. You must learn to serve Germany in other ways. Do your job.'

'My job! Nursemaid to Germans living abroad who

don't give a damn about their country. To the pathetic American Nazi organizations!'

'They're valuable,' Wiedemann said.

'Rubbish. They're comic. Have you seen them? They can't sing and they can't march. They're inarticulate and ineffectual.'

'They are a reminder,' Wiedemann said quietly, 'to every German living here, to every American of German descent, that in the United States the Reich has people in uniform and on the streets. I promise you that every person with German blood feels the pressure – '

'On their bladders,' Von Galen interrupted rudely.

Wiedemann remained patient. 'You're a fool, Von Galen,' he said. 'I have a certain sympathy because you want to fight and you can't. That's bad luck. But you have to learn to face it. You'll have to learn to fight from behind a desk.'

'No.'

'Or accept the consequences. I think Herr Bohle means what he says. How *is* your vision?'

'Improving.'

'Then let's see if another six months helps. Settle down and do your work. It's February now. Have another medical test in July or August. If, by then, there is further improvement, I will support your application to go back.'

'What about my car?'

'Its return,' Wiedemann said, 'will depend upon your performance.'

The letter was in his in-tray, part of a backlog he had allowed to accumulate. The *Auslandsorganisazion*'s job seemed to Von Galen to consist largely, though not exclusively, of welfare work. As the Party department responsible for Germans living abroad, it had meetings and membership applications to arrange, but much of his work was handling requests to trace families who had moved, in one country or the other.

There were several of them now in his in-tray. He

47

sorted through them resentfully: this to be sent to the city authorities in Kassel, that to Hamburg, the other to Frankfurt-an-der-Oder. A widow not receiving her pension, a cousin who had not written in three years.

The letter went through with the others: into the outtray, marked: 'Forward as instructed.' Miller would have escaped if Karen Hanzer, Von Galen's secretary, had been less alert.

It had begun with Dot calling through from the kitchen of their little apartment, 'Weather forecast, honey.'

Miller glanced at his watch, switched on the radio receiver, saw where it was tuned and called back: 'If you're going to listen to all that stuff, retune the set afterwards, will you!'

'Sorry, dear.'

He turned the dials and by the time the set warmed, heard only the last words of the forecast. Dot came through, drying her hands. 'You'll get the Air Corps in a minute or two.' She kissed his cheek. 'I won't do it again, promise.'

He swatted at her backside and missed, and she said, 'You're slowing down, kiddo,' and went back into the kitchen, laughing.

Miller grinned and began hunting for the Air Corps forecast. He caught the words '. . . fight over the Chann . . .' from some station and tuned back.

'. . . third sortie that day,' a voice was saying, 'and of course we were all a little tired, but then we saw a flight of British Hurricanes fifteen hundred metres below and so we were tired no longer.'

Miller frowned. It was a German accent. What the hell was *this* station?

It was propaganda, but well done. He learned gradually, listening hard because the short-wave transmission surged and faded, that the voice belonged to a young German fighter pilot flying ME 109s. His description of the fight was plain and modest. The German fighters had had height and surprise on their side. They lost one, the British two.

'. . . I saw my friend go down. An hour before we had been drinking coffee. It might have been me, but it was Joachim and I had avenged him. He had died for Germany and would be proud to do so. I was proud of him.'

The Hurricanes had dashed for home. The young German did not impute cowardice: the Hurricanes were low on fuel and he said so. The ME 109s had followed, but the fight was over. 'We returned to our base in France. I wrote to my friend's father. It was important to write at once because tomorrow could be my turn. That is the way of war.'

'You have been listening,' said an announcer's voice, 'to Leutnant Heinz Zoll, a *Luftwaffe* fighter pilot based in France. Last week, Leutnant Zoll received, from the hands of Reichsmarschall Hermann Goering, the Iron Cross First Class. Heroism runs in the family. He is the grandson of a colonel of infantry who won the same decoration in 1915. This is Deutchlandsender on bands . . .'

Miller rose, switcheed off the set and stumbled to the bathroom so Dot wouldn't see his face. He came out a few minutes later with some degree of self-control re-established.

'What was that you were listening to?' Dot asked.

'Description of an air fight, that's all.'

'You missed the forecast.'

'I know,' he said. 'But it doesn't matter. Nothing much changes in San Francisco.'

'Fog does,' she said, 'and you're flying tomorrow.'

'Not if it's foggy I'm not.'

She said, 'Promise?' and grinned at him.

Lying next to her that night, snug in a double bed, he listened enviously to the regularity of her breathing. His own mind turned over and over, trying to absorb, to cope, with the extraordinary fact that it was his own son's voice

49

he had heard, and that his son was a *hero*, a fighter ace! Somewhere over there, six or seven thousand miles away, his own *son* was flying Me 109s . . . receiving the Iron Cross – and from Goering, no less . . . *Goering!* In Miller's mind, he was not the Fat Hermann of the cartoons, but the man who'd taken over the Circus from Von Richthofen; one of the true aces of the Great War.

A cataract of emotions roared through his head: intense pride, astonishment, a deep regret that he could tell no one; above all shame. The announcer had made a point of family heroism, the Iron Crosses. But between the two heroes lay the unmentionable generation: the Zoll convicted of cowardice. *Him.*

Why hadn't Gretel written? Because it was *good* news. Gretel had written three times, over the years, but only with news of death: his mother, his uncle, his godfather. He'd always let her know his address, wherever he moved, but there had been only the three notes, each as brief as she could make them, even the paper on which they were written cut to a thin slip, as though to use more paper were in some way to make a concession.

God, but he wished he could tell Dot. Could he? He turned his head to look at her in the dimness, sleeping with all the peace in the world. Nothing on Dot's conscience, and not likely to be. The best thing that had happened to him, in his entire life, without any doubt at all, was meeting Dot. How many men had a wife like her? The day swam into his mind, as it often did: he'd come into a stray, dirt airfield in Oklahoma one day with the canvas shredding on his wing and taxied over to the tin hangar, needing canvas and dope and skilled hands and expecting to find none of them. And Dot had come out. She took one look, laughed and said, 'So that's what a wing structure looks like underneath.'

'Can you fix it?'

'I think so.' And she'd done it fast and beautifully; you wouldn't get it done better in a factory, maybe not as well. Then she'd listened to the engine and said, 'It's running retarded, you know that?' And fixed that, too: another hundred revs coaxed out of the motor.

He'd watched with amazement and pleasure: the more so because she wasn't just skilled, she was the prettiest girl he'd seen in a long time; and, as it turned out, the nicest.

He couldn't tell her, though. He'd do anything for Dot except tell her two things: that he was German, and that their marriage, *her* marriage, was bigamous. That would destroy her.

But he couldn't do *nothing*, couldn't fail to acknowledge that the son he'd never seen had fulfilled his own dreams. If he wrote to Gretel, would she pass the letter on? No, she'd tear it up, no question.

In the end, he climbed out of bed and went into the spare bedroom he used for office work, and wrote the letter. After a certain amount of thought he'd decided that if Gretel wouldn't send it, maybe the radio station would.

'We just forward it?' Karen Hanzer asked Von Galen. 'You think that's enough?' She looked at him hopefully. He was an attractive man, injured in the service of the Fatherland: she wished he would take more notice of her.

'It's what my notation says.' Von Galen looked at her sourly. She was a strongly-built blonde who would one day be statuesque, with braided hair wound tightly round her head; he thought she looked like something off a *Hitlermädel* poster. She probably thought so too.

'I know. But it's interesting, isn't it, that – ?'

He said, 'This Consulate is, in part, a damned post office, Fräulein. Let's make it an efficient one.'

She said quickly, 'He's not on the phone, the writer of this letter.'

'So?'

'Well. No phone number and no address.'

51

'What do you suggest?'

'Let's at least find out who he is?'

'I imagine we can find out by opening the enclosure.'

'I have your permission?'

'Do as you damned well like, Fräulein.'

She steamed the letter open. It seemed to her improper to tear an envelope addressed to an authentic hero.

Dear Heinz,

I heard you on the radio the other day and was very proud. You will probably be surprised to hear from me, and may not even know that I exist. If my name has been mentioned, I'm sure it cannot have been in any affectionate way. All the same, you may be interested that your father is alive and that he's a pilot like you.

I have lived in America for many years and flown dozens of aircraft types and by now I doubt very much whether I'm quite the same person I was when the events you may have heard of took place in 1918.

Listening to you, I envied you. You're everything I once hoped to be, and hearing your voice brought a lump to my throat.

If you feel able to write to me – even a few words on a postcard – it would be generous.

My congratulations on your Iron Cross. I can't tell you how proud of you I feel!

                                        Ernst Zoll

She thought for a few moments before replying. San Francisco postmark, no telephone listing, the only address a post office box number: he was concealing something. No good German had the right to do that. She sat at her typewriter, wound in a sheet of stationery and wrote:

Dear Herr Zoll,

There is a letter for you, here at the Consul-General's office, if you wish to call and collect it.

With an impishness Von Galen would not have suspected, she then signed the letter with his name. If Zoll did turn up, she'd learn of it before Von Galen, and knew already what she would do. Karen Hanzer was ambitious to become something more than a secretary. Her application for Party membership, recently made, was currently being considered. Von Galen might think of San Francisco as the deadest of dead ends, but Fräulein Hanzer spied opportunity there and, being intuitively certain that Herr Wiedemann had an intelligence role in addition to his consular duties, was busily bringing herself to his notice. She found it exciting to prise reluctant Germans out of their comfortable hiding places, to remind them sharply of their responsibilities, and to draw them eventually to Herr Wiedemann's attention.

Von Galen was wondering how many of these damned meetings he would have to attend before Wiedemann condescended to return his car, which was still in the custody of the Police Department. Wiedemann had told the police it might have been sabotaged, and the police had willingly agreed to subject it to minute and prolonged inspection. It was an unusual piece of co-operation, and afforded both sides a good deal of quiet satisfaction.

Von Galen accordingly had to go to Daly City by taxi: no great hardship in itself. He suspected, though, that it would be far from easy to get a taxi back, especially if the forecast rain came.

As he limped through the doorway into the hubbub of the crowded, drab hall, he was brusquely stopped by a big florid-faced man in the doorway. 'Don't think I know you,' he was told.

He looked with distaste at the gaudy silver shirt stretched taut across the man's gut. One deep breath and there would be a fusillade of shirt buttons. 'I am from the Reich Consulate-General.' He handed the man his card.

The manner changed at once; it always did. 'Yes, sir. Seat right over there. I'll tell the Pastor you're here.'

'Don't bother. I'm here to observe.' He made his way to the seat.

This time there was something more than the usual half-dozen flaming torches. The evening's speaker was the notorious Pastor Joseph Jeffers from Los Angeles, and not surprisingly the hall was packed. Jeffers had been acquitted, at a sensational trial not too long before, of certain unconventional practices of a highly immoral nature with members of his congregation, and wherever he went people flocked to gawp both at him and at his extremely attractive young wife. She had also been the subject of startling testimony.

With Jeffer's appearance, a flame was put to a wooden cross doused in paraffin. Looking round, Von Galen saw a few figures in the audience had put on the tall white headdresses of the Ku Klux Klan. Dirty smoke from the cross was marking the ceiling; the audience stamped and cheered every predictable cliché. Von Galen, not for the first time, reflected that the Führer's racial policies gave Germany some undesirable friends.

He left as the speech ended and before the singing began. In the doorway he found without surprise that it was raining heavily. At least he'd brought his umbrella. He was putting it up when a woman's voice beside him said, 'Haven't we met?'

'I don't think so.' He barely looked at her.

'Oh, but we have!' She was middle-aged, carmine-mouthed, gushing at him. 'You came to a reception we had. It's Mr Von – er?'

'Von Galen.'

'Don't you have a car? – you're going to get awful wet. If you're going into San Francisco, I can give you a ride.'

It was an uninviting choice: a soaking – or a boring twenty minutes. He elected to be bored, and shortly afterwards wished he hadn't. Bridget Mahoney was a member of the Women's Committee to Keep the United States out of War – another of the groups which talked a great deal and did little. It frequently seemed to Von Galen that their pro-German stances came from anything but pro-German feeling. Mrs Mahoney was a case in point. She was Irish, bitterly anti-British, and about as interested in Germany's triumphant rise as she was in last year's hat. But she was unstoppable. She invited him to her home; he declined. She named another date, then another, until there was no escape beyond real rudeness. And since she knew Wiedemann, rudeness was impolitic.

At her home, he met Joseph O'Hara.

They stood looking out from her terrace over the lights of the city and the velvet black of the bay: the only men present, and the only two possessed of anything like youth. 'Ten minutes more,' Von Galen said, gulping his cognac.

O'Hara laughed. 'I'll come with you.' He was a tall young man, bespectacled and earnest-looking. 'I'm only here because she's been nagging me for weeks.' Mrs Mahoney apparently hailed originally from Boston, as did O'Hara, and she knew his mother.

Then, leaning on the terrace rail, O'Hara said, 'I'll never understand why you people stopped.'

Von Galen knew what he meant: they'd been talking about it over dinner. Why hadn't Herr Hitler invaded Britain last year, when he had the chance?

He said, 'Because the Führer decided. I don't know his reasons, but I trust his judgement.'

'Given his record, so do I. But I'm as bad as the old biddies in there. I want to see the British *smashed*.'

There was a crushing emphasis on the final word, an unlikely vehemence that abruptly transformed O'Hara's mild manner.

'Why?' Von Galen asked. 'Because you're Irish?'

'In the main, yes,' O'Hara said. 'I'm Boston-Irish so

55

the anti-British feeling's hereditary. You ought to see a diary we have at home of the Famine. But it was only general, you know. Then it got personal. Want to know why?'

'If you like.'

'It was in 'thirty-eight. I'd been to Germany. Enjoyed it a lot. Then I was on my way to Ireland to visit with some relatives. Landed from the German boat at Harwich and the customs man found a couple of bottles of Irish whiskey in my trunk. Those and a copy of *Mein Kampf*. I can see the look on his face now! You ever had a body search?'

'No.'

'Hair to toenails. Every inch. Probes into every crevice and orifice, and not gentle, believe me. Then he started on my clothes, sadistic bastard. Unpicked the linings of my suits, took the heels off my shoes, cut up soap and toothpaste tubes. I was left with a pile of junk. Toy car I'd bought for my nephew was taken to bits. Then when he'd finished, he confiscated the whiskey and said, 'Enjoy your stay in the Irish Free State. *Sir*.' Oh boy, the way he said those words! That was when I knew. I said: "Were you by any chance a Black and Tan?" He didn't answer, just grinned.'

'Uncomfortable,' Von Galen said. 'But if you hate them so much, do something about it. Isn't there an Irish Republican Army? Or there's a small Irish volunteer unit attached to the *Wehrmacht*. Join one or the other.'

'I have pronounced astigmatism and a prolapsed spinal disc,' O'Hara said. 'I couldn't even drill with a rifle, let alone shoot straight. If I could, I know who I'd shoot.'

'Who?' Von Galen asked, a little wearily. Another minute or two and he'd leave.

'Roosevelt.'

Von Galen glanced at him. 'Why?'

'He's going to take the United States into the war – *and* on the British side. That's why.'

'Well, it might be useful. Pity about your eyes.' Von Galen put down his glass. 'Good night.'

But the next words halted him. O'Hara said, 'Oh, I *am* going to get him.'

'Roosevelt?'

'Yeah. I *mean* it.'

'How?'

'I'll find a way. Somebody's got to stop him. Might as well be me.'

Von Galen frowned. Was this man drunk, or what? 'Why are you telling me? I have an official position here – possibly a duty to report what you say. Germany and the United States are not at war.'

'Not yet,' O'Hara said. 'Want to bet they won't be inside a year?'

No, he didn't *appear* to be drunk, nor from his demeanour was he a braggart. And he wasn't one of the pointless, flatulent malcontents who went to the meetings. All Von Galen knew was that O'Hara came from a rich Boston-Irish family, and that he was standing here threatening, apparently seriously, to murder the President of the United States. He controlled a smile: the thing was unreal. 'If you killed him, what do you suppose would happen afterwards?'

'To me? I'd get the chair,' O'Hara said levelly.

'That's not what I meant.'

'I know.' O'Hara became serious. 'Okay, I can tell you what would happen. There's nobody to take his place, and a hell of a lot of powerful people who would break their goddam backs to keep America out. With Roosevelt gone, it'd be goodbye to all the others, Hopkins, Sumner Welles, the whole crew. The influence would shift straight away to people like Senator Taft and Joe Kennedy. You people could take your time over Britain, and Britain wouldn't have American arms.'

'Very tempting.'

'Just one thing. Hands off Ireland.'

'I doubt very much,' Von Galen said, 'whether the Führer would be interested in Ireland.'

'That's right, he wouldn't. He's interested now because U-Boat bases in the south-west would be strategically vital in the war against Britain.'

O'Hara, he thought, was at least well-informed. He said, 'The Irish won't allow that.'

'The Irish,' O'Hara said, 'have just got rid of foreign troops. It's taken several centuries. They're kind of leary about any more.'

'Yes, well . . .' Von Galen nodded. 'It's all very interesting.' This time he *would* go. He began to turn away.

Then O'Hara startled him again. 'There's a chance of getting Churchill too.'

This time Von Galen couldn't stop himself laughing. 'With the same shot?'

'Depends who fires it. You want to hear?'

'I don't think so, Mr O'Hara.'

'You think it's impossible?'

'Unlikely, at any rate. They're three thousand miles apart. It would,' Von Galen said, 'be quite a shot.'

Once again O'Hara startled him by saying quietly, 'They're going to meet.'

'Churchill and Roosevelt? Are they really? How do you know?'

'That,' O'Hara said, 'needs explaining. Do you want to hear?'

'I suppose I'd better,' Von Galen said, amused. 'This should probably be reported to Berlin.'

'Don't make fun of it. I'm serious.'

'I see you are.' This would be either the intelligence coup of the century, Von Galen thought, or half an hour wasted; with very heavy odds on waste. Still, it would be intriguing. 'Tell me.'

'No. Not here. I'm at the Bedford Hotel. Come and have dinner with me tomorrow night.'

'I'm afraid – '

'Of ideas?' O'Hara said. 'I see you are.'

Von Galen was nettled. 'All right. What time?'

Having used Von Galen's name once without his knowing it, Karen Hanzer did not hesitate to do so again: she inscribed it on the request to *Luftwaffe* Records Office for information on the father of the heroic Leutnant Heinz Zoll. The inquiry might have taken months to process, but she was lucky: a diplomatic courier was in San Francisco to make the fortnightly collection of material, with the result that her request was not subject to the usual long waits both there and in Washington, and went to Germany quickly in the diplomatic bag. Further, she had marked it Most Urgent. *Luftwaffe* Records helpfully replied by signal. In a mere nine days Fräulein Hanzer had the information.

She read the signal and smiled to herself. It was now only a matter of waiting for the fly to walk into the spider's parlour.

But for that she had a longer wait.

Miller was in Long Beach, working hard. As the equipment was gradually packed into the first Canso there were endless difficulties with weight distribution and its effect on handling and instruments. The Canso felt different every time it was flown and Miller and Alec Ross were engaged with the Martingale engineers in a dawn-to-dusk search for compromise between the rigid demands of the equipment and the no less unforgiving requirements of aerodynamics.

'Give us time,' Martingale kept saying, 'and we'll lick this thing.' Or that thing, depending on the problem. His highly qualified technologists often laboured all night seeking an answer to a difficulty unearthed the previous day, or to some trouble that had been beaten once, only to recur as the equipment was readjusted. The hope had been that Project Cull would move up to Canada quickly, but the early days of March saw them all still in Long Beach, still sweating.

'What the hell,' Martingale said one day. 'Enjoy the sun while you can. It's cold up there in Ontario.'

The fly arrived in early February, its coming signalled by a call from the public counter.

'A man here to see Herr Von Galen,' the counter clerk reported.

'Name?' Karen Hanzer asked.

'Won't give it. Says he had a letter.'

Her heart thumped pleasurably. 'Ask him to wait,' she said. 'Then, in five minutes, tell him that Herr Von Galen isn't here today.'

'But he is. I saw – '

'Please do as I ask.'

She looked out of the window. Fog so shrouded the city that the higher buildings seemed to be pillars supporting a vast blanket of cotton woool. Misty tendrils drifted down into the streets, carrying rain with them.

Karen Hanzer was well prepared. She slipped on her raincoat – an American-made mackintosh, reversible in blue and fawn – picked up her umbrella and the light canvas shopping-bag ready by her desk, went down the stairs and looked through the glass panel in the door of the reception area. Only one person sat waiting: a small-ish, square man in his early forties. She left by the side door and darted across the road to the cab stand. No cabs were waiting, but after two or three minutes one pulled in.

'Where to, miss?'

She gave him three dollars. 'I only want to shelter,' she said. 'I'm waiting for my husband.'

The cabbie shrugged and switched on the meter.

She had to wipe condensation off the window to keep the entrance in sight, and because she was keyed up the minutes dragged. When the man emerged, he stood for a

60

moment or two on the sidewalk, then turned up his coat collar and walked away.

As she got out, the cabbie said, 'You only used twenty cents, miss.'

'Keep the change.' She took the blue rain-hat out of her shopping-bag and followed.

He hadn't liked the whole thing. Come and collect, the letter had said, and it sounded so easy but hadn't turned out that way. He'd told the counter clerk what he wanted and been told to wait, and they'd kept him waiting: five, six, seven minutes before he was called.

'Have you identification, please?'

'Well, no, but I was sent this letter.'

'We have to be sure it's being given to the right person. Anything will do – cheque-book, driver's licence.'

He had identification, sure enough, but nothing he was going to show in *there*. 'Isn't it proof enough that I have this letter?'

The answer was no. It must be understood there were rules. The Consulate had a responsibility. But there was really no difficulty: he need only return with some everyday form of identification. The clerk was polite but implacable, even in the face of a sheet of Consulate stationery bearing an invitation to come and collect.

He was irritated, but unsurprised. From the moment he'd had the letter he'd thought it strange. If his son had replied, the letter ought to have gone direct to the PO box, without any intermediate nonsense with the Consulate. But the temptation of something actually *there* had been too much to resist; and anyway, how could he be compromised? He couldn't – nobody knew who he was.

Now he stood on the sidewalk outside, turned up the collar of his coat against the persistent rain, and looked around. If the newspapers were to be believed, a lot of people of German origin were having pressure put on them. There were lurid stories about spy rings, blackmail,

61

men in raincoats turning up on doorsteps demanding contributions and support for this and that. Probably just newspaper talk, most of it, but recruiting *was* going on, no doubt about that.

If they'd opened the letter to his son, they'd know he was a pilot, and he'd heard of a guy called Langendorf at Lockheed who'd been told he ought to be back in Germany fighting for the Fatherland and that if he didn't volunteer there could be trouble.

Yes, he'd known, but still he'd come here, the complete innocent, knowing they could be wondering about him, chancing it. All the time he'd sat inside, he'd been thinking they might take a picture of him, something like that. But he'd felt reasonably secure because there wasn't any way they could know his identity.

Now he wasn't so sure. The thought struck him that all it needed was somebody to follow him home. Would they go that far? Probably not, but he daren't take any chances. If anybody did follow, he decided, they'd have to follow a hell of a long way. Taxi maybe? He could take a cab somewhere, up Powell Street, somewhere like that, then get out and do some complicated walking. He glanced towards the cab rank; only one taxi there, and it was taken.

He turned and began walking.

Half an hour later he was crossing Union Square, heading west, then climbing, feeling the pull by now on his leg muscles. Several times he'd glanced back, without spotting anybody consistently behind him. The streets were quieter than usual; people were staying indoors out of the rain. But there were still plenty about, most of them rain-coated and wearing hats. He wished he'd worn a hat: rain was running down inside his collar.

He turned left along California Street, busy at any time, walked a few blocks, then took another left into Taylor and began running down the hill, finally dodged into the big tobacco emporium and stood panting for a minute while the smooth assistant politely waited for him to get his breath back and buy something.

She almost lost him when he began running, hesitating too long, then having to run faster herself, feeling conspicuous and too far back. By the corner of Geary he was out of sight and she stood in confusion, looking round anxiously, then heaving a sigh of relief as he came out of a shop along Geary and quickly set off west. Hurrying after him, she took off her coat, turned it inside out and put it on again, blue side outwards. She was soaked instantly, but with a change to the brown rain-hat she was a different person. He turned uphill again, and went into a hotel. If there was more than one entrance she could lose him here. As he went into the coffee shop, she picked up the house phone, keeping her finger on the button, and began an animated and imaginary conversation.

She couldn't stare through the doorway from there, not directly, but there was a mirror on a pillar that gave a view. As she jabbered she kept her eye on it, unable to see him, but keeping the door in sight. When he came out he stood for a moment, then turned towards the north entrance. She managed to be just ahead of him, dashed out, let the door swing back at him and stopped to buy a paper from a newsboy on the sidewalk outside.

He began pounding up the hill again. She put up her umbrella and followed. The rain was darkening her coat and the umbrella shielded her face. She was wet and uncomfortable, but pleased with herself. There could be no doubt the man had something to hide: nobody would behave as he was doing otherwise! Already they had walked three or four kilometres, pointlessly, in the rain.

At Washington Street he caught the cable-car, scrambling aboard as it moved off, and she was very lucky indeed: a cab was just halting and she pushed in front of the elderly man who'd hailed it, saying, 'Excuse me, but it's extremely urgent,' then told the taxi-driver to stay behind the cable-car because she'd seen an old friend board it.

The man stayed aboard right the way down to the terminal; but she'd paid the driver in advance, got out quickly and watched from across the street as he hurried away down Market. Now she crossed too, watching him from the other side. She was shivering, wet to the skin, but when he stopped in a doorway she found another doorway and reversed the coat again. Some stupid man coming out of the shop said, 'You're getting far too wet, young lady,' trying to pick her up, and she said, 'I like being wet, you idiot!' and left him gaping. But it gave her an idea. As her target began moving again she watched for and finally found a youngish woman walking quickly, came up behind her and said, 'Want to come under my umbrella?'

'Why, thank you!'

Two hundred metres, then the woman left her, but it had been two hundred metres with another person, and once the target had glanced back.

She felt she couldn't lose him now.

He'd spotted nobody. Half an hour ago he thought he'd seen a man, *had* seen him, a hundred yards or so back, ploughing on through the rain, and the guy had stayed there for a while, but next time he looked there was no sign. Then there'd been a woman in blue with an oilcloth rain-hat, going faster than most girls would walk and seeming to stay with him. He'd wondered sharply about her: about using a *woman* to trail somebody – would that happen?

But then she'd gone. Now, though he couldn't be sure, of course, it didn't *seem* as though anybody was following. And he was drenched. It was time to go home.

As he cut up Leavenworth, then along Pine, the rain stopped and a few minutes later the sun found a break in the cloud and the streets glittered. It seemed like a signal and he felt a lot happier, pretty confident now that even if he had been followed, he'd shaken off whoever had had the job. He was tired, legs feeling the strain of the slopes, but it had been worth it, even if he'd been paranoid about the whole thing. If nothing else, it set his mind at rest.

Just before he reached the apartment block he looked around again, then circled the block once, to be sure, before he went in.

She'd seen him glance up at the building, pause, then turn, and there was something in his manner, some relaxation of his posture which seemed to suggest that he was home. But he looked up again, then turned and walked off along the street. She was a hundred yards behind and didn't dare follow: this was a residential area, the roads quiet. She hurried up the hill, tired now, and more than a little worried, and when she came to the intersection looked along the street and couldn't see him. And now it was raining again. He must have turned. She half-ran up the hill, the length of the block, her muscles protesting, and looked left again at the next corner. No sign of him! She set off once more, still climbing. At the very next corner she'd have to turn and run that way, or he'd really get away. But by the time she'd crossed the street she saw him on the edge of her vision, coming round the corner a block away, then turning towards her. She kept going, up the hill. A delivery truck was parked at the kerb and she moved behind it, waited, watched as he came into view.

He stood on the corner, surveying the street. She'd been right – she *knew* it!

He went up the four front steps of the apartment building.

She waited twenty minutes before she went in. It was a small block, only four floors high, and while she'd been watching only one person had emerged: an old woman who looked like a cleaner. Karen Hanzer's heart was thumping. If the man came out again and saw her, he'd probably guess and then have to do something about her, maybe something violent, because he'd been trying hard to protect himself and would know he'd failed. Rainwater dripped from her coat as she stood in the lobby; it pattered on to the polished linoleum. She glanced down at it, and saw his drying footprints leading to the stair. She walked up. The footprints petered out, but there were drops of water that had fallen from his coat, just a few; enough. By the third floor they'd almost vanished, but she saw a scuff mark on the newly polished lino, and outside one of the doors a little scatter of drops as though he'd shaken his coat before going in. Brass figures on the door gave a number: 3B.

She went quickly down the stairs and read the name on 3B's mailbox. One more for the German-American Bund, she thought to herself. She was becoming good at this work, and it gave her *great* satisfaction. No German had the right to hide away with his country at war, and this man was her fourth.

'You should have joined the Gestapo, Fräulein,' Von Galen said bad-temperedly. That morning he had received a letter from his uncle, repeating and underlining the earlier threats. It told him to stop behaving like a half-witted infant, and gave instructions that the Horch be sold and replaced with a smaller, cheaper vehicle appropriate to his status.

Karen Hanzer stood dripping on his carpet and said defensively, 'At training school we were instructed always to be on the look-out for people who might be useful to the Fatherland. I now have a full dossier on this man.'

'What makes you think he's important?'

'If you read the dossier,' she said, holding it out to him, 'you'll see.'

He put it at the side of his desk. 'Go change your

clothes before you get pneumonia.' She went obediently. Von Galen was being foolish, she thought. Fortunately, Herr Wiedemann was far from foolish and would hear about this before long.

Von Galen resumed his study of the automobile advertising in the *San Francisco Chronicle*. The thought of parting with the Horch dismayed him, but things were not quite as bad as they might seem. Uncle Willi knew nothing of American cars. Something cheaper would not be hard to find; though something smaller would. There was, for instance, a Lincoln convertible at half the price of the Horch . . .

He telephoned the dealer, who was not in the least interested, told him nobody wanted fancy foreign cars, and offered him roughly half what the Horch was worth.

When Von Galen finally read Karen Hanzer's small dossier, he was feeling thoroughly spiteful and Zoll, or Miller, or whatever his name was, provided a tailor-made target for idle venom. He reached for the telephone, then thought better of it. Let the man think his subterfuge remained unbroken: yes, leave it a few hours; the shock would be greater.

It was.

Miller, at the phone in the hallway, felt his face go stiff. He glanced at the sitting-room door, checking it was closed. 'Sorry, you have the wrong – '

'I don't think so, Mr Zoll.'

'Who *is* this?'

'I think we ought to talk.'

'What about?'

'Mutual interests.'

Miller said desperately, 'Look, I told you, you have the wrong – '

'We could, for example, talk about marriage. In an hour I shall be in the restaurant and bar beside the Pickwick Hotel, eating baked clams. Greet me as "Jack", but not before I have finished.'

Miller was trembling as he hung up. How in *hell* had he been traced? He went and sat at his desk, striving to think rationally. He'd always been terrified of something like this; now it had happened, and through his own stupidity.

There was no option: he'd have to go. He made himself smile at his wife. 'I'm taking a walk, Dot.'

She looked up. 'Okay, honey.' The walk was nothing unusual. She caught sight of his face. 'Are you okay?'

'Touch of indigestion, that's all.'

'You're not going to be sick? You look sweaty.'

'I'll be okay.'

Von Galen said, a little more loudly than was necessary, 'The baked clams, I think. And a salad. Roquefort dressing.'

He enjoyed the meal. A number of men, solitary drinkers, sat at the bar on the other side of the room. One of them would be Zoll – which? He took his time over the clams.

As he was wiping his mouth, a voice said, 'Jack?'

Von Galen raised his head. 'Good evening.' He picked up his bill, left a tip on the table and crossed to the cash desk, Zoll following. 'Shall we talk as we walk?'

Outside, Zoll was predictably belligerent. 'What in hell *is* all this?'

'It must be clear to you. I am able to address you as Zoll, so I know about your past. I was able to telephone you, therefore I know about your present.' Sidelong he watched the man. Until that moment some small hope might have survived. Visibly, in those few seconds, hope died.

Zoll said, 'Was it the first time you called?'

'Why?'

'You haven't spoken to my wife?'

'Your bigamous wife.'

'No, she's – '

68

'Your real wife, Anneliese Zoll, still lives in Hanover with your father and your sister.'

'It was the letter?'

'Yes. Foolish of you.' Von Galen found he was rather enjoying himself. He'd thought Fräulein Hanzer's enthusiasm childish, but there was satisfaction in applying pressure like this. 'It's perfectly understandable, of course. When a coward like you has a son like yours – it is bound to inspire complex emotions.'

'What do you want?' Zoll demanded hoarsely. 'I haven't much money.'

Curious, Von Galen thought. Here was a man who actually *hoped* he was being subjected to financial blackmail! 'Not money.'

'Who are you?'

'You could say,' Von Galen said, 'that I am your country. Germany is at war and all kinds of people may prove useful. Even cowards.'

Zoll, he thought, looked abject now.

Von Galen said, 'You are living under an assumed name. You have committed the crime of bigamy. You are an illegal immigrant in the United States.' He was not certain of that, but it was more than likely and Zoll did not deny it. 'I know everything important about you, but there are a few gaps. I know that you are still flying aeroplanes, but not what they are. That might be interesting.'

'It's *spying*!'

'I know what it is. By the way, I think it's a mistake to call you Zoll. Who knows, we might encounter some friend who knows you as Miller. How, by the way, did you pick on that name?'

Miller had had three weeks to plan. He was amazed that this guy Von Galen hadn't called him again, hadn't demanded information on the work he was doing – that was important enough! But he hadn't. For a day or two

69

he'd felt like a butterfly pinned to a board, but then his mind had begun to work. When the project moved up to Canada he'd have the only opportunity he was ever likely to be given to disappear from Von Galen's surveillance. To do it he had to cut everything clean – go, and leave no trace.

He made arrangements to sell his aerobatic biplane, at a ruinous price, to an aviation broker happy enough to buy knowing there was a good profit to be made. He spent a morning visiting the electricity supply company and paying his bill a month ahead, saying he might have to move quickly and there wouldn't be time for proper notice. He told the same story to the city taxation office and the phone company. It cost him quite a bit, but it was worth it to get off *this* hook.

There remained Dot, but he was confident he could manage things with Dot. She was accustomed to fast moves, had made them all their married life, regarded them as a challenge. The way they lived, a move meant packing a few suitcases and calling a cab.

The days passed, but the fear did not. All it would take was one call to the apartment. Dot would cheerfully hand out the number of the hotel he was using in Long Beach, and he dared not warn her. And next time Von Galen wouldn't walk away without asking. Next time, Miller knew, he'd find himself talking about anti-submarine warfare, and *that* was the start of a road with a brick wall at the end of it. A brick wall – and a bullet.

THREE

Von Galen entered Joseph O'Hara's suite at the Bedford and looked around him in astonishment. The place was like an operations room: two big blackboards on easels, maps spread on the floor, books lying open. The long curtains were drawn.

'Hang the Do Not Disturb on the door handle,' O'Hara said. 'We don't wany anybody walking in.'

'You seem extraordinarily well prepared.'

'Prepared?' O'Hara, pinning something to one of the boards, turned. 'You think I'm crazy, don't you?'

'Ambitious.'

O'Hara looked at him closely. 'Kind of a smirk on your face.'

'I'm sorry.'

'Don't worry. I intend to wipe it off. I do my research. Example: you are not just a third secretary: you are the nephew of Ernst Wilhelm Bohle who, in addition to being Minister of State at the Reich Foreign Office, is Gauleiter of the *Auslandsorganisazion*, and an honorary major-general of the SS.'

'Whom did you ask?'

'That's all I did, sure. I asked. I asked a correspondent in Washington of the *Berliner Boersen Zeitung*. He's a financial writer, and my family's in finance. I also looked Bohle up. You can find out a lot from reference books. Example two, still on Bohle: he's the only member of the higher ranks in the Government who was born abroad. In England, as a matter of fact. I can give you the date, the place.'

'What does all this prove?'

O'Hara selected a drawing-pin and finished pinning the map. 'It proves there's a lot of information around.'

'Damn it, you can't assassinate Roosevelt with – '

'Information? Sure you can. Plenty of politicians have been ruined by information getting out. But I'm not talking about that. Let me ask *you* a question. What happened on January 3rd?'

'I don't know.'

'And you a member of the Foreign Service?' O'Hara said reprovingly. 'I'll tell you. Franklin Roosevelt changed his mind. He decided he was going to send Harry L. Hopkins to London after all – to talk to Churchill. You remember?'

'Yes.'

'Remember anything else?'

Von Galen felt irritated. There was more than a touch of the schoolroom about this. 'Hopkins and Churchill are supposed to have got on well together. It was announced shortly afterwards that war material would be supplied – '

'Right! Now, what about Wendell Wilkie? Name ring any bells?'

Von Galen sighed. 'He was the defeated candidate in the Presidential election.'

O'Hara said, 'He went to London too – in the same month. What did he take with him? He took a message. A sheet of paper in Roosevelt's own handwriting. A poem by Longfellow, part of it, anyway. Here's what it said: . . .'

'Poetry!'

'Listen. It goes like this: "Dear Churchill, I think this verse applies to your people as it does to us:

> ' "Sail on, O ship of State,
> Sail on, O Union strong and great,
> Humanity with all its fears,
> With all its hopes of future years,
> Is hanging breathless on thy fate." '

72

'You're trying,' Von Galen said incredulously, 'to draw some conclusion from that!'

'Let's look at it. It's emotional. Roosevelt's doing a lot more than supplying a few things. Right there, he's putting his arm round Churchill's shoulder and saying, "We're worried about you, but you can rely on us." Now – did you read *this*?' He passed Von Galen a newspaper cutting. It came from the *Washington Post,* from a gossip column, and two or three lines were underscored. 'Eleanor Roosevelt told somebody over tea the other day that she just *knew* how much the President would like to meet Winston Churchill. She was sure they'd be real friends. Bad news, maybe, for isolationists?'

Von Galen handed the cutting back. 'All this is totally inconsequential.'

'Think about it. Roosevelt's sending people close to him to see Churchill. His wife says he'd like to meet him.'

'It means nothing.'

'Let me offer you a simple statement. Those two are the big men of the English-speaking world. They're moving closer to an Alliance, or what in hell's the Lend-Lease Legislation about? They're going to want to meet, and there's nothing in the whole wide world to stop them. When they do – and they *will* – Roosevelt will be consorting with Germany's legitimate enemy. You people have every right in the world to attack with everything you've got. Turn the pair of them into ground beef.'

There was something infuriating in the young American's certitude. Von Galen said, 'If they *do* meet – no one will know where, until it's over. If it's here in America, as it would be, any attack within a neutral country would not be legitimate.'

'They won't meet here. They can't.'

'Why not?'

'Practicalities,' O'Hara said, 'and protocol.'

'Rubbish,' Von Galen said, rising. 'This is adolescent day-dreaming. I really see no purpose in listening.'

O'Hara blinked at him through the heavy glasses. 'You're absolutely wrong, but I'll just say this. Keep your eyes and ears open. Think about what I said. I'm going to be here in San Francisco for a couple of months more. And you, my friend, will be back.'

'I doubt it.'

'You will, believe me.'

Ernie wasn't supposed to be home for the weekend, but he arrived Saturday night, having hitched a ride on an Air Corps plane to Oakland. He looked tired and under strain, and on the Sunday morning Dot let him sleep and slipped out to the food market. Ernie liked steak for Sunday breakfast, so steak he'd get, plus eggs and hash browns, plus fresh rolls, plus iced tomato juice with a dash of pepper sauce. He liked that.

As she reached the store, a girl was going in, wheeling a small baby in a big perambulator, having trouble with the swing doors.

'Here, let me hold it.'

The girl smiled. 'Thank you. I am not used to this yet.'

Dot looked into the pram. 'You're new, young fella?' The baby wore blue. 'He's beautiful.'

'Thank you. But he cries so much.'

'They all do. I haven't any kids myself, but that's what people always say.'

They chatted as they waited to be served. It emerged that the girl and her husband were Norwegian and that he was a ship's officer on a regular run between the West Coast and Yokohama. She'd come out to marry him a year earlier and now, with Norway occupied, was stuck in San Francisco. 'So you see, here I am and here I must stay. It's lonely sometimes with only me and the baby. Georg, my husband, does not get back so often.'

She seemed on the verge of tears and Dot said, 'I'm alone a lot myself so I know that feeling. Listen, why don't we have a cup of coffee one day?'

'Oh – I would like that *very* much.'

'No trouble. A real pleasure, in fact. Be nice to have that little fella around sometimes.' Dot ripped a page from her shopping notebook. 'Here's my address and number – it's just a couple of blocks away, and *my* husband's away the whole week. Why not bring that little fella to see me tomorrow? I'm Dot – short for Dorothy.'

'My name is Karen.'

As Dot walked away with her bag, Karen Hanzer began to push the pram back towards its owner's apartment. The baby was the son of a commercial officer at the Consulate, whose mother was only too delighted to let somebody else wheel him up and down San Francisco's demanding terrain. There would be no trouble borrowing him again, and Karen Hanzer was determined to find out still more about the Zoll/Miller family. Herr Von Galen, attractive as he was, was lazy, and deep down she had a feeling that she had found something of a prize.

The move north from Long Beach to Kingston, on the north-eastern shore of Lake Ontario, was scheduled for March 15th. Miller collared Ed Martingale in the hangar washroom, the only place Martingale stood still long enough to talk.

'I hate to ask, Ed, but there's not much for me to do in the next few days. I know it's not in the contract – '

'Got a problem?'

'Well, Dot seems kind of low. Been alone a lot. I'd like to give her a little break before the work starts.'

Martingale began to wash his hands. 'We'll be five days or more bolting Canso Ring Two down. I don't see why not. Thinking of anywhere special?'

'Palm Springs, maybe.'

'Good idea. Desert air will do her good.'

'Thanks, I'll check with Alec.'

'He's out on the field. I'll tell him I okayed it. Just call your wife.'

75

On the phone he said to Dot: 'How'd you like a surprise?'

'What kind?'

'The nice kind. How about closing the apartment up and getting on the train down here. I miss you.'

She laughed. 'What's all the hurry?'

'I want you here, that's what the hurry is.'

'Ernie, there's things to *do!* Give me a couple of days.'

'It'll cost you.' Me too, he thought, if you don't move fast!

'What'll it cost me?'

'A few days in Palm Springs.'

She whistled. 'You're not fooling?'

'No, but the schedule's tight.'

'Well, there's the rent to settle. Electricity. Phone.'

'I settled them all.'

'Ernie, you're a crook!' She was delighted. He knew now it was going to work!

He said, 'Tell you what.'

'What?'

'I've ten bucks say you can't make the afternoon train. Leaves at four-thirty.'

'You lose.'

'Hey, Dot. Pack my radio carefully, huh?'

'Don't I always? Listen, get off the line. You're just keeping me talking to make ten bucks. Sure you paid all the bills?'

'All of them.'

'Okay. You'll meet me?'

'We'll stay in Los Angeles tonight, head out tomorrow.'

'*Hasta la vista,* pal. I got things to do.'

He hung up smiling but his hands were sweating. She'd had plenty of practice at the quick move, but even for Dot this was short notice.

Dot had finished the packing and changed her clothes and now took a final, systematic look round the apartment in case something had been missed. The pride, even amusement, that she felt in her own slick efficiency, warred inside her with a measure of regret. Other people had to have a big truck, or even two, to make a move, but all she and Ernie ever needed was a couple of hours and a taxi. It would really be nice, one day, to choose carpets and curtains and wall-coverings, buy them, make them, hang them, and be surrounded by things that belonged to *her*, not to some apartment rental operator. Still, *this* way she got the trip to Palm Springs!

Yes, everything was done. Time to call the cab. Picking up the phone, she remembered the Norwegian girl and at once felt guilty. The poor kid had come over twice for coffee and company: a nice girl and an *adorable* baby, and now she was running out on them; couldn't even phone to say goodbye because Karen had no phone: didn't need one because she knew nobody. It was so *sad*. Dot opened the blue case she always used for their papers, found a sheet of stationery and an envelope and scribbled a swift note:

Dear Karen, We're leaving in a hurry on account of Ernie's new job. Don't know what my new address will be, but I'll write and let you know and we'll keep in touch. Give young Olaf a kiss and a hug for me, huh? Love, Dot.

She stopped the cab at a mailbox on the way to the station.

Von Galen had virtually forgotten about Joseph O'Hara. For two weeks he had not thought either about the man himself or about the absurdities of his notion. Then, on a Sunday morning, and almost entirely by chance, he heard a broadcast. He was in his bath at the time and the radio was playing in his living-room; he had left it on to hear the final few minutes of a concert. When it ended, there came the inevitable advertisements and brassy music, and

Von Galen debated with himself whether to endure the next programme, or get out and turn it off. While he was hesitating the announcer intoned: 'We go now to the Shrine of the Little Flower in Royal Oak, Michigan . . .'

That settled the question. He relaxed in the warm water: it would be Father Coughlin's weekly broadcast, and he ought to hear it at least once. Coughlin, an Irish-American priest, was thought by many people, in the foreign service and outside it, to be Germany's most potent friend in America.

Coughlin was a phenomenon. Having got into broadcasting in its earliest days, he had built for himself an audience of millions and was arguably one of the two most influential voices in America. He had once supported Roosevelt, but did so no longer, defiant of church and state.

Von Galen listened with growing surprise. The virulence Coughlin displayed was extraordinary, his loathing of the British as strong as O'Hara's. The broadcast was a total contrast to anything else he'd heard on the pap-filled airways of America.

Coughlin ended:

'You will say: but did I not support Franklin Roosevelt? To that I plead guilty. I did support him. When millions of Americans were unemployed, he was creating work and nobody spoke for him more loudly than I.

'But things change, my friends. It is said that power corrupts. I must tell you that it *has* corrupted the President of these United States. I must tell you that he no longer looks inward at the troubles that afflict this nation. His attention is elsewhere. He listens to the voice of the Anti-Christ.

'And who, my friends, *is* the Anti-Christ? I will tell you, for he *is* a man. He is a man whose deep and disgusting dream is to tempt America, to persuade America, in the end to *force* America into war!

'His name is Winston Churchill. Oh yes! *He* is the Anti-Christ. And, my friends, he is winning!

'Did Roosevelt promise that no American boy would die defending foreign soil? You know he did. I challenge him now to say it again. I have made this challenge many times, but has he spoken? No. Will he say it? Again, no.

'Instead he sends his friend, his witch's familiar, his comrade-in-disgrace, to talk to the Anti-Christ, and to ask what is now *required* from America. Hopkins, my friends. Hopkins, who furthered and fathered the New Deal. And who now conveys to your President the instructions of a foreigner – Churchill.

'We are told they became friends. Hopkins, supping with Satan, used a short spoon and fell beneath the spell. He returns singing praises of the Anti-Christ!

'It is even said that Hopkins was given the task of arranging a meeting, of bringing *our* President, whose task is to *defend* America, to a table with the man who wants America at war.

'Let a great shout rise, my friends. Let us tell Roosevelt, so loudly that Churchill will hear and tremble: America must stay at peace!'

By that time, Von Galen was lying in cooling water and thinking hard. It was one thing for Joseph O'Hara to postulate a meeting; quite another for it to come from Coughlin, who was notoriously well-informed. He'd thought O'Hara mad. But was he? O'Hara was saying that if Roosevelt chose to meet Churchill, an opportunity might occur to kill them both. That was self-evident if anybody knew where they were. And that, of course, was the point: nobody would ever know. Such things were announced afterwards: at the time secrecy would be intense.

Then, on 19th March, something occurred which again set Von Galen thinking: Roosevelt set off on the yacht *Potomac* for a fishing cruise in the Bahamas. It was officially described by White House spokesmen as 'a carefree fishing trip', but Von Galen noticed that Harry L. Hopkins accompanied the President.

And then, on the following day, the newspaper political correspondents were speculating publicly, if not very seriously, that the fishing trip was a cover for some other activity of greater importance. One writer, in the *Washington Post*, even mentioned Churchill, and pointed out that the Bahamas were British possessions, governed by the Duke of Windsor, brother of the King.

Suddenly Von Galen had a vision: a white yacht on a calm blue sea, two men at a table, one smoking a cigar, the other with a cigarette in a long holder – and then a single fiery blast. And after it, no Churchill to oppose the Führer: no Roosevelt to march America towards conflict.

It would do no harm, he thought, to listen once more to O'Hara.

Infuriatingly, and perhaps inevitably, O'Hara gave a little chortle of triumph on the telephone. 'You thought it was happening right now, didn't you? Sure, come on over.'

'Before I do, there are two questions to be answered. Otherwise the visit is pointless.'

'I know what you're going to say – you want to know *where* and you want to know *when*.'

'Precisely.'

'That,' O'Hara said, 'has to be worked out.'

'I thought so.'

'But it can be done.'

'How?'

'Brains,' O'Hara said. 'And available information.'

When Von Galen walked into the suite, O'Hara was holding a newspaper. 'You see today's development.'

'What is it?'

'Well, it shows the way the wind's blowing. There's been a *coup d'état* in Jugoslavia. The Regency, which favoured you people, is out. King Peter is in.'

'I scarcely see that it's relevant.'

'Let me tell you what happened when FDR heard. He turned the *Potomac* around and high-tailed it back to Port Everglades. There's a German ship there.'

Von Galen knew about that ship. *Arauca* had lain in harbour for a year after being chased into port by a British cruiser.

'The FBI has told Roosevelt there's a plan for Axis ships in American ports to be scuttled by their crews to disrupt port traffic,' O'Hara said. 'So now the Coast Guard's boarded *Arauca*, how d'you like that? They've taken off the crew "for safe-keeping" and they've hauled down your flag – no Swastika flying there now!'

'That is certainly an outrage,' Von Galen said primly. 'But no doubt it will be handled through the usual – '

'It's a declaration of war,' O'Hara replied. 'Not overt, but near enough. He hauls down your flag and nails his colours up, wouldn't you say? Well, *I* say he's got to be stopped!'

'You were going to tell me where and when.'

'Not exactly. I'm going to make a few predictions.'

'All right, predict.'

'Roosevelt can't and won't go to Europe.'

'If that isn't a statement of the obvious – '

O'Hara smiled. 'That's the beauty of it. Roosevelt *won't* cross the Atlantic, so Churchill *must*. Question for you. How old is FDR?'

'Sixty?'

'Fifty-nine. Physical condition?'

'Well, he's crippled.'

'Right. Had polio. Legs are no good. He can stand, he can walk a few paces with a lot of difficulty. What's he do for relaxation?'

'Apparently he goes fishing.'

81

'Right. Or he goes to Warm Springs, Georgia. He has pain in those legs. He likes warm weather. What do you know about Churchill? *His* age, *his* idea of fun?'

'We're not talking about fun,' Von Galen protested.

'Play along for a while. Tell me.'

'He's older. Late sixties. I believe he paints.'

'Absolutely. Yes, he does paint. He goes off into the sunshine and he paints in Madeira and in Morocco.'

'You're saying they'll meet in a warm climate?'

'Yes, I am.'

'You've heard of fires? Of central heating?'

'Look, Baldur, they're powerful men, these two. They don't have to listen to some hard-ass telling them a little discomfort's good for the soul. They can choose.'

'You may have a point.'

'I have more than one. Recapitulate for a moment. Roosevelt won't go to Europe because there's only Britain and if he goes there he's in danger and in any case the American public wouldn't tolerate it. Churchill must therefore come this side, and when those two get together they'll want a little comfort. That's all I'm saying. That by itself puts big limits on the available places.'

Von Galen shook his head. 'You're in a dream world. You say X is so, therefore Y follows.'

'Stay with me.' O'Hara picked up a map, unrolled it. 'Look at this. We've already eliminated all of Europe and a hell of a lot of North America. What we have left is the south and the Caribbean.'

'What is wrong,' Von Galen said, 'with Washington?'

'You really don't see it? Okay. Imgine Churchill comes to Washington. Do you think for one second that he could do *that* in secret?'

'Does he have to?'

'Sure he has to! If those two are going to talk they aren't going to want the entire American press speculating what they're talking about. They don't want big demonstrations outside the White House. And Churchill would have to go back, remember, with every U-Boat in the Atlantic waiting for him! And if he flies – well, for one thing it's risky, and for the second he might get shot down. They wouldn't risk *any* American city.'

'You're overestimating the influence of the press. Secrecy can always be – '

'In your country, maybe. Not in this one. News would be all round the country in ten minutes, believe me. No, they're going to choose somewhere quiet and comfortable. They *could* have been cruising round the Bahamas the last few days. I thought they were for a while. But that's the general area: the West Indies, the Bahamas, maybe Bermuda.'

'A lot of territory.'

'We can rule some of it out. Bermuda's attractive, but too many people. Word would get round fast on a small island. You may have agents there, I don't know. And Bermuda's mid-Atlantic. U-Boat country. That's true of much of the Caribbean. Convoys muster there.'

'How do you know?'

'I can *read*, damn it! Read the papers – they tell you a hell of a lot. Where was I? – yes, the Caribbean. All right, those islands with really good harbours have big populations, too. Same problem with secrecy, maybe the same problem with U-Boats. You follow me – the range of possibilities gets smaller.'

'I'm sorry. You're building something in the air. It doesn't really exist. What exactly are you suggesting I do?'

'Tell Berlin.'

Von Galen laughed. 'Make a fool of myself?'

'How much does that matter – making a fool of yourself?'

'Look, there is nothing to *tell* Berlin except that an American of my acquaintance has a theory.'

'What's wrong with theory? What the hell was *Mein*

Kampf but theory? Do you imagine Germany's not looking for ways to kill Churchill and keep America out of the war?' He sighed. 'No. I – er – I understand how you feel. I've lived with this for quite a while. You haven't. But maybe there's something we can get out of *your* mind. Give me a few minutes more.'

'I really see no purpose.'

'Please. You're in the foreign service. You know about protocol.'

'I'm hardly a specialist.'

'Tell me what protocol governs any meeting between Roosevelt and Churchill, remembering that one is a Head of State and the other isn't.'

'It's not my department. I don't know.'

'Well, protocol's involved. Who greets who and where. Guns get fired for Heads of State. I think, for instance, that protocol is one reason we can rule out all of Canada. If they met there, they'd be stuck with the Canadian Prime Minister, and they wouldn't want him. Not those two. Two whales inviting a tiddler to their meeting, no sir! But they couldn't *not* invite him – that'd be a hell of a snub!'

'Yet Canada,' Von Galen said, his eyes on the map, 'is by far the nearest point in North America to – '

'Ah,' O'Hara said. 'Got you interested!'

'An observation,' Von Galen said.

'Why don't we leave it there?' O'Hara rose. 'I've told you some of it. Let it lie in your mind, see if it doesn't grow on you. You're a highly intelligent man. Bet you'll think of considerations I haven't.'

'I doubt if I'll think about it at all. It's just a mirage.'

'A mirage,' O'Hara said, 'can come in two classes. This is a superior mirage. That's something normally invisible below the horizon that comes into view because of prevailing conditions.'

* * *

Meeting Dot, Miller said, 'I was wrong about Palm Springs.' Her face fell. 'We're going to Flagstaff instead.' He grinned and held the tickets up for her to see. 'Tonight we're at the Hollywood Roosevelt Hotel. Home of the Stars! Maybe you'll see Cary Grant. Then tomorrow first thing we're on the train.'

She was hugging him when the porter came alongside with the barrow. He counted. Seven suitcases and a packing case. 'Which of these goes with us?'

'These two. The rest get sent ahead. Oh boy, Ernie, was I in a *rush*.'

He kissed her. 'Nobody else could do it, kid. Here's your ten bucks.'

He had tickets already and there were no problems about the forwarding. They left five cases and the packing case at the station and took a cab to the hotel.

Next morning at seven they were on their way, in Arizona by evening, and Miller was breathing more easily. After almost a month of feeling like a rabbit with its foot in a snare, he felt a free man again. Their rail tickets ran clear through to Kingston, via Kansas City, Chicago and Toronto; but they stayed in the warm for three days, then did the travelling in a long, two-and-a-half-day burst.

When they arrived, Ross was waiting. He'd flown Canso Ring One up from Long Beach the previous day, and been busy checking arrangements. Now he picked Dot up, swung her round and said, 'Did you ever think about a nice little white house with a picket fence?'

'Did I!'

He put her down and held out a bunch of keys. 'You've got it. Not precisely prime waterfront property, but you can see the lake.'

He had a blue Royal Canadian Air Force car outside complete with driver. Twenty minutes later, Dot was moving purposefully from room to room.

'That's a great girl,' Ross said. 'She really is.'

'Absolutely right,' Miller agreed. Ross had been best man at their wedding, and Ross's then wife had been Dot's attendant. 'Matter of good judgement.'

Ross pulled a rueful face. 'Most expensive mistake I made in my life.' He'd married a leggy California blonde nine years earlier; she'd taken him for every cent he had and was still doing so. 'I should have met Dot first.'

Miller said smugly, 'She'd still have married me.'

'I heard that.' Dot put her head round the door. 'And I'm not as sure as you are. You never gave me a house like this. You should see the kitchen. Anybody want coffee?'

They began work, not without misgivings, on April 1st. A series of metal buoys had been sunk in Lake Ontario, of different sizes and moored at varying depths. Initially they were trying simply to locate them with the equipment. The sets worked: that was already known. A ship on the surface produced frantic blips and major variations as the Canso flew over. But any Mark One Eyeball could spot a ship on the surface too. By fine-tuning the design and operation, they were seeking to increase the depth at which a sub might be found, and to widen the track a search plane could cover in a single pass.

They were embarked on weeks of flying. Miller and Ross and their crews flew endless hours, working out optimum heights and improving search patterns. They were long, dull, professional days, and improvement was slow – far slower than any of them had hoped.

Dot saw the lines of weariness deepen around Ernie's eyes, and kept waiting for him to make one of his breaks; but he didn't. Either he was getting more than enough flying already, or there simply wasn't a stressed aerobatic plane in the vicinity. He remained unusually steady-humoured: no bouts of sudden enthusiasm, no sinkings into mild depression.

Miller was, in fact, enjoying himself in a job that might have been made for him. His idea of happiness was to fly all night after he'd flown all day, then eat one of Dot's lovingly prepared meals, chat with her for an hour or two while she knitted or sewed, then sleep, preparatory to flying some more. Hours of concentration came more easily now, in his forties: the house was a haven, the two Cansos were splendid airplanes beautifully maintained.

By far the best thing of all – he'd escaped! From the moment of arrival he'd been wary as a cat, praying that the quick exit from the San Francisco apartment had shaken Von Galen loose, but scarcely willing to believe it. Now days were lengthening into weeks without the smallest indication that the German knew where he was. Damn it, how *could* he? They were in Canada now! Not only that: money was going steadily into the bank. At the end of the six months, when this contract was up, he'd have enough, with a bit of luck, to go south into Mexico, and if necessary further south still: way out of the German's range; soon he'd be almost immune from threat.

Yet there were occasions now when, paradoxically, he would find himself thinking as a German. The reason, he recognized, was his son. Every time he read in the newspapers about the air war over Europe, he found Heinz in his mind: the son he'd never seen, about whom he'd heard nothing more. For the first time, in moving to Kingston, he had failed to send an address to Gretel, and Heinz could even have been killed without his knowing. He ached to send that address, but dared not. If Gretel had it, Von Galen would be able to get it. In his mind there was a picture of the man, furious at Miller's disappearance, determined to find him again, and to put him to work: a spider who'd seen a fly escape and now waited for some faint quiver in its web to say, 'He's here. *Here!*'

FOUR

In truth, Miller could scarcely have been further from Von Galen's thoughts. To Von Galen's vast annoyance, O'Hara's idea had taken root in his head and now wouldn't go away. Twice he found himself daydreaming: seeing again a big white yacht exploding on a blue sea. Then the damned fantasy entered his dreams, and he began to waken with his mind full of destruction and glory. He told himself repeatedly that O'Hara was wildly impractical, that the whole thing was an intellectual fraud. How could any such meeting be predicted? And if, by some miracle, an accurate prediction were made, what could be *done*?

Yet it stayed with him. To annoy him further, a word entered his consciousness, a stupid word he could do without. *Destiny*. The Führer believed in destiny. Well, *he* didn't. And yet – the accident that had cut out his flying; the posting to America; the meeting with O'Hara; the implanting of this ridiculous notion: what was all that?

Not destiny. Just a chain of circumstances.

Yet almost hourly he found himself looking speculatively at maps. There were plenty to see: in his office, in Wiedemann's, in the commercial department, the culture office – maps were on every damned wall.

Was he going mad? Why was this thing inescapable? O'Hara didn't even get in touch with him, but his presence seemed everywhere: and his confidence that somewhere Franklin Roosevelt was going to be in the same place with Winston Churchill; and that the opportunity would then occur to destroy them both, to blast to pieces the two men who stood most staunchly in Germany's way!

88

Paranoia, Von Galen told himself. No one man could achieve it.

More to try to exorcize the troublesome notion than to forward it, he began to read, and to study; to draw up a list of possible meeting places so long it would demonstrate the fatuity of the entire concept.

Soon he had a list of more than seventy, a list he proposed to send to O'Hara: with a note attached which said thank you and goodbye.

But, reading, he came across mention of the bases. In a summary of the terms of the Lend-Lease Act, reference was made to a deal the previous year in which America had handed over fifty ageing destroyers to the British in exchange for the right to lease naval and air bases in eight territories: British Guiana, Bermuda, Newfoundland, the Bahamas, Jamaica, St Lucia, Trinidad and Antigua.

Protocol, he thought. O'Hara's damned protocol. Yet those bases *would* technically be American territory on British soil: and of the eight, seven were in the warm climate O'Hara swore would be chosen. O'Hara had also specifically excluded several of them because populations were too big or for some other reason. He sat for several minutes staring at the list, realizing angrily that he was getting in deeper rather than escaping.

He thought of Bohle. To forward all this nonsense formally to Berlin, or even give it to Wiedemann, would be insane. But there might be another way to get rid of it: a letter to his uncle. 'I have met a young Irish-American with a curious idea which might amuse you, particularly since you've met Churchill.' Yes, that was one way. Bohle *had* met him, three or four years earlier, in London. 'Would you imagine from your knowledge of him, that Churchill would act so predictably?' And then set out the whole plan. Certainly no advocacy, but set it out. Let Bohle trample on it. If he knew his uncle, a tart note would come back telling him not to waste his time. But he would have passed the whole stupid business onward and upward, would himself cease to be involved. Yes, he'd do that.

'What the devil have you been doing?' Consul Wiedemann demanded when he called Von Galen into his office several days later. 'For you,' he said, handing him a long signal. 'And it is marked Most Secret – Addressee to Decipher.'

Thoroughly puzzled, Von Galen took the day's cipher sheets into his office and set to work. Soon he was trying to adjust to the knowledge that Bohle had taken him seriously. Bohle had called some kind of gathering of experts and put the possibility to them; he'd found people who knew both Churchill and Roosevelt, asked naval and air specialists; he'd gone deeply into the whole crazy thing!

I must tell you [the signal read], that there was general agreement such a meeting is very likely. Furthermore, there are circumstances which suggest it might happen soon. I congratulate you on your perspicacity in recognizing the possibilities in a piece of thinking which at first seems so unpromising.

Then came the orders.

There must be no delay in following-up. Travel forthwith to the Embassy in Washington. Instructions already sent to provide any assistance you need.

Had Bohle taken leave of his senses? And *what* were those mysterious circumstances which suggested Churchill might meet Roosevelt soon?

Von Galen worked on. The last paragraph, deciphered, read:

Kriegsmarine will not act without very strong probability of target. Every effort must be made to determine place, and date, *at whatever risk*.

90

Von Galen read those final words and swallowed.

The impression given to Von Galen that Berlin throbbed with excitement and urgency about the O'Hara idea was, in fact, a long way from being accurate. Ernst Wilhelm Bohle, his uncle, stood firmly in the second rank of Party and government, was keenly aware of it, somewhat resentful, and determinedly ambitious. As a man who rated intelligence highly, and especially his own, the wide preference given to nincompoops offended him. His own master, Ribbentrop, was a prize example, equipped with a rich wife, indolence to match his arrogance, and little to be said for him save a gift for presenting the work of others as his own. That – and the Führer's favour.

Such favour did not fall upon Bohle. He knew he was seen merely as a valuable functionary: an able man, but not one of the Party élite. In June the previous year he'd had high hopes: Britain was to be conquered and he was almost certain to be its ruler. Britain being the country of his birth, that prospect had had particular sweetness, and when Hitler called off the invasion, the disappointment was accordingly greater. Instead of being master of a country, he sat at his desk in the Foreign Ministry, hoping the future held something better than the past. The present was, for him, a hiatus.

So Von Galen's letter provided more than a moment's interest. At the time of Roosevelt's fishing trip, Bohle too had thought it might be a cover for something else. He had said so but Ribbentrop had pooh-poohed the idea and it had withered on the vine.

Now, he reflected, it was perhaps worth cultivation. Bohle knew a great deal about Winston Churchill, had met and talked with him, and was certain that Churchill would love nothing better than to play political chess with a man of Roosevelt's quality. Churchill saw himself as a figure in history, a manipulator of great events, and would see a journey across the hostile Atlantic as high adventure.

Also – one day they *would* meet; they were bound to; and nothing was more likely to trigger such a meeting than the now-imminent attack upon Russia. When that took place Churchill and Roosevelt, both implacably hostile to the Soviets, would have a great deal to talk about. And he, Bohle, if he postulated a meeting and forecast where it would happen, could collect kudos when, inevitably, it did.

His actions, therefore, accorded more with a bureaucrat's determination to advance his career than with a military opportunist's to attack. Bohle, in fact, was merely assembling a file. Already it contained Von Galen's letter and the minutes of a conference he had convened at his house in Wannsee to discuss it. Now a further piece of evidence lay on his desk: a letter from one of the participants in the Wannsee meeting, a psychologist from Berlin University.

The letter made two points:

There is a significant coincidence in the careers of Churchill and Roosevelt. Twice Churchill has been First Lord of the Admiralty – in charge of the Royal Navy. Though his own service was as a soldier, he appears to have a deep sentimental interest in naval affairs, evidenced by the clothing he often wears. The same seems true of Roosevelt. He held the post of Assistant Secretary of the Navy from 1913 onwards and in 1918 had already resigned to become a serving officer, but the Armistice then came. He is credited, within those years, with having transformed the American navy. *This was his first political success*. It is probable that he, too, therefore has sentimental feelings about the navy.

This, I suggest, may have the effect of biasing both men towards travel by sea rather than by air, and towards a meeting at sea, or at least aboard ship.

As it would, Bohle thought. Here was his opportunity to involve the *Kriegsmarine*!

He made an appointment to visit U-Boat Command at Wilhelmshaven and talk to Admiral Dönitz.

Dönitz was polite, puzzled, manifestly busy. 'What can I do for the Minister?'

Bohle told him, compressing it. He handed over the typed brief, described the nebulous calculations, admitted the difficulties. He was simply seeking advice. Though much remained to be done, a classic and historic coup might be achieved.

'That's all you have, these few theories?'

'Yes, at this stage.'

'Well, I understand the attractions of a great coup, none better. We've had one or two ourselves. You'll remember Prien sank the battleship *Royal Oak* at anchor in Scapa Flow?'

'Precisely why I came to you. I'd like your attitude to what is, after all, only an idea.'

Dönitz looked at him coolly. 'It's not a matter of attitudes, but of resources. You must be clear about my position. I neither agree nor disagree with what you suggest. Do I want to kill Churchill? Of course I do. It would give me intense pleasure to blow him into a million pieces. But I am fighting a war in the Atlantic and I have not enough boats for it. You seem to be suggesting a permanent watch on half a dozen different places. That would be quite impossible.'

'What *would* you need to act?' Bohle asked.

'To act? More than you have or are likely to get. A date, a place, a target.'

'Admiral, it's not likely I will ever be able to offer a certainty. What degree of probability would you accept?'

Dönitz smiled. 'When *you* feel certain, tell me. I'll consider it then.'

Bohle rose. 'You'll tell me, will you, if anything occurs which might have a bearing?'

'Yes, of course.'

On his way back to Berlin, Bohle wrote out a minute of the conversation for his file. Next he involved another old sea dog. This particular admiral was no longer connected with the harsh practicalities of naval warfare: Admiral Canaris controlled the intelligence service, the *Abwehr*. Like everybody else of importance in Berlin, however, Canaris was busy. Lights burned late these days as the final details of the invasion of Russia were decided. Bohle himself was working on the final draft of the treaty of friendship with Turkey, designed to safeguard the *Wehrmacht's* southern flank when the *blitzkrieg* began. An appointment proved difficult to arrange.

Bohle, however, finally contrived to chat with Canaris at the close of a long session in the Wilhelmstrasse. He suggested a revivifying glass of champagne in his office. Canaris liked champagne, and sipped appreciatively as Bohle began to outline the scheme, then said, 'It's a pretty bubble, you know. Chase it and it will burst.'

'Are you sure?'

'Oh, it all seems believable now, but it isn't. I agree they may meet, but if they do the secrecy and the protective cordon will be impenetrable, wherever they may happen to be.'

Bohle said, 'Both have long-standing naval associations. As you have. Don't you think they'd meet at sea, for instance, and that it's worth some effort?'

'Oh, it's beguiling enough.' Canaris smiled, toying with the glass. 'I can play happily with these things all day. You could, for instance, work backwards. Think of the propaganda value afterwards – to *them*, I mean – the vast barrage of publicity, especially if they met at sea. Churchill the bulldog under the guns, Roosevelt the cripple in a bosun's chair. If they're together on a Sunday, a religious service on deck and those two old hypocrites singing naval hymns. You couldn't match *that* on land. *Ergo:* they will meet at sea. The whole thing sounds delightful. But at the risk of spoiling the game, here's the other side. Suppose you did succeed in finding out in advance? Suppose the *Kriegsmarine* were to attack – and fail? What have you *then*, Herr Bohle? Leaving aside such losses as we sustained, and they'd be heavy, you'd have made Roosevelt and Churchill yet bigger heroes and turned American public opinion against us even more strongly. And it's bad enough now.'

'All the same,' Bohle said, 'the possibility may exist. I simply feel it would be wrong not to take the matter as far as I can. If a prediction *can* be made . . .'

Canaris nodded. 'I take the point. No harm in a prediction.'

'Will you help?'

'How can I?'

'I assume you have people in Britain. Anything you hear of Churchill's movements may be indicative. Will you let me know?'

Canaris put down his glass. 'Anything *I* hear is invariably in the past tense. But yes, if I do, I'll tell you. Meantime, take an old man's advice – don't spend too much time on it.'

When he'd gone, Bohle added a further minute to his file. All reactions negative, he thought pleasurably; and only *he* took the positive line. When the time came, there would be advantage in that.

Von Galen was emptying his desk, preparing to move to Washington, when Karen Hanzer came in with his cup of coffee. Glancing up absently to thank her, he saw she was also carrying an opened brown-paper parcel. 'What's that?'

She was smiling – no, smirking. 'An item of clothing for a baby,' she said. 'It's called a matinée jacket. It's hand-knitted.'

'Really.'

'You may be interested to know where it came from, Herr Von Galen.'

'Where?'

She told him it had been knitted by Zoll's wife, in Canada. He was not much impressed. Fraülein Hanzer decided she was quite glad he was going. He had his attractions, the aristocratic 'von' strong among them, but he was too indolent, had very little imagination, and apparently no dedication at all.

An hour later Von Galen left the German Consul-General's office in San Francisco for the last time and was driven to the airport. O'Hara would be on his way, now. It must be very pleasant, he thought, to have O'Hara's advantages. When, the night before, he'd told him of the reaction from Berlin, O'Hara had been predictably enthusiastic, only too anxious to assist. If anything finally came of O'Hara's notion, Von Galen thought, the British customs man who'd searched O'Hara's rectum would have a lot to answer for.

He'd said, 'But what about your work here?'

'I'm the boss's son, remember. I do as I like!' O'Hara had simply called Western Union and dictated a wire to his office for morning delivery, saying that he was going away, perhaps for a few weeks. 'Now – what d'you want me to do?'

'The Bahamas,' Von Galen said. 'Roosevelt's been there once. Nobody'll think it odd if he goes there again. We need to try to find out – '

'How'd you like me to *go* there?'

'Well, certainly, if you can.'

'Sure I can,' O'Hara said.

'You'll have to be careful. But it's the atmosphere that may be interesting, if anything's being prepared.'

'Let me see, who do I know there? Yeah, I know some people.' O'Hara laughed with sudden pleasure. 'Baldur, we're going to get those bastards – I feel it in my bones!'

* * *

The evening was beautifully balmy; in the fine garden, moonlit now, palm trees swayed only gently in a breath of sea-scented air. The two men, having dined, had taken their cognac into the spacious library. Joseph O'Hara, seeking his tidbits of information, had come to a prime source: Sir Harry Oakes was, perhaps, the most influential of all Bahamian citizens. He was a financier, a philanthropist, and had recently been host to the ex-King, now Duke of Windsor and Governor of the islands. Indeed, this very house had for a time been the home of the Duke and Duchess, while Government House was being expensively adapted to Her Grace's relentlessly exacting standards. And, the world of finance being what it is, Sir Harry knew O'Hara's father, his trust company, and its interests.

Joseph O'Hara, as he usually did on such occasions, presented himself as impressionable, content to listen to the views of those older and wiser. His private conviction was that it was here, in these islands, that Churchill and Roosevelt would find it most convenient, and most comfortable, to hold their inevitable meeting. The ex-King had standing enough to greet a President, but could not expect to participate in discussions between Roosevelt and the Prime Minister.

With the usual inquiries about health out of the way, O'Hara asked with careful naïveté if the royal couple had really lived right here, in *this* house? He was disconcerted by the reply.

'You mean, this hovel,' Sir Harry said.

'I'm sorry – ' O'Hara looked round him at the impressively luxurious room. 'I don't quite understand.'

Sir Harry laughed. 'That's what the lady said. Not to my face, naturally, but those were the words. Oh yes, she said it was remote and provincial, too.' It was clear, despite the laugh, that the words had stung.

'But that's crazy! I mean – '

'I know what you mean. Cigar?' Sir Harry Oakes

unfastened his white dinner-jacket and pushed a silver box across the occasional table to his guest.

'No, thanks. But I just can't imagine how anybody could say that.'

'She isn't just anybody, my boy. She thinks that by rights she's a queen-empress, and the superlative in everything is only just good enough.'

Sir Harry Oakes, it seemed, was in a mood for indiscretion. So much the better. O'Hara said. 'What's *he* like?'

'The Duke? Under the thumb, as we used to say. She frowns and he shrinks. Put it another way: he's besotted. Like an adolescent with his first pretty girl.'

'But a good governor, I expect?'

'Well – ' Oakes paused, lighting the cigar carefully – 'he's certainly trying. Some would say – ' he gave a wicked little grin – 'that he's *very* trying. No, to be fair, he does a lot of good work. But this is a small place, Joe, and things get noticed. He's got pretty decided views about the blacks, you know, inferior race and all that, and he doesn't seem to care who knows. Not very wise, not in these islands.'

O'Hara probed on, astonished that a man like Oakes should be so ready to gossip, and he learned a great deal. It was much resented in the islands that the Duchess visited Miami every week to have her hair styled; that she bought at least two new dresses every week, at a reputed $250.00 each, and had them sent specially from New York.

But it was when O'Hara introduced the name of Churchill into the conversation that the real jewel came. 'Winston's out of patience with the pair of them,' Oakes said.

'Why? I thought he'd supported him very strongly.'

'So he did. But he thinks the Duke should be back in England, lending support, not skulking like some of us in a tropic paradise. But the Duke won't go. Can you guess why?'

'No.'

'Because they won't agree to make his wife a royal duchess. So nobody would have to curtsey to her. What do you think of that?'

'Is it really true?'

'Well, it's what the Duke told me. He says he hardly hears from Winston now, and when he does the letter's short and ratty. I suppose the truth is that he's an embarrassment nowadays.'

Travelling north, two days later, O'Hara brooded over the conversation and particularly over the final phrase. *An embarrassment nowadays*. Would that make a difference? Did it really matter? There were two ways of looking at that fact, if fact it was. Would Churchill regard an imperious wife who demanded curtseys as a serious impediment to a meeting in the Bahamas? It was, after all, a trifling matter. On the other hand, there was nothing trifling about demonstrating a support Churchill no longer felt; nor would Churchill, burdened as he was, be looking either for further embarrassment or additional burdens.

On balance, he decided, Churchill would be likely to avoid all of it: after all, Churchill had a choice – so why seek out difficulties? But O'Hara was deeply aware that it was an uncertain conclusion.

He was still fretting when, with the train halted at Raleigh, North Carolina, he stepped off to stretch his legs and buy fresh reading matter. It was while he was reading a story in *Time* magazine about, of all things, fish, that his feelings about the Bahamas as a rendezvous at last crystallized. He was suddenly sure that the uncertainties of the Bahamas could be forgotten. The article about the troubles certain fishermen were experiencing seemed suddenly to be a bright signpost, pointing directly. It was in those fishermen's waters that the whales would appear. There the whale hunt must take place.

To Baldur von Galen, the whole thing remained a fairy tale; but he accepted that Berlin must know a great deal more than he, and Berlin had issued orders. With that silly and uncomfortable word 'destiny' rooted in his brain, he was still unable to decide whether he was a man with a mission, or one chasing a very wild goose.

The first few days in Washington did nothing to help him. The more he stared at the list of possible meeting places, the more difficult it became to see any one of them as having advantage over the others. He checked each for harbours, out-islands, places of concealment. Some had them; some did not. If he favoured anywhere, it was the Bahamas, but that was a product of a vague instinctive feeling, no more.

And even that disappeared with O'Hara's return. Von Galen, warned several times that the Embassy was now under FBI surveillance, used it very little. He was living in a small hotel, unwatched as far as he could tell, and it was there that O'Hara called him. When they met, shortly afterwards, O'Hara was bursting with news. 'Churchill won't go near the Bahamas!' He explained why.

Von Galen listened, then said, 'I still don't think that you've ruled out the Bahamas. I wish you had.' He looked, and sounded, disappointed.

O'Hara grinned at him, enjoying his moment. 'On the other hand, I reckon I have the *real* answer. I know where it's going to be.'

'Where?'

The grin widened. 'The one place we didn't really think about seriously. It isn't warm and sunny. It isn't inviting. But I'll bet you a thousand bucks they'll be there inside a month or two.'

FIVE

Newfoundland.

Von Galen stared warily at the word. He'd gone into the Embassy Registry, written it on a pad and begun to answer the questions. Now, much against his will, he felt excitement growing in him, and surprise, too: that he was turning quickly from sceptic to believer and couldn't explain why. He reminded himself that he'd had a *feeling* about the Bahamas, and not long before *that*, he'd regarded the whole thing as the product of O'Hara's wild Irish imagination.

Question: was there an American base in Newfoundland? The United States undoubtedly had a treaty right to lease such a base, but had they actually done so?

When he found the answer, they had. Not one base, but *two*!

He made himself assess it calmly, tried to look at Newfoundland from both British and American viewpoints.

Now the list of advantages grew steadily. From St John's, Newfoundland, the first non-stop, trans-Atlantic air crossing had been made more than twenty years before – *because it was the nearest point to Europe in the whole of North America!*

Secondly, it had an American *air* base.

Thirdly, it had an American *naval* base. *And both were United States territory on British soil!*

Fourthly, in addition to being the closest point to Britain, Newfoundland was easy to reach from the Eastern seaboard of the United States.

Fifthly, it was a vast empty landscape of deep sheltered

bays and excellent harbours, where nobody except a few fishermen would see anything.

Sixthly, there would be no security problems. Newfoundland was at war, and wartime conditions and regulations must certainly prevail: censorship, out-of-bounds areas, troops and all the rest.

And *lastly*, Von Galen noted, lastly but most important of all, there was Newfoundland's freedom from the bedevilling toils of protocol. No Duke of Windsor, no Canadian Prime Minister, no complications at all.

Seven reasons *for*. But – what were the reasons against?

He laboured, playing devil's advocate to the limit of his capacity, and could find only the climate. Old men and warm sun? – would the climate really matter? In the winter, it might, but this was June. Reference books quickly told him that summer temperatures in Newfoundland were actually pleasant.

Sure, now, that he was close, he postponed sending Bohle his conclusions, deciding he would let it lie in his mind for a few more hours. But his mind refused to let it lie. Whatever it was that heated O'Hara's imagination was now warming his own. Every instinct, every rational process, seemed now to convince Von Galen that one day soon, somewhere in Newfoundland, the chance would come to destroy two men – by far his country's most dangerous enemies.

He took a sheet of paper and began to write his signal, setting out his points carefully, saving his trump card till the end:

Finally [he wrote], there is the political status of Newfoundland. In 1934, due to the collapse of the market for Newfoundland fish, the island ceased to be self-governing. It is now governed by a Commission appointed by the British Crown. It is therefore a colony: it is *British*, not Canadian territory.

When he'd finished and enciphered the signal, he went out to tell O'Hara. 'I have reported to my superiors,' he said, as they walked across the grass by the Washington Memorial.

'What do you think they'll do?'

'They'll want verification.'

For the first time since he'd known O'Hara, he saw disappointment, and thought to himself, I was right from the start: you *are* naïve!

'How *can* we verify, Baldur? I mean – '

'I doubt if we can, but we have to try.' It was clear to him now that O'Hara, for all that early bold talk about pulling a trigger, had really been interested in an intellectual problem, expecting somebody else to take it over eventually. Well, Von Galen thought grimly, that was not going to happen. He said, '*You* began with just an idea. Now we have something far stronger. Those two men are going to meet, and we know it's going to be in Newfoundland, probably on a ship. Very well. Somewhere up there something will exist. A clue, an indication. It may be small but it's vital, or Berlin will do *nothing*!'

'They must!'

'You,' Von Galen said, 'will have to go there to find the thing that's missing – one solid piece of evidence.'

'Me – to Newfoundland?'

It was odd, Von Galen thought, how control had changed hands. It was O'Hara's scheme no longer, but his. 'Tomorrow,' he said crisply. 'Time's slipping away.'

Next day he was glad he'd acted. Bohle's reply to his signal was in terms that worried him:

Look at it coldly [Bohle had written], and from the point of view of Admiral Dönitz who, I remind you, must be convinced. A young man, inexperienced in military or diplomatic matters, offers a theory about a spectacular opportunity. Asked what evidence he

103

has, he produces another theory: a theoretical meeting is to be held in Newfoundland for theoretical reasons.

You may have convinced yourself. You have more than half convinced me. But I am certain neither of us could convince the *Kriegsmarine*.

You must produce evidence and do so rapidly. If this meeting takes place – and it may be taking place *now* – the whole course of the war may be changed. Being right is useless if nothing is achieved.

So Bohle was now only half-convinced, was he? Von Galen's lip curled. A few months at the Consulate had taught him something about the official mind and he seemed to sniff cunning emanating from this paper. His mother had always said Bohle was a user of people. Perhaps, now, he was using *him*, in some kind of political ploy. But Bohle was right about one thing: it would be a spectacular act of war.

And one way or another he'd see that it did not finish up in some damned waste-basket in Berlin!

Dot, hearing Miller in the hallway, smiled to herself, put her knitting aside and went to finish the preparation of his supper.

'Had a good day?'

'Not bad. Any beer in the ice-box?'

'Help yourself. Making any progress?'

'It's slow – maybe a little. You know.'

He sat at the table eating. 'You had supper already?'

'An hour ago. I was hungry.' She picked up the knitting and he said, 'What is it?'

'This? A blanket.'

'Who this time?' She was always knitting for somebody: old ladies, young babies, the Red Cross.

She glanced at him. 'I didn't have to buy any wool, Ernie. It's just stuff I had. You see, it's kind of patchwork.' She held it up. 'Like it?'

'Yeah, it's nice. Any more coffee?' Money, Miller thought: he'd gone on too much about money and now Dot was worried about a buck for a ball of wool. He'd been laying it on too hard.

'Hey, Dot.'

'What?'

'We can afford a few balls of wool.'

'We can? That's a relief. How'd you like a great big warm sweater?'

The trip to Newfoundland was proving futile. Nothing was going to drop into his lap, and there was an air of oppressive secrecy which made casual inquiries impossible. Everybody seemed guarded about what they said. Joseph O'Hara stood alone at the bar of the Newfoundland Hotel, a glass of beer untouched in front of him. Aftr three days in St John's not only did he seem to be getting nowhere, he was also beginning to feel awkwardly conspicuous: an aimless American civilian all too obviously doing nothing in a place which bristled with the activity of war. He had made only two contacts. The first, a banker with whom O'Hara Trust Co. had very occasional dealings, was professionally welcoming, but barely troubled to hide his surprise at Joe O'Hara's presence. O'Hara had devised a thin cover: he was prospecting – after the war Newfoundland would become increasingly important in trans-Atlantic aviation, and O'Hara Trust Co. wanted to be in on the ground floor. The banker agreed, as he would, but looked puzzled and said little.

The second contact seemed to have even less potential. The previous evening in the hotel lobby, a noisy crowd of Navy ensigns heading for the exit had included Simmonds, an old schoolfellow from Choate, who'd paused briefly and said, 'It *is* Joe? Hey, let's have a drink tomorrow if you're here.'

O'Hara was waiting for Simmonds now. The bar was almost empty, making him feel even more conspicuous, and he stared into his beer glass, his foot on the brass rail, to avoid looking round and round the room.

'Hello, Joe!' Simmonds was beside him. 'What are you doing in this God-forsaken spot?' O'Hara made himself smile, told his story as convincingly as he could and prepared himself stoically for an hour of 'whatever-happened-to-so-and-so?' Simmonds had never been a particular friend anyway, and –

'Join you fellas?' Another officer stood beside them.

'Recognize him?' Simmonds asked, smiling.

'Hey, now. No games. Just introduce us,' the officer said.

O'Hara thought he *did* recognize him. 'Just a minute . . .'

'Let's just stop this, huh?' The young man held out his hand. 'I'm John. I don't use the other half in public.'

'Joe O'Hara. From Boston.' Hell, yes. He knew *now*! Somehow he controlled his astonishment.

'What are you doing here, Mr O'Hara?'

'In theory, a little business. In practice, very little. You?'

'As you see, serving Uncle Sam.' The young officer laughed. 'The rest is dark and devious and you're not allowed to ask.'

'Am I allowed to ask if you'll have a beer?' Heart thudding, O'Hara waved for the barman. As he waited to be served, he could see the young officer's reflection in the mirror behind the bar. It would wipe the smug smile off your damned face, he thought savagely, if you knew what I'm planning for that debased crook of a father of yours.

After the beer arrived, they talked for only a minute or two before a group came in and the officer excused himself to join them. He was serving, Simmonds said, in a US destroyer on escort duty in the North Atlantic. 'This place is going to turn from a British colony to an American one,' Simmonds went on. 'You're here – that's

106

American business. And two of *them* – that's American politics. Jeepers, but the writing's on the wall for the Newfies!'

'Two?' O'Hara said. 'You don't mean – '

'Hell, no. John's brother. He's up at the airfield at Gander.'

As soon as he could, O'Hara went to the hotel's reception desk. When, he demanded urgently, did the next ferryboat sail?

The diplomatic courier, newly arrived from Berlin via occupied France, Madrid and Lisbon, carried a letter from Bohle for Von Galen. 'We are becoming suspicious that the Americans are monitoring diplomatic traffic,' Bohle wrote. 'I therefore feel it safer to send this by hand of courier.' Included was a résumé of the Wannsee meeting, a report of his conversations with Dönitz and Canaris, and almost nothing by way of encouragement. He ended by saying, yet again, 'The *Kriegsmarine* is helpless without precise details. Do all you can to furnish them.' Von Galen slapped it down bad-temperedly on his desk. Damn the *Kriegsmarine!* Damn Bohle, too, who pretended to take him seriously and didn't.

Then came the call. It was late in the long, frustrating day and O'Hara sounded excited. 'Can you meet me?'

'Usual place. Six-thirty.'

He muttered sourly to himself, as he hung up, that it was a pity some of O'Hara's enthusiasm couldn't be transferred to Uncle Willi and U-Boat Command; then he made his way to the Drake Hotel.

O'Hara could barely contain himself. 'Have I got something for you!'

Von Galen waited.

'It clinches the whole deal,' O'Hara said. 'Guess who I met up there?'

Von Galen said irritably, 'We're not playing games.'

'Sorry. Well, he's a naval officer, and his name . . .'

107

Von Galen at once returned to the Embassy. Nobody could ignore *this*: not Bohle, not Dönitz. O'Hara said it was the clincher and so it ought to be.

The signal on Bohle's desk early next morning set his bureaucratic heart beating just a little faster. He stared at it, calculating briefly, then reached for the phone. 'I wish to speak to Admiral Dönitz,' he told his secretary. 'He's probably at Wilhelmshaven. If he isn't, find him.'

She found Dönitz at home and at a very bad moment. Dönitz had been up most of the night, listening for responses to the late evening transmission to all U-Boats. Bayer in U-179, one of his young lions, had again failed to respond and it was now nine days. The first asterisk, which meant 'missing', already hung beside U-179's number on the operations board, and Dönitz had himself placed the second beside it: the asterisk that meant 'lost'. This year, he'd lost too many U-Boats, and every loss was painful. But some hurt more than others: Prien and Kretschmer in March, and now Bayer.

'Yes?' he said grimly.

'Scrambler phone, please, Admiral,' Bohle said.

Dönitz pushed the button. 'What is it?'

'You'll remember our conversation?'

'Too well. Minister, is it more of the same? Because –'

Bohle broke in. 'We have further indications.'

'About?'

'Newfoundland.'

Newfoundland, Dönitz thought wearily. Bayer had been patrolling off the Grand Banks, hunting a convoy newly out of Halifax. He said, 'Go on.'

Bohle said, 'I now know that two of Roosevelt's sons are stationed with the American forces in Newfoundland!'

'Herr Bohle, have you got a time and a place?'

'Not yet. But –'

'These sons of Roosevelt. You say there are two?'

'Correct.'

'How many sons *has* Roosevelt? I seem to remember he has four.'

'Yes, he has.'

'Where,' Dönitz said, 'are the *other* two?'

Bohle hung up and wrote his careful minute.

The starboard engine of Canso Ring One had given trouble on and off for more than a week, running inexplicably rough and retarded. Now, with the replacement fitted, she was ready for testing. It was early on a bright Sunday morning when Ross signed the amphibian out and they took her up from Kingston to swing out over the lake, Miller acting as co-pilot and flight engineer. They were at five hundred feet several miles short of Galloo Island when Ross spotted a sailboat brightly ablaze on water below. He brought the Canso round to circle the boat.

'What d'you make of it?'

'Two people in the water,' Miller said.

'Lifejackets?' Ross looked out. 'Bet it was bottle gas in the bilges,' he diagnosed, 'and some idiot dropped a match.'

'No lifejackets.'

'Sunday people,' Ross said. 'They're all the same. Sailors, pilots. If they're out Sunday look for trouble.'

'I don't see any other boats, Alec.'

Ross looked down. 'Hell!' he said. The boat was burning fiercely, the two swimmers detached from it. 'We'll have to pick 'em up. Thank God for smooth water!' He swung away, turned the Canso into what wind there was and began to let down. 'Let's hope the damn hull's still watertight.'

He kissed the flying-boat down, dropped her off the step, and taxied towards the swimmers. Miller had moved to the hatch, and was clipping the ladder in place and readying the lifebelts, waiting for Ross to turn and bring the sailboat into view. When he saw the swimmers they were clearly in distress, mouths wide and arms flying. He wriggled down the crawl-space back to the flight deck and yelled, 'They're bad, Alec. I'll have to go in.' He took off his flying jacket and boots.

Ross nodded, cut the engines, left his seat and followed Miller back through the fuselage tunnel.

Getting the swimmers aboard wasn't too hard, but Miller came back soaked and had no spare clothes. The two in the water had badly burned hands and arms, and were exhausted.

'Hospital,' Ross said.

Miller nodded. 'Where – Kingston?'

'Toronto'd be better. Hour and twenty maybe. Ambulance can meet us if we radio ahead.'

Miller applied acriflavine and gauze to the burns, talking soothingly but deeply resentful. 'God, we'd have drowned!' one of the swimmers said. He was in his sixties, grey-haired and wearing ruined but expensive leisure clothes. 'We're in your debt, mister.'

'All in the day's work,' Miller said, wondering how much the burning sailboat was worth, not to mention the man's life. He thought: *How would it be if I sent you a little bill? What's your life worth? How about enough to get me to Mexico and keep me for a couple of years? How about my life – Ernie Miller, spy?*

Instead, he said, 'We'll go straight to Toronto. You'll be in good hands soon.'

Ross already had the right engine running as Miller slid dripping into the co-pilot's seat. His hand worked the starter for the left, and he swore.

Miller didn't need to ask; he knew that sound. 'How many hours on the engine and the goddam starter's unserviceable!'

Ross tried again. Nothing. The starter motor was dead. For a moment they sat numbly: what a hell of a mess! They couldn't be sure of lifting off water on one, not this heavy; get her up and she'd *fly* on one, but –

Miller said, 'Radio, Alec. Get some help here.'

'It means bringing the other Canso in and there's service work being done. Then they have to round up the engine fitters.'

'No other way, Alec.' Miller's hand was on the radio.

'Wait a minute!'

'Alec, we have to. Those burns –'

'Just give me a minute.' Ross was looking up, his gaze moving from the spinning blur of the right propeller to the stationary blades of the left. 'It'll take an hour at least to get a plane in,' he said. 'That's if the Canso's available. If they have to track a float plane down – Ernie, do me a favour. Don't talk for a minute.'

'You're the boss.' Miller gave him the minute, timing it. At the end, he said, 'So now we radio.'

'Hold it.' Ross's eyes moved from gauge to gauge. 'Listen, Ernie – it's just the starter.'

'So?'

'We crank it.'

'You think you're King Kong? You couldn't hand-crank that thing if you were ten men.'

Ross said, 'We crank it with the other engine.'

'Huh?'

'Look up there, Ernie. There's nothing between the engines. They're up high. Get the tow hawser, quick!'

Baffled but obedient, Miller scrambled from his seat as Ross cut the running engine. The towline was three-inch-circumference hemp, in a coil back near the tail. Going for it, he passed the burned swimmers.

'Why's the engine stopped?'

'Little trouble,' Miller said. 'You just relax.'

'Can you fix it?'

'We're trying.'

Ross came fast through the crawl-space.

'Got that line?'

'Here.'

Ross unfastened the hatch clasps, swung up the cover,

111

then climbed acrobatically out on to the top of the fuselage. Reaching down, he said, 'Hand it up to me, then come on up.'

Miller followed, struggling a little, the wrong shape for gymnastics. As he stood on the fuselage, Ross was scrambling up on to the wing.

'What in hell *are* you doing, Alec?'

Ross pointed. 'Nothing but air between the two propeller bosses, right?'

'Well, yeah.'

'So we run the line round them like a drive-belt. Tie it tight as we can . . .' He began uncoiling the rope.

'Start one with the other?' Miller said disbelievingly.

'Why not?'

Miller shrugged. 'No reason, I guess. It's just – '

'Not in the manual, I know. Stop arguing, Ernie. Let's just see if it works. Over here, now.'

Miller found himself standing gingerly on the hot cowling of the left engine, heat scalding through the soles of his wet flying boots. He reached past the propeller blades to loop the rope round the prop boss.

'Okay?' Ross called across.

'It's in position, for what that's worth.'

'Keep it there.' Ross was struggling with the two ends of the heavy rope, trying to find some way to tie them tightly; the rope's own weight caused a sag. He looked across at Miller. 'How do I keep it tight without a finger on the knot?'

'You need King Kong's finger.'

'It'd work if we – '

'Wait,' Miller said. He swung down into the Canso's belly, grabbed his wet leather flying jacket, climbed back up, and called to Ross, 'We tie the rope tight as we can, then pack the space. Okay?'

'We can try.'

'Feed it in and drag it round,' Miller said. 'Simple friction ought to do it.' He folded the jacket, leather side

112

out, and found the friction too great: the wet leather clung too hard to the surface of the prop boss. Turned, with the lining against the machined-smooth metal, and Miller hauling the rope, the packing was gradually and painfully worked in. Miller, biting momentarily at a broken fingernail, said sourly, 'Float plane could have been on its way.'

'If they could raise one. This *ought* to work.'

'Maybe.' Miller stood up and looked at the still-sagging rope and the flapping arms of the trapped jacket. 'And if it does,' he said, 'things are going to fly in all directions. Ropes, jackets, goddam engines for all I know. How will you rig it?'

'I've been thinking about that. Let's get back inside.' Ross had almost forgotten about his passengers. Now as he climbed down through the hatch, the old man's pale sweaty face gaped up at him. He said, 'We'll soon know.'

A minute later, when they were side by side in the cockpit, Ross said, 'The way I see it is this: magnetos on –'

'Are we running a start-up check?'

'Talking,' Ross said. 'Listen a minute. Magnetos on. Fuel booster pump on. Mixture rich. Prop full fine. Okay so far?'

'Trotteau crack,' Miller said.

'Hell, yes. A quarter?'

'Okay.'

'Anything else?'

'Crossed fingers.'

Ross gave a tight grin. 'Okay, we'll crank the right engine. Cross 'em.'

They knew the first crank was likely to spin the jacket away; that after that the rope would almost certainly be too slack to sustain the drive.

Ross pressed the starter and both watched the blades of the left propeller anxiously. It moved slowly, once; faster, twice, then dissolved into the familiar spinning blur: suddenly both engines were roaring. Miller pointed up. 'Okay, genius – what do we do about the rope?'

'Let nature take its course. Or maybe you'd like to go back up and cut it.'

'Not me.'

'No,' Ross said. 'Too dangerous. If it breaks it'll cut you in half.'

'Maybe safer than flying like this, though.' Miller took the fire axe from its clip. 'Think this'll do it?'

'It should. The rope's not moving now. Good luck.'

'Yeah.'

Miller was half way through the crawl-space when he heard Ross's shout, turned and saw the arm waving him back.

'Okay,' Ross said, 'the blades sheared it. We can go.'

Miller went back and closed the hatch.

In the cockpit, as Ross brought the Canso round on two healthily roaring engines, Miller said, 'You ought to tell Consolidated about that little trick.'

Ross gave him a grin. 'Little bit of aviation history, you mean? What do we call it – the Ross-Miller rotating line start-up?'

They took the swimmers to Toronto, and by early afternoon had the starter motor repaired. But that wasn't the end of it. Ross got clearance to send a report to Consolidated Aircraft Corp. in Long Beach. With dozens of PBYs patrolling the world's oceans, and often landing on them, it might well save lives, and since no mention was made of the nature of Project Cull, security was hardly likely to be endangered. The report was simply about the aircraft.

It was received with interest, and its contents quickly circulated to Consolidated's customers. One copy reached the aviation correspondent of the *San Francisco Examiner,* who chased up additional and personal details from a friend at Consolidated for the sake of human interest, and wrote up the story of the two pilots who had performed a rescue with such old-fashioned American ingenuity.

On June 18th, 1941, Fritz Wiedemann, German Consul in San Francisco and Von Galen's erstwhile superior, came to Washington for one of his regular briefings at the Embassy. He was told nothing about the event that was to shake the world three days later; nor was any other member of the staff.

So, like Von Galen, he was astonished by the bombshell of the June 21st *blitzkrieg* attack on Russia. Unlike the younger man, however, he did not allow the news to make any difference either to his outlook or to his plans. Wiedemann intended to have a few days' vacation in New York, and to New York he went as soon as the briefing was completed.

Von Galen was more than astonished: he was both thunderstruck and deeply unhappy. Knowing the depressing *Kriegsmarine* response to the news about the two Roosevelt sons, his determination and his feeling of futility were at war. He was obsessed now, able to think of nothing else.

The new thought struck with, it seemed, the elemental force of the *blitz* itself, as he stared for the thousandth time at a map of the North Atlantic, his head awhirl with the knowledge of the fighting, of Churchill's prompt declaration that 'any enemy of Nazi Germany will be our ally'. Now Churchill and Roosevelt *must* come together, and when they did they must be killed. Both of them. The Washington newspapers rang with questions: what would the United States now *do*? Would Roosevelt supply Russia?

He would, Von Galen thought, and there would be more convoys, more reasons for the *Kriegsmarine* to say no! The one man who could blast President and Prime Minister into butcher-meat was too blind to see that this single attack could be the most vital of the whole war!

115

His eye ran over the map. Distance, he thought: distance was the curse. Newfoundland and Washington were too far from the scene of battle. If U-Boat Command were *here*, they'd see it, see how easy it could be. Or if not U-Boats, the *Luftwaffe*. In Europe –

He stopped and his eyes moved to the window, staring out unseeing as his mind raced. All along, he'd thought of *naval* attack. Newfoundland – anywhere this side of the Atlantic – was out of range of the *Luftwaffe*.

But it wasn't out of range, was it? *Not for an aircraft setting out from America!*

Air attack! The very last thing that would be expected. Launched from the least likely direction!

He closed his eyes and tried to tighten his mind, all too aware now of his tendency to daydream about the enormous impact of two men's deaths. Was it *possible*?

Questions flooded forward. Aircraft? Where could an aircraft come from? Bombs? Difficult, but perhaps . . .

He reached for the telephone. 'Where is Herr Wiedemann now?' In New York, he was told. 'Can Herr Wiedemann be reached?' Yes, he was at the Plaza. 'Give me the number!'

By the time Wiedemann returned two days later, Von Galen had been very busy indeed. Germany had friends, here in the United States, and he, Baldur von Galen, intended to harness them.

They were two days in which Von Galen had felt exalted. The knowledge throbbed in him that now, at last, he could fight again – and could even be the engineer of a triumph of German arms. He would damned well demonstrate to those idiot *Luftwaffe* doctors, to the blind, bureaucratic *Dummköpfe* who couldn't see a chance when it was thrust beneath their noses; he'd show them what youth and vision could achieve. If the proper strike force was not prepared to act, then others *must*! It was the old men who were at fault. But the Führer's young men knew how to fight – and to die if necessary!

He now knew exactly what he needed: three things, and the first already under way. He found an angry satisfaction in using Bohle's *Auslandsorganisazion* as the tool.

SIX

Contemptuous of bureaucracy as he was, Von Galen now became grateful for its detail and precision. There were tens of thousands of cards: the Washington bureau of the *Auslandsorganisazion* covered the entire Eastern seaboard, plus all territory as far west as Cincinnati, where the Chicago bureau's fiefdom began. Without effective cross-indexing the task would have been long and tedious; as it was, he was able to hunt through listings by profession, by location, even by age group.

Quickly he had several cards: within twenty minutes one which tempted him greatly:

METZHAGEN, RICHARD b. Nov 16, 1890.
Charleston, W. Virginia

Prof:	Mining Engineer
Address:	1694 Holyoake, Davis, W. Virginia
Member:	German-American Bund, Knights of the White Bamellia, American Nationalist Confederation
Telephone:	DAVIES 714897 Phone code clearance: Fly-fishing
Notes:	Third-generation American of pure German descent
	Specialist in blasting techniques underground
	Married Ushi Reitz (b. Kassel, 3 April 1899) 1921
	Metzhagen volunteered for Imperial Army 1914, rejected: medical grounds. Volunteered again 1939, rejected: age.

'I want to inquire about fly-fishing,' Von Galen said.

'So. I get my husband.' Metzhagen's wife still had a thick accent; somehow the fact was reassuring.

The receiver rattled and a man's voice said, 'Fly-fishing?'

'Can we meet and discuss it?'

Von Galen took a train from Union Station to meet Metzhagen half way, at a town called Winchester. The name, with its overtones of rifles, seemed a good omen.

Metzhagen was a smallish, quiet man in his early fifties, with a pipe in the corner of his mouth, and a studious air. He saw Von Galen's identifying copy of *Field and Stream* and nodded. Von Galen climbed into his elderly Buick.

'Do I get to know who you are?'

'Not yet. I simply want to ask you a question.'

'Fire away.'

Von Galen smiled. *Fire away* – he liked the image! He said, 'Would you be able to construct a bomb?'

'A bomb to do what?' There was no surprise. Metzhagen was driving calmly, eyes on the road.

'I can't tell you.'

'Not what I meant, son. I can build a bomb, but there's all kinds. What does it have to blow? Is it a pound of dynamite or a half-ton – concrete, steel, earth, what?'

'I was thinking of an aerial bomb.'

'Aerial huh?' Metzhagen drove along in silence, turning off at last into an empty picnic place in the woods outside the town. Then he said, 'It's not my field. You need aerodynamic casings and that means a design job, metal castings. That's factory work.'

Von Galen's optimism fell away a bit. 'I should have realized.'

'Hold it, son. Maybe I can figure out something.'

Metzhagen applied a match to his pipe. 'Aerial bomb has to drop accurately, so that would be the problem. What kind of height?'

'Difficult to say. Probably low.' Von Galen felt increasingly foolish. He was talking to an expert technician, a man who needed data, and he had none.

'You'd have to have some kind of bomb bay. Simple bomb sight, release mechanism,' Metzhagen was saying.

'Yes, I see that now. I'll have to consider it more carefully. Perhaps I could come back and see you again?'

'Any time.'

Von Galen looked at him and Metzhagen smiled. 'Son, you have something you want to do. I know where you're from because you know about the fishing. That's enough for me. Now – I'm real sorry to disappoint you – an aerial bomb just isn't my field. But explosives are. Think whether some kind of static charge won't do the job. I can do just about anything with explosives, *except* make an accurate aerodynamic casing.'

'Thank you. I will give it more thought.'

'There's something else,' Metzhagen said. 'I've been more than twenty-five years wanting to do something beyond talk. I thought today was the chance. So I'm disappointed too.'

'Thank you.'

Metzhagen took his pipe out of his mouth and said quietly, 'Heil Hitler.'

Von Galen blinked. The familiar words struck a strange note in this peaceful place.

'Heil Hitler,' he said. 'I'll call you again, as soon as I can.'

When he returned to Washington, Wiedemann was back. Von Galen suggested dinner. It had been a mistake to telephone the Consul in New York and he'd realized it, thank God, before the call went through, and cancelled. Wiedemann mustn't be alerted.

Their conversation was inevitably somewhat formal and Von Galen made it deliberately wide-ranging: the war, America's position, the state of public opinion, only towards the end, when a good deal of wine had been drunk, did he allow it to become more personal. He inquired about his car, and then, almost as an after-thought, 'By the way, what happened to that pilot – the one who wanted a letter sent to his son?'

'I have him.' Wiedemann chuckled and poured himself a second glass of old *Weinbrand*.

'He's working for you?'

'Not yet.' Wiedemann sniffed at the brandy. 'But he will.'

'I'm glad he'll be useful.'

Wiedemann chuckled again. 'He tried to run away.'

'What do you mean?'

'Oh, it was very elaborate. He made arrangements to disappear.'

'You found him?'

'I didn't need to look. The ground was prepared. Karen Hanzer kept in touch with his wife. A good girl, that. And then there was this.' Wiedemann took out his wallet and passed over a newspaper cutting. 'Read it.' He was much amused.

As Von Galen read, Wiedemann said, 'You see, it's all there. He's flying PBY flying-boats in Ontario. The American press is wonderful, you know. They tell us everything. Quite soon Herr Zoll will get an unpleasant surprise.'

'You mean he doesn't yet know . . .?'

'Read the cutting again, Von Galen. You'll see it actually mentions "a government project". I'll want to find out what the project is. No, he doesn't know.'

'But you,' Von Galen said, 'know precisely where *he* is.'

'I have his address.' Wiedemann sipped the *Weinbrand*. 'In Kingston.' He paused, frowning. 'Why so interested?'

'If you remember, I dealt with his letter.'

'So you did, so you did.'

When Wiedemann went off to bed, Von Galen made himself busy. He found the Bell Telephone System's information operator very helpful and remarkably quick. When he'd hung up, he visited the air attaché's office, which was locked. It didn't matter: a few minutes later, in the Registry, he found the necessary reference books. As Wiedemann had remarked, the press really *was* very helpful.

For German diplomatic representatives in Washington, after the invasion of Russia, life was proscribed even more and contact with other embassies limited. The Americans were cool and distant, the other English-speaking countries already enemies, the Communists likewise. The neutrals became more carefully neutral, but friends still remained, particularly among the South Americans, and it was to Argentina in the glossy person of Roberto Heines, a man whose name reflected his mixed descent, that Baldur von Galen appealed. Heines had a reputation as a Lothario, and it was on the basis of romance that Von Galen made his pitch. He was in love, he told Heines, with a Swedish girl who worked in Ottawa.

'But if the girl is Swedish,' Heines said at once, 'she is perfectly free as a neutral to come here.'

'Not as often as I'd like. It's expensive – and anyway I want to be able to see her more often.'

Heines grinned knowingly. 'My friend, Washington is *full* of women.'

'Not like this one.'

'You're mad, you know. If they catch you in Canada, you'll be shot as a spy.'

'I'm willing to take the chance. It's worth it. Anyway with an Argentine passport . . .'

Heines looked at him pityingly. 'All this for a *woman*?'

'For this one.' He felt, and was sure he looked, anything but a lovesick swain. 'She is able to come here only every three months. It's a long time.'

'And you propose to go back and forward to Canada, taking this stupid risk?'

'Yes.'

Heines examined his nails. 'It never fails to amaze me, my friend, this madness that strikes the heart. It doesn't strike mine. I hunt happily in a city teeming with game –'

'Will you do it?'

'I don't know. The reason is so – pathetic. Frankly, if you were engaged in some patriotic duty, I'd be far more inclined . . . Anyway, if you are caught, it will reflect badly on us.'

'I won't be caught. Please – *will* you?'

Heines smiled. 'Well . . . we're under instruction to be discreetly helpful to German interests in general. A Swede, you say. Is she blonde?'

'Long, blonde hair. Very beautiful,' Von Galen said. Her name is Ingrid.' He tried to look soulful, and wished savagely that Heines would say yes or no.

Heines looked at him, frowning. Then, 'All right. You'll get your passport for three months only.'

Von Galen tried to frown; inwardly he was exulting.

'After that you must hand it back and make other arrangements. Marry her, perhaps. But by then you'll find another fish.'

Von Galen thanked him.

'Shall I tell you why I'm doing this?' Heines said. 'It's not because you look like a man in love, Baldur. Don't ever try to earn a living on the the stage, or you'll starve. I think you have a mission.'

Von Galen blinked angrily.

'I thought so. Good luck.'

'There was a phone call,' Dot said when Ernie got home. 'Hung up when I answered. Ernie, could it be that burglar?'

123

The Kingston newspaper had recently carried stories about a thief who telephoned to check a house was empty before breaking in. He said, 'It'll just be a wrong number, Dot. We haven't a damn thing worth stealing!'

'I suppose.' She sounded doubtful.

'Don't worry about it. I'm home nights.'

Dot smiled at that. 'I know. That's what's nice about this job. Ham for supper, okay?'

'Done how?'

'Braised.'

'Better than okay.'

He was drinking coffee, smoking his second cigarette, when the phone rang again. 'Be Alec, honey. I'll get it.'

But it wasn't Alec. An unfamiliar and slightly accented voice said, 'It was interesting to hear of your exploit, Herr Zoll.'

His heart seemed to stop. Desperately he said, 'You have the wrong – '

'You will leave your house now, Herr Zoll. In half an hour you will meet me at the foot of Brock Street, at the waterfront.'

'Look – '

'Be there. Do not make me remind you of your position. Half an hour.'

Miller hung up. Glimpsing himself in the mirror by the phone, he barely recognized the haggard face as his own. His brain was racing madly. Was there time to run? Where to? Christ, his money was in the bank! Half an hour: less now. He couldn't run, not tonight. Tomorrow, maybe, he could withdraw the cash, take the car, try to drive clear through to Mexico. But what about Dot? Vainly he searched for answers and found none. Half an hour, the voice had said, and the threat had been clear: 'Do not make me remind you of your position.' Miller needed no reminding. He'd just have to go. Maybe he could make time enough to act – he'd have to try.

He half-opened the door. 'I have to go out for a while, honey.'

'Okay,' Dot said. 'Just so you're here when the burglar breaks in.'

Brock Street ran down to the lake shore. Miller parked at the top and walked down the short, steep hill. The town was quiet behind him, the landing deserted ahead. He stood looking at his watch: ten-twenty, and the beat of his heart faster than the tick of the watch. His eyes swept the seemingly empty hill, then moved to the water, as it lapped softly at the piers of the jetty, and with a sudden, grinding sense of hopelessness he saw himself jumping, sinking . . . there would be no problems down there on the bottom of the lake. The temptation was almost overwhelming.

Then a footstep. He swung round. A man in a raincoat and cap had appeared from some patch of shadow and was approaching, limping. 'There are better things than that,' the man said, halting seven or eight yards away, his back to a street lamp, his face in deep shadow. Miller felt black rage erupt suddenly inside him. His fists clenched. He knew who the man was, the limp gave him away. *Von* something, the supercilious little bastard in San Francisco who'd sent him the letter. He took a sudden step forward and then another. If he *killed* this guy . . .

'Don't be a fool,' the voice said, so contemptuously, so commandingly, that Miller hesitated, then stopped. 'Do you think I'm the only one who knows about you?'

No, Miller thought dully, he wouldn't be the only one. His name would be in files; there'd be plenty who knew. He said, 'Can't you leave me alone?'

'To work against us – why would we do that? Herr Zoll, there is work to be done. No, Herr *Miller*, isn't it? I must remember.'

'Please go away. Please *leave* me!'

'No. It is a simple answer. Face it – and come with me.

125

We will take a walk, and talk as we go.' He limped off up the hill, turning his head after a moment. 'Come.'

Miller glanced again, almost with longing, at the smooth water, and seemed to see Dot's face on its surface: if he ran, Dot would be left with barely a cent. He moved reluctantly up the hill, leadenly aware that this slope truly led down, not up: down into torment, down to a brick wall and the crack of rifle fire. Or the noose – this was Canada.

The man did not speak for a while. For Miller the silence was threatening, unbearable. He burst out, 'Look, Mr von – '

'Applejack. You will call me Applejack. It's a drink, I believe. Useful as a code name.'

'What the hell do you *want*?'

'Not what you imagine.'

Miller stopped. 'I don't understand.'

'This flying of yours, this "government project". I'm not interested in it.'

Miller was astonished. 'What, then?'

'A flight.'

'What kind?'

'Just one. A single flight.'

'Where to?'

'Not yet.'

Ernie Miller said, 'Where – *here*? This is Canada, and you're German.'

'So are you!' Applejack said. 'Bound by oaths to the Fatherland, both of us.'

Silence then, extending, and only their footfalls in the quiet night. Now Applejack said, 'One flight, a very important one, *and* for Germany. Your country demands it. You have a chance to atone for your disgrace.'

'What is this flight?'

'I told you: not yet. When the time comes, you will know.'

'And after that – I mean, what happens? I'll be in gaol, I'll be shot – *what*?'

Applejack seemed to hesitate for a moment. 'I will not trouble you afterwards.'

'You mean I'll be in the clear?'

'We wouldn't call on you again. You have my word. Now, Mr Miller, there are two things. The first is something you must do. You must rent a small storeroom here, best of all a garage with a strong lock.'

'You want to fly from here?'

'Secondly,' Applejack said, 'I myself am a pilot. I would require you to instruct me in the duties of a flight engineer on the aircraft you fly.'

'The Canso?'

'Yes, the Canso.'

'Hell, you can't use that – it's – !'

'You will instruct me. We will spend tomorrow – '

'I can't, not tomorrow!'

'You can be sick, make excuses.'

'No, there's a man coming. He's – he'd expect me there.'

Applejack halted and faced him. 'I could insist.'

'Don't. It would look bad.'

'Very well. Sunday.'

'May be bad, too.'

'Sunday,' Applejack said firmly. 'And this time I do insist. Now go.'

Miller went back to his car. He drove home badly, his mind whirling. A single flight in the Canso – carrying something, must be, otherwise why the need for a store? He couldn't possibly get away with that – take the Canso and the whole world blew apart!

But what was it Von – he couldn't remember the damn name! – what was it Applejack had said? Afterwards . . . *'We wouldn't call on you again.'* And he'd given his word, too – for what *that* was worth.

What if he took the car tomorrow and drove along through Toronto and over the border at Niagara Falls, then just kept heading south till he got to Mexico? Applejack would never find him. No, but he'd be stopped. The Saturday visit hadn't been a lie. Ed Martingale was coming in, and if Miller didn't show at the field the sequence was easy: they'd phone home, Dot would say he'd left in his car. They'd call the cops in case there'd been an accident, and when they found there'd been no accident, well, *then* a pilot on a secret project would be looked for pretty hard. He'd be stopped at the border, if not before – no doubt about it.

One flight, he thought. Then, abruptly, the hair on his neck prickled as comprehension came.

Well satisfied, Von Galen watched him drive away. He had no doubt that Miller was the right man or that Miller would do as he was told. Miller might wriggle, but there were too many holds upon him to allow him to run away again, including one threat Miller had probably not even imagined. Not, Von Galen thought with grim amusement, that he was in any position to carry out that particular threat, but that didn't matter: Miller would *believe* he could.

On his Argentine passport, Von Galen had crossed the border at Niagara Falls and travelled via Toronto to Kingston by rail. Now he caught the night train back to Toronto: he had a fancy to see the Falls, and a day to spare. Next day he stood for a while on the observation terrace on the Canadian side, watching the vast, endless, hurtling torrent of Niagara, then went downstream to visit the museum of barrels and photographs from the many attempts to challenge the water's power. As he looked at yellowing paper and rusting metal he reflected that challenges made with forethought and courage did sometimes succeed, and those who succeeded became heroes.

Later, when he had returned to Toronto and was looking for a restaurant in which to eat, he chanced to pass a store which sold central heating equipment. Von

Galen stopped, struck by an idea, saw that much of the equipment was American-made, and thought about it as he walked. Then he persuaded a newspaper-seller to change three dollar bills into nickels and dimes. If he was careful in his choice of words, he could now tell Metzhagen exactly what he needed, and Metzhagen could start work . . .

In the summer of 1941, apartments in Washington were hard to come by, but – then as ever – money talked. So, since money was one thing Joseph O'Hara did not lack, he had succeeded without too much difficulty in obtaining a short lease on a penthouse in Arlington which, though enormously expensive for what it offered, none the less had one priceless asset.

It had a view.

O'Hara, with a telescope mounted on a tripod just back from the open window, was not admiring that view. Though he could see clearly all the way from College Park to Fort Belvoir, he was concentrating on one small sector: the telescope was trained directly on the US Naval Station on the opposite bank, where the Presidential yacht *Potomac* was tied up. If *Potomac* moved, Franklin Delano Roosevelt would be moving.

SEVEN

Ed Martingale, for the first time since Ross had known him, seemed disheartened. For an hour he pored over the accumulated results, plots and graphs. When he raised his head, his brow was deeply furrowed. 'What do you think, Ernie, honestly?'

'We can find a sub in Lake Ontario,' Miller said. 'Problem is, they're operating in the Atlantic.'

'Yup. Brutal but it's true. Science ahead of engineering, the way it always is. We need ten years of development in six months, and it's not happening. Alec?'

Ross said, 'We're better than we were; let's not sell this thing too short. A Canso equipped like this *does* have more chance of locating a sub. Two together – '

'Two don't double the chances, that's the whole trouble,' Martingale said. 'If we had the equipment we'll have a few years from now, then okay. At the moment it costs too much and isn't effective enough to justify the extra.' He was operating against a lifetime's habit, putting more and more money into something he no longer wholeheartedly believed in, because two navies were pressing him hard.

'Calling the whole thing off?' Miller asked. It had occurred to him suddenly that the removal of the Cansos and cancellation of the project was now the best thing that could happen. Without them, Applejack might back off, give him a chance to work something out.

'Nope,' Martingale said. 'The Navy wants this thing to work. Anyway, we're on to a new wrinkle.' Characteristically he'd stepped sideways to find another way forward. 'We're working on a buoy – sends out sonar impulses

130

under the surface and has a radio on top to communicate with airplanes . . .' His enthusiasm picked up as he described the communication and dropping techniques, sketching quickly with a pencil on the back of a plot.

Next morning, Dot, hearing Ernie describe his gut-ache to Ross on the phone, said as he hung up: 'I ate what you ate, and I'm okay.'

He put his head round the bedroom door. 'I'm taking a day off, that's all. Going to take a drive, then maybe a walk.'

'Oh, like that? I thought maybe you were going shopping.'

'Huh?'

'My birthday,' she said.

'When did I ever forget?'

She giggled. 'And when did I forget to remind you?'

He made himself smile. 'You'll be twenty-six, right?'

'Oh, sure!'

Soon, with Applejack beside him, he was driving out of town, westward, into empty country. On the bench seat between them lay the pilot's notes for the Consolidated PBY, otherwise known as the Canso, otherwise known also as the Catalina.

It was a long day of technical talk, mainly in English, sometimes in German, when Applejack's English wasn't quite up to the technicalities. At the end Miller said, 'Well, if you've got it, that's the theory.'

Applejack nodded. 'I have it. Where are the keys to the garage?'

'In my pocket.'

'Give them to me. How many are there?'

'Two. Why?'

'Because I need them both. You are not even to go near.'

Miller handed over the keys.

'And now,' Applejack said, 'I have to go back. When I

131

telephone it will always be at nine o'clock at night. Make sure you answer.'

He caught the evening train to Toronto and the over-night sleeper from there. By midmorning he was in Washington and on the phone to Metzhagen, asking anxiously about progress. The answer was more than satisfactory.

He now had everything he needed. It meant an almost immediate return to Kingston, and this one would be tricky. But when it was over, he'd be ready to *act*.

Von Galen had an absolute conviction that the long wait was over and that his chance would come very soon. But he had no foreknowledge of an unpleasant experience ahead . . .

The plywood packing case sat in the back of Metzhagen's pick-up truck. Stencilled red lettering on the scuffed wood said, 'Domestic water boiler. Soft copper. Ballards are best.'

'There's a consignment going over from Oswego to Toronto,' Metzhagen said. 'I fixed it with a couple of men in the Bund. This one gets offloaded on shore by tender. Night's good and dark.'

Von Galen climbed into the passenger seat. 'The whole bomb is complete?'

'Yup. All there, except the fulminate sticks. They're under my seat, gift-wrapped in cotton waste and candy-stripe paper. We're going to drive good and slow.'

It was a long drive, and an almost silent one. Metzhagen kept the pick-up at a steady forty as they wound north, driving watchfully, keeping clear of other traffic where he could. They stopped for a brief meal at a roadside diner near Shenandoah, then pushed on past Scranton and up to the border with New York State, and on north.

Black cloud had been gathering for some time as they approached the small town of Cortland. Just inside the town limits the storm struck with startling fierceness: big raindrops driving like lead shot against the roof and windshield of the pick-up. Metzhagen prudently pulled over, killed the engine and began to fill his pipe as summer lightning flashed through the loaded sky. 'Too heavy for the wipers,' he said, 'and we sure as hell don't want to hit something we don't see coming.'

'Agreed.' Von Galen tried to match his patience. He was often surprised by the violence of America's weather, by the extremes of chill and heat, the awesome humidity. Now, as they sat, the pick-up was rocked on its springs, every few seconds, by tremendous wind squalls.

'Won't last,' Metzhagen said. 'These things are like that guy said about life – nasty and short.'

'Good.' Windshield and side windows were almost opaque, so great was the weight of rain, yet Von Galen felt an abrupt urge to move on despite it, and an obscure apprehension that something was wrong. He recognized the stupidity of the feeling and kept quiet as Metzhagen smoked contentedly at some sweet-scented tobacco.

Twenty minutes later, peace came. The last of the water ran down the glass and the sky ahead was blue and filled with bright, white cloud. Metzhagen started up and the truck moved forward. A mile or so on, there was flood-water at a dip in the road and the truck was up to its axles as it chugged through. The little town lay behind and the road stretched empty ahead when a policeman unexpectedly appeared in front of them, arm upraised, and Metzhagen stopped and wound down the window.

'Okay, let me see your driver's licence.'

Metzhagen took it from the pocket of his checked shirt. 'Something wrong?'

The cop looked at the licence. 'Where you going?'

'Oswego.'

'Where you from?'

'Washington.'

'You got Virginia plates.'

'I was in Washington before I came up here.'

'That right?' The cop walked round the truck and they heard the thumps as he kicked at the tyres.

'What's this about?' Von Galen asked softly.

'He's bored, I reckon. Looking for a little trouble,' Metzhagen said. 'Don't worry about it.'

The cop was at the open window again. 'What's your load?'

'A water boiler,' Metzhagen said. 'The order's here if you want to see it.' He held out the papers; an order from Kingston, a shipping-space reservation. 'Is something wrong here, Officer?'

The cop didn't reply for a moment. Then 'Metzhagen,' he said. 'Sounds like a German name.'

'My grandad, that was. Me, I was born in Charleston.'

Metzhagen's calm was not shared by Von Galen. The sense of unease he'd felt earlier was now back and growing, and the cop's next question increased it further.

'Who's your passenger?'

'Just a friend,' Metzhagen said.

'Can you identify yourself?' the cop asked Von Galen.

He nodded. 'Certainly.' But it was a problem. He had both passports with him: German diplomatic, and the other, his Argentine one. He handed the Argentine passport across.

'Looking for somebody, huh?' Metzhagen asked, as the cop turned the pages.

'Maybe. Carrying your passport – you going somewhere?'

'Kingston,' Von Galen said. 'I have a sister there. The boiler's for her.'

'Sure is a long way to take a boiler,' the cop said.

'It's a replacement,' Metzhagen told him, 'for the one she's got.'

'Argentina?' the cop said.

'Yes.'

'Me, I'm a Polack.'

'I see,' Von Galen said politely. He didn't know the

134

word. Metzhagen, realizing it, said to the cop, 'You were born in Poland?'

'Came to the US when I was a baby. From Poznan.' The cop added deliberately, 'Germans sure kicked hell out of Poland.'

Von Galen felt sick. The cop seemed to *know*.

Metzhagen said, 'Sure hope we don't get mixed in it.'

'Hmm.' The cop's flat stare was almost palpably hostile now. He said, 'Took you a hell of a time to stop. We better check your brakes.'

'They're okay,' Metzhagen said.

'We're still gonna check. I'm gonna go down the road and you're gonna get up to thirty and when I signal like this – ' he made a chopping motion with his hand – 'you hit those brakes, right?'

He left them, got into his car and drove two or three hundred yards, then halted.

Metzhagen said quietly to Von Galen, 'He's really looking for trouble, God knows why! Knows we came through water back there and the brakes'll be wet.'

'What do we do?'

'What he wants. We'll have squeezed some of the water out of the linings when we stopped. Anyway the truck's okay. But can't take chances with the fulminate. Take the box and walk along behind. And for Christ's sake be careful!'

Von Galen reached carefully beneath the seat and eased out the small box, gift-wrapped in green-and-white striped paper. 'He's guessed I'm German.'

'You're from Argentina, son. Passport says so. I just hope it's a good job.'

'It's genuine.' Von Galen climbed down, holding the package gingerly, and watched the truck start up and move slowly off. Metzhagen's foot would be on the brakes, squeezing. It accelerated towards the cop, and stopped abruptly. By the time Von Galen reached it,

135

Metzhagen was out of the cab, unfastening the canvas cover that protected the load.

'He wants to see the boiler,' Metzhagen explained briefly. 'Brakes are okay.' Then, pulling the cover back, 'It's a sealed carton, Officer, as you see. Packed for export.'

The cop looked at it. Three hundred pounds of dynamite, Von Galen thought. Could the cop demand the seal be broken?

Apparently not. He turned to Von Galen. 'What's in the package?'

'A present for my sister.'

'I said, what's in it?'

'A piece of china.'

'That's why you got out and carried it, right?'

'I didn't want anything to happen to it.' Von Galen was desperately conscious of how non-American his speech sounded: how the 'w' he'd worked so hard to master still emerged as a 'v'.

'Can I put this cover back?' Metzhagen asked.

'Go ahead.' The cop was still staring at Von Galen. 'She likes china, your sister? Collects the stuff?'

'A little. When she can.' *Venn she can. Damn!*

'What kind is it? Did you buy it?'

'Yes, it's a little vase.'

'What kind? Where's it made?'

Oh God, he knew nothing about china. 'I don't know.'

'Got the receipt?'

'No, I don't think so.' He could feel the colour mounting in his face. 'Threw it away, I think.'

'Maybe I ought to take a look.'

Metzhagen said, 'Aw c'mon, Officer, it's just a little present for his sister. He had it gift-wrapped.'

'Won't make no difference to Canadian customs if it's gift-wrapped or not,' the cop said. 'Let's see inside it, fella.'

136

'Aw, Christ,' Metzhagen said. 'We've done nothing, we're just on our way to Oswego.'

'Don't know about that. Seems to me there's something a little suspicious here. Reckon I better take you in.'

Metzhagen, still polite, said softly. 'You do that and I'll raise an almighty stink. We're law-abiding people.'

'Threatening me, huh?'

'No. Just – '

'Okay, lean on the bonnet, the both of you.'

'This is goddam ridiculous!'

'Lean.' The cop was unfastening the leather cover on his revolver holster.

Metzhagen obeyed, spreading arms and legs. Von Galen said, 'The present?'

'Put it on the ground.'

Von Galen did so and Metzhagen said, 'Do as he says. We've done nothing. What could he find?'

But there *was* something. Metzhagen didn't know Von Galen's diplomatic passport, his ultimate protection against trouble, was in his jacket pocket. Heart thudding with anxiety, Von Galen leaned.

While the cop frisked Metzhagen, Von Galen's mind worked frantically. If the passport was found, the cop would have to be killed: there was simply no alternative. But he had no weapon, and neither, he was almost sure, had Metzhagen, whereas the cop *was* armed. He glanced up and down the road. There was no traffic in sight, but there were a couple of houses two or three hundred metres away.

Metzhagen was saying; 'You're not entitled to go through my pockets. Not here. If you want to do that, do it at the station.'

'Save it, fella.'

Von Galen felt the hands on him, under his armpits, across his chest and his back, down each leg in turn, then entering his side pockets and, finding nothing there, the inside pocket of his jacket, actually touching the diplomatic passport. He felt himself trembling.

The cop must have felt it also, for the hand lingered before it withdrew. Von Galen felt the passport snag on the lining as it came out, and he tried to whirl fast, but the leaned-over position had long ago been worked out to counter just such a move.

The cop was standing back from them now, his revolver out, his eyes flicking from the passport to Von Galen. He read the words softly: 'Deutsches Reich . . .' in a tone of surprise turning to satisfaction. 'What's *this*?'

Von Galen said stiffly, 'It is a diplomatic passport, as you can see.' He must now use the immunity it gave him. He began, 'And I am under its protection according to – '

The cop interrupted him. 'Your pal ain't, though. That right?' He said to Metzhagen, 'You got one of these?'

'No.'

'Oh boy, I just *knew*! Right from the time I heard you talk, I knew. You're a German, you bastard.'

'I am a diplomat properly accredited and I demand to be treated accordingly.' The cop had taken another pace back: he was a least four metres away, and the gun, immunity or not, was pointed at Von Galen. To rush him, he must get the gun turned away. He said, 'You have no power to detain me, and I warn you that my government will make the strongest protest.'

'Yeah.' The cop was grinning openly now. 'A pair of Germans with a little cargo for Canada. Christ, I wonder what we're gonna *find* in there.'

The gun hadn't moved. Von Galen glanced at Metzhagen, saw his imperceptible nod, and said in German, '*Zusammen*!' Together.

The cop at once stepped back. 'I speak it, too. Don't try.' He looked at them with unconcealed pleasure. 'What you're gonna do, you're gonna get in that truck *zusammen* and you're gonna drive back into Cortland, and I'm gonna

138

follow you, make sure you don't drop nothing out the window.'

Von Galen said again, 'I remind you –'

'We'll sort this thing out at headquarters. Get in the truck and turn it around.'

As they climbed in, Metzhagen whispered, 'I'll try to run him down.' He put the pick-up into gear, gunned the engine, glanced round, and swore. The cop was beside them, and there was no way to catch him any kind of blow.

'A spanner,' Von Galen said urgently. 'Something to hit him with.'

Metzhagen shook his head. 'There's nothing. When we're moving I'll try to –'

'Turn it around,' the cop shouted. 'And don't try anything. Pull in right over there, on the other side.' He pointed with the pistol.

Von Galen said, 'Could we go faster?'

'Than a police car? No – we'll just have to try to crash him on the road, when he's behind us.' He swung the pick-up round, then stopped, looking back.

The little green-and-white parcel lay at the roadside where Von Galen had left it, and the cop was walking towards it, bending as though to pick it up, then straightening, standing for a moment looking down at it.

They didn't hear the cop say to himself, 'China – from Germany maybe!' But they saw him draw back his foot, saw the vicious little kick at the parcel, and felt the explosion that plastered the cop all over the grass verge.

Metzhagen slammed the pick-up into gear, swung it round and drove off rapidly. 'Our lucky day,' he said grimly. The road was still deserted, and he drove fast; no fulminate to worry about now, and the dynamite in the copper boiler was safely inert. Through Syracuse and Fulton he slowed and drove with obsessive care; he had no means of avoiding either place. But there seemed to be no alert. They saw one police car in Fulton, window down and cigarette smoke drifting out: in a way it was puzzling; the cop's body must by now have been found. All the same, they reached Oswego without further alarms.

There the boiler went to join other deck cargo on a small lake trader with the odd name of *Ontario Turk*. Twenty-nine similar plywood cases were stacked with it.

Metzhagen, having introduced him to the owner/skipper of the *Turk*, then held out a hand and said, quietly as ever, 'I'll supply more detonators, don't worry. And whatever the target is, good luck!'

'Thank you for all you've done.'

Metzhagen took the pipe from his mouth, glanced quickly round him, and murmured: 'Heil Hitler.'

Solemnly von Galen returned the tribute. For a moment it seemed as weirdly out of place here as it had in the woods outside Winchester; but all the same he felt the words stir him. The Führer, he was certain, would approve of any man who, when absurd rules denied him the chance to fight, could yet seek to spill the enemy's blood.

Turk sailed an hour later. She made no more than eight knots and the trip towards Kingston, a mere fifty-five miles away, would take most of the night. That fact met his requirements exactly: a deserted lake shore in the hours before dawn was the perfect place to unload his bomb.

The packing case was taken ashore by tender at four o'clock in the morning, and by six was locked safely in the garage half way between Kingston and the airfield. Von Galen wished he could stay with it, could remain here and wait for the signal; but that wasn't the way it would happen: like everything else, the signal would have to be looked for, *willed* into being.

When it came, it would come in Washington. Not in Berlin: he had no hopes now of Bohle. No, when it came

– as soon it must because events dictated it – it would come in the capital.

Deep in his bones, Von Galen *knew* that it would happen, that his chance must come; and he exulted in the knowledge. He had not always believed, but it was far more than belief now. He thought of the package of fulminate that had decimated the cop the day before.

'You're next, Mr President,' he murmured savagely to himself, 'and you, Mr Verdammte Churchill!'

He didn't know it, but already there were indications; didn't know, but would not have been surprised. The feeling that he was part now of the inexorable march of great events dominated his every movement.

Ernie Miller, too, felt himself absorbed into the relentless movement of time. His every footstep became the swing of a metronome, his pulse-beat the tick of some remorseless clock. He had to get *moving* – but he was in as bad a situation as could be.

'Please, Applejack,' Miller prayed to himself, 'stay off my back for just a little while.'

It was July 31st.

EIGHT

While Von Galen in Washington and Miller in Kingston both seethed with impatience, Bohle in Berlin did not. He had administrative matters on his mind, and a stream of paperwork moving across his desk. When, in the last days of July 1941, he thought of Von Galen at all, it was only to note the uneventful passage of time.

The hiatus ended that day, Thursday, July 31st, with a morning priority signal to the Foreign Ministry from the German Ambassador in Turkey, the redoubtable and dangerous intriguer, Franz von Papen. Von Papen had learned 'from usually reliable sources in Ankara' – and Bohle grimaced at the hackneyed phrase – 'that Harry Hopkins, personal envoy of Franklin Roosevelt, has just flown to Moscow'. The news was important for a variety of reasons. Three *Wehrmacht* army groups were tearing the guts out of an unprepared Russia and there could be no doubting Hopkins's purpose: he was asking Stalin how America could help. If Hopkins had travelled to Russia via Britain, he would undoubtedly be reinforcing Churchill's message to Stalin that all enemies of Germany were friends of Britain. The alliance Germany most feared could be coming into being.

Bohle spent the morning with Ribbentrop and top echelon Foreign Ministry officials attempting to produce a swift analysis of the consequences. He returned just before lunch to his office to find that, in his absence, there had been a telephone call from Admiral Dönitz in Wilhelmshaven. He returned the call, intrigued.

'I wondered,' Dönitz said, 'whether you had discovered anything more.'

'No. The fact is,' Bohle said, 'that other matters – '

'We all have those.' There seemed to be a trace of reproof in the cool voice. 'I said I would let you know if I found any pieces for your jigsaw puzzle.'

'And have you?'

'Possibly. A Condor reconnaissance aircraft risked a trip over the British naval base at Scapa Flow yesterday. There was low cloud and bad visibility, so it got back. Photographs show, among other things, that the *Prince of Wales* is there.'

'Prince of? – there isn't one now.'

'A ship, Minister. A battleship. She was damaged in the action in which *Bismarck* was lost and has been undergoing repairs. We did not expect her at Scapa. So the question is, *why* is she there?'

'Why shouldn't a battleship be at fleet headquarters?'

'Ignore the naval aspects, Minister. I see two possibilities. The first is that a convoy of supplies may be being assembled for Russia. But there is a possibility of something else.'

Bohle said, 'Roosevelt's man, Hopkins, is in Moscow.'

'Which lends support to the convoy theory,' Dönitz said. 'I thought I'd mention it. The *Kriegsmarine* does keep its word.'

Bohle hung up, frowning, conscious of a small frisson of excitement. After all these months, could it *possibly* be happening? Seemingly it could. In which case it was no longer a matter for a file. He drafted a quick signal to Von Galen in Washington demanding that any further hint, no matter how slight, be instantly reported, then he left for his afternoon meeting.

Twenty-four hours later, another piece of the puzzle edged forward. Like the rest, it was anything but conclusive. The phone call was from Admiral Canaris. 'I wondered,' he said, 'how your little scheme is coming along?'

Bohle thought the word 'little' unnecessarily patronizing. 'Have you a contribution to make?'

'I wouldn't call it a contribution,' Canaris said. 'You know what intelligence is. People think we rush round hiding under tables and planting bombs. All we do is try to piece together unrelated trifles.'

'Have you something?' Bohle asked flatly.

'I don't know. In Britain they have collections for charity. They call them flag days.'

'I remember them. Old ladies with collecting-boxes.'

'Last Wednesday, Churchill was photographed buying a flag. In Downing Street.'

'He can afford it.'

'It seems,' the Admiral went on quietly, 'that the particular flag day is not until the tenth. You do see what I mean?'

'Thank you, Admiral,' Bohle said. 'I see very well.'

That Saturday, in faraway Washington, Baldur von Galen, almost sick with tension, had decided to escape for a few hours to attend a reception at the Argentine Embassy. He knew within minutes that he would not enjoy the evening, and after a second glass of champagne, left in a cab.

He returned to the Embassy to find his phone ringing.

'Yes?'

Joseph O'Hara's voice: 'The caravan seems to have moved along.'

'*Gone*?'

'That's right.'

Von Galen hung up. Where the devil was *Potomac*? Gone – that was all he knew and all he could hope to learn. He turned his chair and looked again at the too-familiar map of the Eastern seaboard. *Potomac* had sailed down the river for which she was named.

Rapidly he composed and then enciphered a signal:

President's yacht has left its berth. Destination unknown. No announcement made.

He glanced at his watch. Eight-fifty. In Berlin it would be six hours later, with Bohle asleep. He added to the signal the three five-figure groups which indicated the recipient must be given it at once, even if it meant waking him. By the time he'd delivered it to the radio-room it was almost five minutes to nine. Von Galen took a fistful of coins from a box in his desk, and headed, limping, towards the nearest public telephone.

It was three minutes after nine when he heard Miller's voice answer.

He said, 'Applejack. Be ready any day.'

Back inside the Embassy, Von Galen warned the duty officer to waken him if any message came, and went to bed, praying that Bohle would now manage to overcome the doubts in Berlin. But lying there, he found his tumbling thoughts turning to Miller. Could he really be certain of him? The pressure on Miller must surely be irresistible, but the sheer weight of it could in itself be dangerous: under that kind of pressure men could crack and behave unpredictably. And Miller had cracked once before . . .

Von Galen lay thinking. After half an hour or so an idea came. He got out of bed and prowled the darkened building: somewhere there must be an accurate description of what he required, but none of the reference books in the library gave the detail he needed. There was one illustration, but he had no means of knowing whether its size was correct. Damn! If he got it wrong, Miller would see it at once. Miller knew what the damned thing looked like. But wait a minute, hadn't he seen one, quite recently – here in the Embassy! He signed for keys, let himself into the naval attache's office, and with relief found what he sought in the top right-hand drawer of the desk. He measured it with great care, then wrote out a detailed description. Shortly afterwards he left the building and telephoned Metzhagen from the public call office.

If Metzhagen found the request surprising, he gave no indication of it. 'I can get it done. No, not myself, but there's a precision engineer I know . . .'

'In the Bund – I mean, is he reliable?'

'Don't worry about that,' Metzhagen said. 'These dimensions. You used calipers?'

'A ruler was all I had. But I was very careful.'

'Yeah. Well, I can find a picture as a guide. You need a box?'

'Can it be done?'

'A few hours' work, that's all. We got all kinds of people. I'll have the whole thing to you some time tomorrow evening.'

Von Galen hung up, satisfied. There was sense in being prepared. At the last moment, Miller's resolve might need some stiffening.

A motor-cycle rider brought Von Galen's signal to the Wannsee house and Bohle, in his dressing-gown, snatched at it bad-temperedly. Its contents cooled his temper and heated his anxiety. It was now – what? – nearly four o'clock. Dönitz, no doubt, rose at six. It would have to wait until then.

He went into his study, took a sheet of paper and listed the evidence, then stared at it, puzzled. Undoubtedly there was a pattern now, yet if he believed it, why did it convince nobody else? Dönitz only half believed him; Canaris was sceptical. Yet, though the pointers were delicate, they *did* point in the same direction.

Or was he merely making facts fit a convenient theory? He went over it again. No – the facts *did* fit the theory. All of them. A battleship in an unexpected place; a presidential yacht no longer in her berth; Churchill carefully being photographed doing something timed ten days ahead.

At six o'clock he put the call through, catching Karl Dönitz at his frugal breakfast.

'Admiral, the President's yacht has sailed.'

'Is he on it?'

'I don't know.'

'I'm sorry. Without something more conclusive – well, you know the situation.'

Bohle dressed and went to his office, demanding from the news analysts and radio monitors in the Foreign Ministry any scrap of information that might come in about Roosevelt's movements. Then he sat at his desk, working desultorily, barely able to concentrate. It was happening: he knew it. And if he could persuade Dönitz into action, the rewards would be enormous for Germany – and for Ernst Wilhelm Bohle.

At that moment the information Bohle sought so anxiously was actually being printed on miles of newsprint, and distributed to newsboys throughout America, ready for the nation's breakfast tables.

A brief announcement late on Saturday night said merely that the President was to take a short holiday. Next morning, Sunday, giving details to the hastily summoned White House corps of correspondents, Stephen T. Early, the President's press secretary, said Mr Roosevelt proposed to spend a few days cruising off the New England coast in the presidential yacht *Potomac*. He needed the sea breezes and a chance to relax after recent strains.

'He's a lucky guy,' one of the correspondents said, fanning himself vigorously. 'Do we get to go with him? *Please* say yes!'

Early grinned. It was a broiling August day, everyone in the room was already sweating, and the day would get hotter. He said, 'What kind of a holiday would it be with you guys along?'

A brief argument developed. The press men wanted to accompany the President, and demanded to know why they couldn't.

'Who's he meeting?' somebody called. 'Churchill or Stalin?'

'Prettier than that, so I hear,' Early replied. 'There may be a princess or two.'

'Yeah? What will Mrs Roosevelt say?'

Early turned frosty. 'She, too, thinks the President needs a holiday. Don't worry, gentlemen. We'll keep you informed.'

The news went straight on the wires.

Having spent a wakeful night, Von Galen fell into weary sleep at six in the morning. Full daylight, spreading across the city, did not penetrate the heavy velvet curtains of his room and it was almost ten before he awakened, sticky and uncomfortable. Rubbing his eyes, he drew the curtains, opened the window, hoping for air. Somewhere in this damned city, he thought savagely, lay the information he wanted. Somewhere within a mile of where he stood. There, in the White House, whose roof he could see. His eyes flickered and refocused. There was movement on the roof . . . men in uniform . . . moving to the flagpole.

As he watched, the Presidential flag was lowered. No need to inquire what *that* meant: the flag flew when the President was there.

It came down only when he *wasn't*!

Von Galen dragged on a dressing-gown and hurried to the Press department, where a bored-looking junior attaché was reading small-ads in the Sunday *Post*.

'Any news about Roosevelt?'

'He's going on holiday. Announced last night. Details are on the wire.'

The attaché handed him a torn-off sheet of teleprinter roll.

Von Galen's eyes raced over the message. 'Leaving today . . . joining *Potomac* at New London, Connecticut . . . cruising off the New England coast.'

'Map.'

'On the wall there.'

He searched with his finger. New London? Where the hell was New London? He found it and his finger traced the route. The wire service report said Roosevelt was going by train, so . . . almost a straight line on the map, probably through New York or round it. Journey of several hours, anyway.

O'Hara! He must set O'Hara on Roosevelt's track!

Limping back upstairs to dress, he looked longingly at the phone at his bedside. But if the FBI were listening, if they caught only a hint . . . no, he daren't risk that. Dressed, he hurried for the side door.

'Oh, Herr von Galen.' One of the secretarial girls stood in his path.

'Not now,' he said.

She blinked. 'But there's a message for you. Just a minute ago. You weren't in your office.'

He stopped. 'What message?'

'An American,' she said. 'He wouldn't leave his name. He said he was – ' she glanced at her notebook – 'off and running. He said you'd understand.'

'What *exactly* did he say?'

She read the words carefully. 'He was off and running. Heading home first. Flying. Then by car.'

Von Galen closed his eyes, trying to picture the map he'd been looking at. O'Hara's home was actually in Boston: so he was flying to Boston, then going on by car.

'Thank you, Fräulein.'

He went back upstairs to his own map. Boston was roughly a hundred miles from New London, but O'Hara was probably right; by flying to Boston, he'd make the journey almost as quickly as Roosevelt.

Von Galen headed for the radio-room.

O'Hara's name got him a seat. The family investment trust had a sizeable share-holding in Eastern, and its executives were frequent visitors to Washington. The booking clerk said, initially, that no seats remained. O'Hara got his at the expense of somebody with no such influence, who was left fuming at the airport.

The spanking new Douglas DC-3 covered the 430 miles to Boston in minutes more than two and a half hours – plenty of time for O'Hara to work out a story to tell his parents. Taking a cab to the family home, he found no excuses were necessary: the housekeeper told him the family was going off to lunch with friends directly after church. She was sure he'd be welcome, too. Why didn't he . . .?

'I can't,' he said. 'Got a date.'

'Oh, that's nice.' She couldn't remember when he'd had a date before.

He left in the open Lincoln his father had bought him, made good time through the quiet Sunday streets, then put his foot down hard as he moved on to the smooth, fast road to Providence. He should be in New London in three hours.

It was mid-afternoon before Bohle saw the Associated Press despatch. His secretary hurried into his office, the sheet held out eagerly. 'Herr Bohle, the President has left Washington!'

He read with satisfaction. Good hard evidence. The *first* hard evidence. But he knew a moment later that in truth it wasn't; or not for anybody but him. Roosevelt was going on holiday, no more.

'Shall I try to reach Admiral Dönitz?'

He didn't reply.

'Herr Bohle?'

He looked up at her, and shook his head. 'It won't convince him any more than – ' and then stopped, struck by a thought. 'Leave me for a while.'

As the door closed behind her, his eyes returned to the report. 'It was announced today by the White House that . . .'

Announced. The word drummed. Last night he'd told himself only an *announcement* would convince Dönitz. Very well, an announcement there would be. It would not be difficult to arrange. Several of his *Auslandsorganisazion* officers abroad had cover as newsmen.

The six o'clock Radio Berlin news broadcast began by reporting smashing gains of Russian territory by the unstoppable *Wehrmacht*. Then:

> It is reported from the Portuguese capital, Lisbon, that widespread rumours are circulating both there and in Washington that President Roosevelt has left for a meeting with the British Premier, Winston Churchill. If so, he has left behind him powerful voices demanding that he go no farther down the road to war. There is informed speculation that they are to meet at sea.

Bohle smiled as he listened. When the announcer switched to another topic, he turned off the radio, and buzzed for his secretary.

'*Now* get me Admiral Dönitz.'

This time he got action, but it was neither as swift nor as easy as he imagined. Submarines on station and on patrol would still not be diverted on the evidence available.

Further reconnaissance would, however, be made as soon as possible.

At an airfield near Stavanger in Norway, a long-range Focke-Wulf Condor had stood ready to take off since six o'clock in the morning, but brutal weather hammering in from the North Sea, squall after squall, with driving rain and low cloud, kept it on the ground. The crew, not unhappy at the delay, relaxed with coffee and cards and made bets on raindrops running down the crew-room window. The pilot, Flugleutnant Keller, was not with them. Keller was keen. Keller was a medal-hunter. Keller's idea of fun was dead-reckoning navigation in foul weather. Keller was not, accordingly, particularly popular.

Characteristically, he spent the waiting hours in the weather-room, eyes on the meteorological instruments, searching for the break that would allow take-off. The met officer, who didn't like him much either, noted privately that Keller seemed uninterested in the duration of a weather-slot; safe return was clearly not in his mind.

They saw the thin band of blue at one-thirty, down on the western horizon with low black cloud crowding ahead of it. Minutes earlier the pressure had increased a little, raising Keller's hopes. Here, now, was confirmation.

He flung the crew-room door wide, letting in a blast of air that scattered the cards, and bellowed 'Schnell!' in his familiar, inviting way. One of the gunners, awash with coffee, pointed hopefully at the latrine door and said, 'Sir,' in a pleading tone. Keller would have none of it.

The Condor was in the air within minutes, climbing scarcely at all before Keller demanded maximum-continuous from the engines and settled her on a course a little north of west. Ahead, the crew knew, lay the usual long flight out over the Atlantic, beyond the British coast, to inspect the convoy routes, to radio any sightings that might be made to waiting U-Boats, then to continue down in a long loop to the French coast.

Tomorrow, they'd fly back again.

Each, in his seat, hoped that in the course of the day they would not encounter one of the freighter-based fighters the British were now using. For two years the Condors had been virtually untouchable, operating out of range of land-based fighters and challenged in the air only by the RAF's Sunderland flying-boats. But now things were different. You spotted a cargo vessel, and suddenly there was a fast fighter buzzing up to attack. Condors were not the joy-rides they had been.

The regular route took them north of the Shetlands to turn out over the Atlantic, grinding out the miles at low level to avoid detection by the radar stations at Orkney and Shetland, or by RAF planes on submarine patrol. These last were the greater danger, and the reason Keller stayed low. The lumbering Sunderlands were slow, but strong and heavily armed, vulnerable only to attack from below. Keller, spotting one, would want to climb to the attack.

The Condor began to make its turn out over the gap between Shetland and the Faroes. Through its ports, the crew's eyes searched grey sea and blurry sky, settling into routine. The gunners fired their bursts, the navigator computed and measured, the flight engineer tracked the levels. 'Nothing, Captain.' Five minutes. 'Nothing, Captain.' The day would pass like that unless ships were spotted.

An hour and twenty minutes after the first turn, the Condor banked again, dropping yet lower, to fly barely above the high, reaching wavetops of an ill-tempered ocean; it settled on a course almost due east.

The crew wondered what the hell was going on – return to base?

But they were not returning. Keller had an announcement to make. They would make a low-level pass directly over the fleet anchorage at Scapa Flow. The camera-gun would be used, but at low altitude its breadth of focus was small.

'It is therefore up to the sharp eyes of this crew,' Keller said crisply. 'What we are looking for is the battleship *Prince of Wales*. She *was* there. We must discover whether she is still. Study your recognition charts.'

Privately, they groaned. Ahead lay fighters, anti-aircraft guns, radar, *and* the extra blessing of massive firepower from whatever warships might be there.

The day was not improving. For nearly four hours they had flown through murk, and were flying through it still as the stark island of Hoy reared suddenly ahead and Keller lifted the Condor's cumbrous nose to roar over the high cliffs. Suddenly Scapa lay below them, and anxious eyes searched its sheltered surface. More than a dozen ships lay at anchor: destroyer, destroyer, frigate . . .

Two battleships!

Almost identical. Same class.

King George the Fifth and *Prince of Wales*.

And *one* was actually moving, white water churning at her stern.

Keller banked for a better look, and just in time – the moving ship was *Prince of Wales*!

Quickly he swung through a hundred and eighty degree turn, tore back over Hoy, climbing on full power now. Anxious eyes strained back, searching for pursuing fighters, until the black cloud closed around them.

Keller circled for two hours. Some of the storm cloud was cumulo-nimbus that could smash his aircraft, but he had to chance that. He'd radioed one word: 'Spotted.' Now he wanted to be sure.

At last he brought the Condor down, walking her like a fly on a ceiling along the underside of the cloud layer, flying a wide circle. From time to time, hanging wisps of dark vapour closed over the huge plane, blanketing all vision, leaving the windows drop-encrusted for moments until the slipstream cleared them. Suddenly the nose-gunner yelled, 'She's there. Starboard, four o'clock!'

Keller took a good long look then climbed back into cloud. In his mind now was a picture of a great ship – and a rough sea that was quickly erasing her wake. But what wake there was streamed east: the battleship's bows pointed west. Three destroyers screened her. Keller took the long course again, maintaining radio silence. At last the Norwegian coast came dimly into view, and soon, triumphantly, he dropped the Condor to the runway.

Two minutes later he was in the communications office, urging speed upon the telephone operator.

'I have the honour to inform U-Boat Command,' he said, when the connection was made, 'that the British battleship *Prince of Wales*, with three destroyers, is now heading west into the Atlantic.'

He wondered, but dared not ask, why his orders had been to return and report, rather than to alert the U-Boats.

The fault lay, in fact, with Dönitz. His orders had been precise: reconnaissance flight over Scapa Flow, an immediate return to base, report direct to his headquarters. In all normal circumstances, if this battleship, or any other for that matter, were spotted at sea, the prescribed action would follow: U-Boat attack.

But his orders had not said so.

'Saw her at sea!' Bohle almost yelled. 'Saw her at sea and did *nothing*?'

Karl Dönitz was not a man given either to explanations or to the eating of humble pie. But now he was at least diplomatic. 'I congratulate the Minister on a remarkable piece of foresight,' he said. 'It seems you may be right, and I was possibly wrong. U-Boat Command will make every effort – '

'Churchill in your sights!' Bohle said. 'In a battleship – and *nothing*!'

'The ship was spotted by an aircraft,' Dönitz said, 'in bad weather conditions. They did well to find her at all.'

'Can the U-Boats find her,' Bohle inquired bitterly, 'in the same bad weather? And can they attack, in the bad weather?'

'They are going to try. Churchill or not, it's a battleship we hunt now.'

They had the battleship's position at a given time. They knew her performance and could make informed guesses at her course. That night, as the Atlantic storm grew rapidly worse, U-Boats rose uncomfortably towards the surface and thrust antennae up into the gale to receive the nightly transmissions of U-Boat Command. Dönitz debated whether to mention Winston Churchill's probable presence on *Prince of Wales*. Such knowledge could drive brave men to suicidal heroics. But finally he decided he should. An old submariner himself, Dönitz knew the temptations of depth when storms were raging. The thought of Churchill would counter those temptations.

Not all the U-Boats received the message. The raging storm centres that ranged across the ocean wrought their usual havoc with radio reception. Some heard nothing, others got part of the signal but couldn't make sense of it. A few received it clearly.

One of those, two hundred miles off Halifax, Nova Scotia, was the command of a young man named Jochen Schrenk.

NINE

Soldiers with fixed bayonets guarded the entrance to the docks at New London throughout that late afternoon and evening. O'Hara, arriving soon after three o'clock, regarded them with a mixture of relief and dismay: they would prevent his getting anywhere near, but at least their presence showed the President had not yet arrived.

A knot of Sunday afternoon idlers waited at the gate. Word had got round of the impending presence of Franklin Roosevelt. O'Hara joined them, to stare at the waiting, shiny *Potomac* as the crew moved around her, putting a final sheen on everything in sight. He found a reporter and a photographer from one of the local papers, disgruntled that they had no passes for the dockside. 'Always the same,' the reporter said. 'Everything for the White House reporters. Nothing for us.'

'Yeah, they're in the conspiracy,' the photographer said sourly.

'What conspiracy?' O'Hara asked, controlling his excitement.

The photographer turned to him. 'You ever see a picture of Roosevelt getting in or out of anything? You sure haven't. *That's* the conspiracy. You see him *in* the car, sure. But you don't see him getting in, and you don't see him getting out. Takes three men to lift him, that's why. They don't want pictures of FDR looking helpless.'

'Free press,' the reporter said angrily. 'In a pig's eye it's free!'

O'Hara went to buy coffee for them, in paper cups, and made himself agreeable, a naïve young man impressed by their worldly wisdom. He also asked cautious questions:

did they know where Roosevelt was going? What kind of fisherman was he? They pointed out the special raised deck from which the President fished, and speculated on its cost. No, they didn't know where he was going.

At 8.15 p.m. the train arrived, and snorted for a while in the dockyard, finally backing to a stop a hundred yards from *Potomac's* gangway. From that moment they saw nothing: the yacht's conversion to FDR's needs included a special entrance in her side for his wheelchair. Dimly they heard the tuneless squeal of a bosun's pipe.

The pressmen, meanwhile, had been badgering the dock-gatekeeper, and kept at it until an aide of some sort appeared to smooth things over.

'Look, boys, it's a holiday,' he said. 'But I'll give you a tip-off. If you're in South Dartmouth tomorrow, you ought to get some nice pictures.'

'South Dartmouth! Jesus, that's sixty miles. It's not even our beat.'

'Be worth it,' they were told.

Bitterly the pressmen watched *Potomac* depart, in the afterglow of sunset, down the Thames River towards salt water.

O'Hara drove the Lincoln direct to South Dartmouth. In August the holiday coast was busy, and hotel rooms hard to find. Again, money talked. Ten dollars bought O'Hara a room in a private house in Tiverton, a few miles away, and from a roadside diner he telephoned a house in Washington, the home of a German-American widow, Hanna Hanssen, whom Von Galen had recruited as a message-passer.

'I'll be using you as a relay,' he told her. 'Get him a message. South Dartmouth, Massachusetts, tomorrow. I'll be there.'

Next morning he was early at the jetty, dressed in shirtsleeves. It was already widely known that several members of the exiled Norwegian royal family were in the town, and again there was a crowd of sightseers. The royals were already in the local yacht club.

Shortly before ten, *Potomac* came into view, and the little crowd buzzed with excitement. It grew louder when a Chris-Craft speedboat was lowered and came roaring shorewards. Roosevelt himself could be seen at the wheel, glasses, famous grin, jaunty cigarette-holder and all.

Three girls appeared on the yacht club dock and climbed into the boat, and the watching women speculated which of the princesses they might be. Then the speedboat stood on its tail in a spin-turn and raced out to sea.

O'Hara asked himself: Why the princesses? Whirling round in a speedboat with pretty girls was a far cry from a meeting with Churchill! He debated making a further report, and decided against it.

Instead he waited. Older royals went out in a ship's boat. Word spread that FDR had taken the princesses fishing. Bluefish were reported to be running in Buzzard's Bay, and FDR liked to get his hook into a fighting blue. It was a long, tense day in the sunshine for O'Hara until, in the late afternoon, the Chris-Craft once more tore into the yacht club dock, and the princesses got out, shiny-eyed and excited. Roosevelt had exercised Presidential prerogative, transporting the pretty girls himself. Older members of the royal party returned by ship's boat.

Watched now by several hundred interested sightseers, the President once more returned towards *Potomac*. Within minutes the speedboat had been hoisted aboard, and the big yacht was under way.

But where to?

'No clue as to destination,' O'Hara reported by phone. 'Nobody knows a goddam thing.'

He found a quiet bar with a radio and few customers, and spent the evening twiddling the dial and listening both to local stations and the networks. As the evening wore on, speculation began to creep into the news broad-casts. Rumours were flying round the nation's capital, it seemed, that the holiday cruise was a brilliant cover for something more momentous. There was even mention of a possible rendezvous with Winston Churchill, but the commentators dismissed it; nobody took that particular piece of whimsy seriously.

O'Hara, however, did. *Potomac* had upped and van-ished over the horizon, and might be anywhere. At midnight, full of the beer he'd had to consume, O'Hara gave up and returned to his sparse lodging and the disapproving eye of the lady from whom his room was rented.

He was awake early next morning, begging the use of her radio set, telling her he was a journalism student writing a story about the President's trip. She sniffed. She knew reporters always drank too much, and this youngster was plainly starting down that path.

At nine the New Bedford radio station said *Potomac* had been seen heading for the Cape Cod Canal. O'Hara, his bill already paid, raced out to his car.

Four hundred and fifty miles west of Orkney, secure in the depths, U-167 waited for the storm to abate. She was one of those who had received only a badly-scrambled signal the night before and her captain, Leutnant Griese, unable to comprehend and therefore unaware, had taken her deep in search of comfort. Near the surface, the sub's long, thin hull had been tossed violently and dangerously by roaring Atlantic waves.

Now, on the morning of Tuesday, August 5th, her listening equipment suddenly picked up the distant throb of engines. Griese stood over the rating as he turned the tuning wheel.

'What is it?'

'Not sure, sir.' The young rating was concentrating

hard, good at his job. A minute or so later he turned his head. 'More than one, I think.'

Griese hesitated, torn between the temptation of targets and the unlikelihood of a successful attack in heavy seas.

'Three, sir, I think.'

Griese decided. 'Take her up. Periscope depth.'

What periscope depth might be was anybody's guess, with forty feet separating trough and peak in the huge, marching waves. U-167 blew tanks and rose.

'Periscope!'

As it came up, Griese gripped the handles and tried to survey the sea; but he got only glimpses. One moment the periscope's tip was metres clear of the water, the next it vanished under a following wave. He worked slowly, trying to be sure one sector was clear before moving to the next.

There! Was that – ?

He waited as the seas swept by, praying the next gap would be a clear one. Another glimpse of something, brief and frustrating because he couldn't be sure. Then, suddenly, as a swell lifted U-167, he got a clear look, and saw for an unmistakable moment the low, sleek shapes of three destroyers.

'Range?' But he knew. They were more than three thousand metres off, and heading away. Not a chance of a shot. In calm water, or if they'd been approaching, he'd have tried but there were only four torpedoes left now, near the end of this cruise, and to try snap shots at fast-moving destroyers would waste them. He wanted ships with those torpedoes.

'Three thousand five hundred metres, sir, at the nearest.'

Griese swore. 'Down periscope.' He looked at the faces turned towards him. 'Three destroyers, and not a chance in hell!'

'Four thousand, sir.'

'Target impossible,' Griese entered in his log. An hour later, coming close to the surface again, he radioed Wilhelmshaven. Perhaps somebody else would get a chance.

'Turned *back*?' Dönitz said. 'Slow the battleship down to let the escort keep up, or drop the destroyers and go on unescorted? But *that's* what they've done. *Prince of Wales* is alone, if we can spot her!'

The night's broadcast carried the news to the waiting U-Boats.

In Berlin, meanwhile, another broadcast, the one Bohle had inspired, triggered a typical response from his master, the Foreign Minister. 'Issue a statement,' Ribbentrop irritably instructed the Press Department. 'Say that any meeting between Roosevelt and Churchill would be a matter of relative indifference to the course of affairs.' He added scornfully, 'The problems faced by *those* two men are not to be disposed of by a personal meeting. Make sure the radio broadcasts that.'

Slowing a little to pass through the old whaling port of New Bedford, O'Hara caught sight of a store sign that read 'Navigational instruments'. He stopped and bought a pair of binoculars. There was no knowing how near he'd get to *Potomac* again. He now had to decide whether to take the new, faster road, or stay close to the water along the older, winding coastal route. He chose the latter.

In Washington, that Wednesday morning, Von Galen sat restlessly by the radio set, anxious for news. There had been nothing from Bohle in Berlin; nothing from O'Hara either, since the call to Mrs Hanssen the previous evening.

Irritably he endured the quizzes, the swing music, the endless advertisements, giving his attention only to the half-hourly news headlines. He knew *Potomac* was approaching the Cape Cod Canal; CBS had said so. But he didn't know if O'Hara was approaching it, too, and whether, if O'Hara did see *Potomac*, they would be any the wiser about Roosevelt's intentions.

He could only wait and hope – and think of Miller, and three hundred pounds of dynamite stored in a garage near Kingston, Ontario, and the fulminate detonators in a cotton-wool-packed box beside him.

For Bohle, too, the tension grew. Ribbentrop could say what he liked: this meeting would have the profoundest effect. It didn't look, at the moment, as though anything could stop Germany's victorious surge, but simple arithmetic said that America's population was two and a half times Germany's; that America's industry was enormously powerful, and that if America *did* enter the war on the British side, Germany's position would be massively changed.

He felt a mild guilt at not informing Von Galen of the state of affairs. But something in Von Galen's last message, a mention of 'possible alternative action' disturbed him. This was a matter, now, for experience and cool heads. Karl Dönitz had both. Bohle didn't want Von Galen running wildly round America trying to do something on his own and thereby earning for Germany further animosity from the American Government.

There it was – the canal! O'Hara had known it from childhood, had passed through it several times when his father's own yacht had gone from Boston to New Bedford, or to summer in Newport. He raced through the little village of Buzzard's Bay, and took up a position, almost out of sight, behind a disused roadside hoarding. He'd passed *Potomac* some time earlier, still well out in the bay, apparently halted. Now he must wait. *Potomac* remained motionless until late afternoon, then moved off. Behind the hoarding, nerves shredded by something between tension and tedium, O'Hara trained his prismatics on the yacht as she entered and passed slowly along the waterway. As she came closer, a small group of men became visible, lounging on *Potomac*'s sundeck. Sightseers, who'd stopped along the road, waved and received cheerful waves in return.

O'Hara examined the scene carefully, his eyes beginning to ache. One of the seated figures wore the white ducks and white hat Roosevelt so often favoured. The bulky, seated figure was half-turned away, but O'Hara kept glimpsing the long cigarette-holder. At least he hadn't lost track. Soon, though, he was bound to lose it, as the yacht passed from the canal into the wide watery spaces of Cape Cod Bay.

She drew level and O'Hara stepped out from behind the hoarding. He yelled, 'Hello, Mr President,' at the top of his voice, and waved. The figure in white turned his head a little, lifted a hand in acknowledgement. O'Hara concentrated on holding the binoculars steady. He stared, and then, incredulously, concentrated the harder. As *Potomac* moved slowly past and away, O'Hara remained rooted, glasses on the white-clad figure, praying for another turn of the head. He was rewarded moments later. And this time there was no mistake.

'You're certain?' Von Galen demanded. He had gone to Mrs Hanssen's home impatient at second-hand messages.

'No doubt at all,' O'Hara said. 'I saw him clearly.'

'You wear spectacles.' It was almost an accusation.

'For God's sake!' O'Hara said. 'I could see him perfectly. Listen, I saw the full rig-out. White ducks, white hat, the glasses, the cigarette-holder. I had binoculars. It was really clear. I could even see the ash on his damned cigarette. *That man was not Franklin Roosevelt!*'

'How do you know?'

'Because it wasn't his goddamned face, that's how. The

rig-out was Roosevelt's. The face wasn't. He's pulling a fast one!'

'Then who was it?'

'How do I know – and does it matter? They put somebody up there to impersonate FDR. Why do that if he's on board?'

Von Galen closed his eyes for a moment. If O'Hara was right, Roosevelt was pretending to be in one place when he was really in another . . .

O'Hara said: 'He was sitting up on deck with his back to the road, but he turned his head twice. I shouted and he turned. *It was not him!*'

This, Von Galen thought, was exactly the kind of thing he had expected, had even forecast. The whole point of sending O'Hara chasing the President had been a hope that he would uncover some subterfuge. A hope, though, *not* an expectation. It seemed to have come altogether too easily.

'Don't doubt me,' O'Hara said a little desperately. 'I've known that face all my life. It wasn't him.'

'Thank you. You've done well.'

'And now?'

'Try to see him again. Be sure.'

O'Hara said, 'He's through the canal now, out on the water: Cape Cod Bay and the open sea.'

'Stay, all the same. He may return. No – listen, go back to Newfoundland. I know it's a lot to ask. But get up there as fast as you can. See what you can learn.'

Von Galen hung up as Mrs Hanssen hovered, coffee-pot in hand. He still felt lingering doubt. '*Potomac* went through the Cape Cod Canal,' he told her. 'Somebody seems to have been impersonating Roosevelt.'

She said, 'Just like the cunning old devil.'

'Is it?'

'Oh my, yes. He's a trickster from way, way back. It's *just* what he'd do!'

165

He saw the excitement in her face and said soberly, 'You really believe that?'

'He'd absolutely *delight* in it!'

Odd, Von Galen thought, that she should be more convincing than O'Hara, who'd seen with his own eyes.

Bohle read Von Galen's new signal with a mixture of excitement and anger. Churchill on his way, Roosevelt on his way. Each with his little stratagems – the flag-buying, the impersonation – to cover departure. And the *Kriegsmarine* now, at last, on Churchill's tracks.

But not on Roosevelt's, damn it! He would inform Dönitz of Von Galen's discovery, but Dönitz couldn't attack Roosevelt at sea, even if he could find him. If they succeeded in attacking *Prince of Wales* – and even *that* was apparently now unlikely, given the weather and the speed of the battleship, they'd still have fulfilled only *half* of Von Galen's scheme. Roosevelt would survive.

What, he wondered, had Von Galen meant by 'alternative measures'? Von Galen didn't even know, yet, that Churchill had left Britain. He deserved to know that, at least.

Bohle replied quickly:

Your signal received. Congratulations on excellent work. Churchill believed to have sailed from Scapa Flow August 4th in battleship *Prince of Wales*, heading westward. Understand ship may have abandoned destroyer escort and sailing alone. *Kriegsmarine* ordered to attack on sight.'

It was now Wednesday. Von Galen, with Bohle's new signal before him, was trying to calculate timings. He had learned from a puzzled naval attaché that *Prince of Wales*, at full speed, could reach Newfoundland in five days. So Roosevelt was ahead: if he'd boarded a big naval vessel as soon as *Potomac* had sailed out of sight of South Dartmouth, he could comfortably be in Newfoundland tomorrow. True, he'd have to wait there for two days: the timing wasn't perfect. But the indications were stronger every moment.

It *was* Newfoundland.

Destiny: again the word surfaced in his mind, and Von Galen smiled wryly to himself. Yes, he admitted, perhaps there was the touch of destiny here. Had it not rained that long-ago night in San Francisco, he would not have met Mrs Mahoney; without her, he would not have encountered O'Hara: but for Karen Hanzer there would have been no Miller, no opportunity for Metzhagen. The necessary elements had all been there, but it was through him alone that they had come together. But for him, there could have been no . . .

Attack, he thought. And this was the moment. Von Galen's stomach tightened, and fear rose in his throat like bile.

She was coming through from the kitchen with a beer from the ice-box for Ernie when the telephone rang. 'Hello. Dot Miller speaking. That you, Alec?'

Silence.

'Hello?' Nobody answered her; she heard only the click of disconnection.

'Who was it?' Miller asked.

She shrugged. 'The phantom burglar again, I guess. He just hung up.'

'Yeah?' Miller sipped his beer. A minute later the phone rang again. 'Okay, I'll get it,' he said.

He's lively tonight, she thought, as the door closed firmly behind him. Usually Ernie gave a little grunt of protest at Alec's nightly call. Must mean they were doing something interesting.

She sighed, reached for a new ounce of wool, and continued work on the baby's jacket. It was always men who got the interesting things to do. Not, she thought contentedly, that she minded. Still, it *was* a pity she'd had to give up her own flying; it had always been such fun. And she'd been good, too, everybody said so, though on that single sneaky trip Ernie'd given her on the Canso, one day when Alec was away, she hadn't flown well. She was rusty, of course, but the controls were so *heavy*! No, she didn't envy Ernie his endless hours in a plane like that one. One day, maybe, there'd be a nice, fast, light twin . . .

'I told *you* to answer at nine o'clock,' Applejack said accusingly.

'She was passing the phone. Not much I could do about it.'

'Don't let it happen again,' Applejack said. 'I think it will be in the next day or two.'

Miller said, 'Saturday's my wife's birthday.'

'Birthday! You talk about *birthdays*?'

'It'll look funny if – '

'I want you to work out a course,' Aplejack said sharply. 'A very accurate calculation.'

'Where to?'

Applejack told him. 'I want to know the duration of a flight in a Canso, full fuel load. Understand? Prepare it quickly.'

'Direct flight, or what?'

'Allow for some delays and diversions. The flight will be clandestine. Plan for that.'

Miller put his head round the door. 'Got a little work to do,' he told his wife. He went into the second bedroom, where he kept his desk and his charts and flying gear. He settled, in agitation, to the calculations.

In the Atlantic, the great storm was abating. Schrenk in U-261 cruised diagonally north-east at periscope depth, feeling the buffeting of the sea and ignoring it. Inside him throbbed the knowledge that the hated Churchill must now be somewhere in his area. The chance was upon him to emulate his hero, Prien.

Schrenk knew well enough that to sight a speeding battleship at night in bad weather in the wide black wastes of the Atlantic would need a miracle. But a miracle was what Schrenk demanded of his fates. He had a deep inner feeling about it, and when those feelings came, they were right. All his life they'd come to him, and all his life they'd been right. As a boy he'd had polio, and been told he'd be crippled. But he'd *known* in some strange way that his muscles would recover and that he'd follow his dead father into the Navy. Schrenk would have laughed at the notion of some kind of spirit guidance; he was an intensely practical man. Yet the weird certainties came: unexplained and inexplicable. Certainty that he must one day emulate Prien was one; certainty that he would die in this war was another. Perhaps it was because it *was* a certainty that he could accept it calmly.

And he was certain now that he would encounter the great enemy in the great ship – and have his chance to destroy them both.

Schrenk's eyes were red-rimmed. He'd hung a long time now at the handles of the attack periscope, scanning round the whole circle of the horizon for hour after hour. His head ached a little, but he'd swallowed four aspirins and a couple of benzedrine capsules, and the ache was under control. It crossed his mind that he might take a brief rest, but that would mean handing over the attack periscope to somebody else, somebody who didn't have his *feeling*, somebody who might lose concentration for a moment.

He could not risk that! When it happened, when the chance came, as he was *sure* it would come, fractions of a second would count and it was vital that he be there, at instant readiness. A battleship moving at thirty knots would offer no second chances.

The night was dark, with heavy cloud cover. Every time he removed his eyes from the attack periscope's rubber pads, the lights at the periscope position affected his vision for a minute afterwards, so he had all but one dim bulb turned off. The microphone connecting him to the sound room remained permanently on. With young eyes and young ears, reinforced by the newest and most sensitive equipment, U-261 was alert as a shark.

Once or twice there was a small alarm. A faint ping on the sound equipment, not repeated: possibly a floating barrel or some other small object; yet quite enough to set heart beating faster and adrenaline coursing. More than once, Schrenk's own tired eyes made out of some wave pattern the shape of a ship, and a shout of warning would begin in his throat.

The long watch at the periscope was anything but recommended procedure. Tired eyes and weary minds were known to produce hallucination; and periscopes could not only only spot but be spotted. Even in rough seas it could happen by chance.

But not tonight, Schrenk thought. Tonight was not a night for the regulations. Tonight was a night for non-stop vigilance, because tonight was *the* night.

His crew grew a little impatient, but it was a kind of affectionate impatience. Schrenk was a successful commander and his methods worked, even if they were occasionally unconventional. This was not the crew's first long vigil based on nothing more than the captain's instinct, and such vigils had produced results before. The sweating, bearded men in the claustrophobic confines of U-261 were more than ready to give him the benefit of any doubt.

Even so, prolonged anti-climax had its effect. The constant readiness for something that refused to happen began to dull the edges of concentration. Schrenk, sensing it in himself, sent for ice from the galley and instructed the startled cook to put it down his neck and rub it across his forehead. Rather hesitantly, the cook obliged and was further surprised to be thanked.

Just before midnight, a sudden *ping* sounded on the

repeater. Hair prickled on the back of Schrenk's neck. 'Well?'

'Trying, sir.'

Schrenk didn't move his eyes from the periscope. 'Bearing?'

Another ping. 'Two-forty, sir.'

He swung the viewfinder round. The ocean was black, the sky above it grey. He searched a twenty-degree arc with great care, then traversed it again, ears alert for word from the sound room.

He waited. Then could no longer be patient. 'Well?'

'Nothing, sir. Seems to have gone.'

Damn! floating flotsam of some kind. *Prince of Wales* wouldn't produce a couple of faint pings and vanish! An ache of tension was knotting the cords at the back of his neck.

Ping.

Schrenk yelled, 'Bearing?'

A moment. Another *ping*.

'Dead ahead, sir.'

'Dead ahead? Range?'

Incredulity in the operator's voice. 'Eighteen hundred, sir.'

'*Eighteen* – !'

Again he swung the periscope and searched the horizon for a long, silent moment. Nothing. It didn't make sense. Not at eighteen hundred.

My God, there she was! He caught a glimpse, lost her as the swell dropped the U-Boat ten metres, then had her clearly in view for a stark moment as U-261 lifted.

Schrenk's stomach turned over. *Prince of Wales* was –

'Sixteen hundred, sir!' Alarm in the operator's voice.

– was bow on, her superstructure high against the dark sky, unmistakable now.

'Bow torpedo tubes!' Schrenk yelled.

'Ready, sir.'

'Fourteen hundred.'

171

'Up a little.' Good Christ, it was going to have to be a bow shot! With the battleship tearing down on her, Schrenk wondered why the hell sonar had not picked her up earlier! He watched. The battleship wasn't turning. She was tearing ahead, straight at them. No course correction necessary. U-261 was perfectly positioned. But she was rolling.

'Fire one.'

A whisper of vibration ran through the submarine.

'Fire three.'

'Three gone, sir.'

'Fire two.' No thought of torpedo expenditure crossed Schrenk's mind. The U-Boat was rolling. Any or all could miss, even at point-blank range like this.

'Two gone, sir.'

He'd have time – just. 'Fire four.'

'Four gone, sir.'

'Dive, dive, *dive*! Down periscope!'

As water tore into the tanks, Schrenk stood rock still, counting the seconds.

'One thousand metres, sir.'

The first would be there by now. They all counted tensely in their minds. No back-bang to signal a hit.

Now, *two*: nothing.

Three. Three would be there now. And still no strike.

Four! Please let four strike . . .

But four did not. 'Two hundred.'

Schrenk's anxious eyes flickered to the depth gauge. It would be close . . . desperately close!

On the bridge of *Prince of Wales*, gazing forward over the long sweep of bow and gun, dark grey gleams against the sea's blacks and whites, Howard Spring, a British novelist and journalist who had been invited aboard as an observer, was drinking a cup of hot cocoa laced with rum, and talking with the master, Captain Leach.

'I was hearing over dinner,' Spring said with a chuckle,

'what the Old Man was asking Professor Lindemann on the train.'

'Go on,' Leach said. Churchill stories were spreading fast all over the ship.

Spring grinned. 'He'd just polished off a pint of champagne, and he said to the professor, "For most of my life I have drunk a pint of champagne a day. How many railway coaches would it require to carry that?"'

Leach laughed. 'A fair number, I'll bet.'

'No. Apparently it would all fit comfortably into one end of the carriage he was in. He was very disappointed. Somebody else suggested Lindemann calculate how many miles of cigars Winston had smoked, but one disappointment was enough, it seemed. He changed the subject.'

Leach grinned back, then peered out through the spinning clear-vue screen. 'Still a mucky night,' he said. 'Look at that!'

Spring looked. The vast steel bow climbed out of the flying-white ocean and crashed down again, burying bow and foredeck under uncountable tons of water.

Neither they nor anybody else felt anything. *Prince of Wales*'s 35,000 tons of steel, racing at 30 knots through rough water, full of vibration from the sea and her own massive engines, sliced so easily through the submarine's plates that no trace of the impact was either felt or recorded. As the battleship forged on, U-261, cut almost in half, was already sinking towards the ocean bed. And far behind, four torpedoes, their motors running down, would shortly follow.

Jochen Schrenk's foreknowledge had proved accurate for the last time.

TEN

There was more than one spectre at the birthday feast. Dot Miller's took numerical form; she was celebrating her thirty-sixth birthday, but forty was the ominous figure in her mind. Only four more years, she thought. And the dress she'd chosen was all wrong, made her *look* forty, and the restaurant lighting was harsh and unflattering.

Alec Ross, best man at their wedding and on this evening their host, was in the classically uncomfortable position of the helpless friend. He wondered if there'd been some kind of marital row; they were being polite to him and each other. In the silences, he reflected idly on a social convention that would not allow people to say, 'Look, we're sorry, we'll be awful company tonight so let's forget it.' Convention said, battle through, however miserable you may be. And this restaurant was no place for a party: barnlike and two-thirds empty, hushed voices and tables far apart. Perhaps its atmosphere was the cause. Ross found himself working at it, resurrecting incidents from the past and mutual friends, hunting hard for laughter and the raising of spirits.

Miller's spectre had a name: Applejack.

On the wall behind Ross's head, an old pendulum clock, brass inlaid into mahogany, ticked audibly and almost mesmerically. Miller had difficulty keeping his eyes off it. He thought resentfully that it shouldn't be like this. That there should be some valedictory gaiety, some show of spirit before . . .

But there couldn't be, of course. Tonight there could be only private realization and public deception. Applejack had disapproved of the party. 'Don't drink,' he'd warned, 'your mind must be clear.' But Miller had insisted on going; to say no to Alec simply wasn't possible. Things must stay normal until the last moment, and anyway it was Dot's birthday and he owed it to her.

He looked angrily at the waiter as coffee splashed into his saucer, then glanced up again at the clock. Twenty after eight. Ten minutes to go. Alec was bending to pick up the gift-wrapped parcel on the floor by his chair, handing it to Dot, wishing her a happy birthday. Miller watched her manufacture excitement to please him, and begin to pick at the wrappings. One layer came off to reveal more underneath, then another layer beneath and another.

Miller thought suddenly: *What if I told them? What if I actually said it, right now, the whole thing – look, I'm not who you think I am. I'm not Ernie Miller at all. I'm Ernst Zoll. I'm not American, I'm German. I have a father who's a German hero and a son who's a German hero who's shot down a hell of a lot of British planes, maybe even including Chuck Stetter. And in a few minutes I have to leave here because I'm being blackmailed into stealing the Canso, and I have to fly this damned Nazi some place for reasons I don't understand, and I'm pretty damn sure I won't be coming back.* What if he said it? They wouldn't believe him, that's what. But when he'd convinced them he wasn't nuts, *then* – well, he'd lose Dot, that was certain. Dot who could tolerate most things, could not tolerate personal treachery like his, and certainly would never forgive it. And Ross would go straight to the phone and call the cops; he'd have to: for Ross there could be no choice, even if it meant his own ruin – as it would, because it was Ross who had chosen Miller, recommended him. It was Ross's duty, and Ross would do it.

Dot was laughing now, struggling with the wrappings.'What *is* this, Alec? I thought it was a shoebox, slippers maybe, but it keeps getting smaller.'

Ross said, 'Some things you have to work at. Earn your fun,' and smiled at her.

Disgrace for Ross, Miller thought, and total despair for Dot. No money, the wife of a convicted, and probably executed, spy, her world shattered, nothing to live for. He swallowed and looked at her. *Nothing to live for . . .*

Dot said, 'Once when I was a little girl, my dad brought my present home on a truck. A wooden crate, it was. Took me forever to find what was in it and by that time the whole room was full of old newspapers and wood shavings. Guess what it was? A silver dollar. It's so much nicer when people take trouble!'

Trouble, Miller thought. If he were gone, if he were dead, she might rebuild some kind of life. She'd always wonder, but she wouldn't *know*, not the detail, anyway, not the care with which he'd deceived her, and it was that knowledge that would destroy her. Knowing how she'd been betrayed, knowing he'd made a mockery of everything she believed in, knowing she was not even a wife when to be a wife – *his* wife – was all she had ever wanted.

No question: Dot was better without him now. And Ross, too. Ross pleading ignorance of a dead Miller would be better off than Ross faced with proof of a living and deeply treacherous friend.

The alternatives were bleak, but seemed clear now, if anything could be clear in the confusion of his mind. And maybe, Miller told himself, it could still be called off. Maybe Applejack would yet release him. Yeah, and maybe pigs might fly. He would go. He had to. It occurred to him that these were his last American minutes. When that clock hung vertically, he became a German again. Again? He'd never been anything else. And this was *Der Tag*.

There were five minutes to go when she got to the little box and opened it and found the gold necklet.

'Alec, you shouldn't; it's so expensive! Hey, I must put it on.' Miller watched the expert female fingers that could

176

fasten small catches instantly at the back of the neck. Dot looked down comically. 'I can't see it. Is it nice?' She was turning the necklet, adjusting it.

Eight twenty-seven.

'Looks great,' Miller said. 'You're a lucky girl.'

Ross asked, 'What did you get from Ernie?'

'I don't know. Not yet.'

Miller forced a grin, hating Applejack's idea. 'Well,' he said, 'it's a little late, that's all.' He looked at his wrist-watch ostentatiously. 'Matter of fact, I have a collection to make right now.' His grin felt taut and false. 'If you'll excuse me for a while.'

'Bad planning,' Ross said in mock reproof.

'Just wait here, huh?'

'But what *is* it?' Dot asked.

'Surprise,' Miller said. He rose, turned away and left them, going straight to the car park, astonished to find, as he put his key in the ignition, that his hands were trembling. For a long deliberate moment, his eyes prickling, he thought of Dot, sitting there in the restaurant, waiting for her surprise. And when it came . . . Aloud, as though speaking the words would somehow help, he said, 'Sorry, Dot.'

And forced himself to put her out of his mind.

As he drove by, he saw Applejack sitting in a pick-up truck parked by the garage. Miller drove his own car well off the road until it was screened by trees, and left it. He was thinking: *It cuts two ways*. As he approached, the door of the pick-up opened and Applejack said accusingly, 'I have been waiting.'

'I'm on time,' Miller said resentfully. 'Right to the minute.'

Applejack swung open the garage doors and backed the pick-up half way inside. He left the engine running as he climbed out. 'The aircraft – it's ready?'

'All gassed up.'

177

'And you?'

'I can fly it,' Miller said shortly. The more he saw of Applejack, the less he liked him. He was too cold, too intense, too ready to be the hard man. Miller felt a tardy rebellion flowering inside himself as, together, they lifted the heavy carton, loading it into the pick-up with care. Applejack secured the tailgate and got into the driving seat as Miller fastened the garage doors.

Climbing into the cab, Miller found Applejack's hand outstretched towards him. 'So now we are ready,' Applejack said, 'and we go. Good luck.'

Miller looked at the hand. 'Now wait a minute,' he said.

Applejack put the engine into gear and the hand withdrew to hold the brake.

'I said, "Wait a minute!"'

'There is no time.'

'We make time. Switch off the engine.'

Applejack stared at him for a moment, then complied. He sat with his hands on the wheel, looking ahead, impatience radiating from him.

Miller said, 'If I don't?'

'You want to go through it all again?'

'That's exactly what I want to do.'

'Very well. You will do as you are told for reasons you know.'

Miller said, 'I can really fix your wagon. You do know that?'

'Can you?'

'You're German, and this is Canada. You're threatening me with exposure as a spy. I can do the same to you.'

'Really?'

'All I have to do,' Miller said, 'is yell for help. Tell the police who you are. You and I wind up against the same wall.'

Applejack gave a little sigh. 'You think it's as easy as that? What proof have you?'

178

'Christ, you're consular staff!' Miller said. 'You're on the record. When the Canadians get you, all they have to do is ask Washington. The State Department – '

'The State Department,' Applejack said, 'would not interfere – *could not* interfere – with an Argentine citizen on Canadian soil. What possible business is it of theirs?'

'Argentine? But you're not – '

'I can prove it.' There was an irritating half-smile on Applejack's face.

'You mean you have a forged passport.'

'No,' Applejack said. 'Unlike you, I have a genuine passport.'

'But damn it – ' Miller's argument was evaporating. He said, 'You're lying.'

'No. I'm well prepared. And if you call for the police – well, there may be a little difficulty for me. Not much.'

'Enough, though. Explosives, conspiring to steal an aircraft loaded with secret equipment. If I blow the whistle on you – '

'You will blow it on yourself. But then you know that. *You* are the spy; *you* are the possessor of another man's passport; *you* are the bigamist. Do you imagine I haven't a story ready? You flew in South America, Herr Zoll, as a German. At that time you had visas. I am merely inquiring into your status on behalf of my Government which suspects impropriety and feels that it should perhaps inform friendly governments of the facts of your case.'

'Friendly? Argentina?'

'Part of the community of nations,' Applejack said. 'But I'm tired of this. You want to refuse to do what is, after all, your sworn duty: to fight the enemies of the Fatherland? Very well. Let me tell you what will happen, what the Reich can do to those who betray it. Yourself you know about. You could try to kill me and run away, as you ran away once before. But that leaves your family. You have a father, a sister, a legal wife, all in Hanover.

You have heard of the Gestapo, heard of concentration camps? You also have a woman here. What would happen to her? Do you think she is beyond our reach?'

'You wouldn't – '

'I told you I'm *prepared*,' Applejack said. 'The instructions *exist*, understand that! If you refuse, now, it will all begin in a few hours. Arrest and interrogation, and after that . . .' The words hung for a long, chilling moment, then he went on, 'And for the woman you think of as your wife – is she not a spy herself? Simple to show that she is, that she connived. And this, as you say, is Canada, a combatant nation. The rope or the firing squad – does it matter which she faces? So there are four lives, Herr Zoll – five, including your own.'

Miller said, 'You'd really do *that*?' He felt sick and helpless; his mind filled with pictures of horror.

'Without hesitation, I promise you. But,' Applejack went on, 'there is another side. All of that is unnecessary. You are a German airman, sworn to fight for your country. Once, long ago, you disgraced your uniform and your service. Now you have a chance to make amends, to restore yourself to pride and honour and patriotic duty, to strike a great blow for the Fatherland.' Suddenly, incongruously in the cab of the pick-up, his voice rang with fervour. 'For Fatherland and Führer,' he said.

'So, if I – '

'*Then* – there will be a proud family, no longer ashamed of you. There will be a heavy blow struck for Germany.'

'And I'll be dead,' Miller said softly.

'Yes.'

A simple, uncompromising monosyllable.

For a moment Miller was silent. 'And you?'

'Also. A hero's death for both of us.' Applejack produced a cigarette case and offered it, and his tone changed. 'It is a matter of accepting orders, no more than that. The pilots of the *Luftwaffe* do not question their instructions. Do you think your son ever questioned his?'

Miller blinked. 'Questioned? What – ?'

'He *died* for the Führer.'

'How, when?' Miller now felt cold, shrunken, appalled. He hadn't even seen his son, yet there'd been such pride that Heinz was a hero. Now a *dead* hero. His eyes closed tight and a small shudder began in his neck and moved across his shoulders.

'Twelve kills,' Applejack said. 'He got twelve. He did magnificently. Believe this – you will achieve even more. Surely you could not do less.' He struck a match, offered it. 'And now, it is time.'

Miller inhaled and said sadly, 'You have me. All ways.'

Applejack nodded. 'All ways.' Once more he put the pick-up into gear, and moved off. 'As I said earlier, good luck.'

'Target?'

'Later. When we're in the air.'

'Now,' Miller said harshly.

'Why?'

'You have a gun?'

'Yes.'

'The target.'

Applejack took his eyes off the road briefly, and his left hand moved to the gun, ready beside his seat. Miller was vital: without him there could be no attack, and Miller knew that. He might go voluntarily, he might go at gunpoint, he might yet try to cut and run. Looking at the pale face with its sheen of sweat, he was looking at a man whose only choice was of the way he died. He said, 'Churchill, the British battleship *Prince of Wales*, and, if we're lucky, Roosevelt too.'

Miller said only, 'The gun is your weakness.'

'Is it?'

'You know it is!' His brain whirled with images: his father, that last awful time he'd seen him; the bright day, long ago, when the vow had been made; Heinz, faceless, a boy in a uniform, a boy he'd never seen, dead now.

And a battleship. And Churchill. And Heinz, again, who would not have questioned orders. And the consequences. And Dot – better without him now . . .?

Applejack's hand was still on the gun. 'Well?'

Slowly Miller nodded.

They drove half a mile in silence, then Applejack said, 'Valhalla.'

'What?' Miller, wrapped in sadness, wasn't sure he'd heard.

'Tomorrow. In Valhalla. This son you didn't know. Maybe you'll meet him there.'

'You're crazy,' Miller said. Yet the crazy thought lodged in his mind, and he sat silent, thinking about it.

Applejack was saying quietly, 'I was once in Japan. There they have a concept of a warrior's death in battle, deliberately chosen. They call it *kamikaze*, the divine wind. To go with that wind is supreme privilege.' His words registered only barely, as perhaps they were intended to, their purpose the reinforcement of the idea of the honour of a soldier's dying, and the inevitability of it.

'Is that so?' Miller had a practical question. 'One thing you didn't say. How do we drop that thing back there? There's no bomb bay, no sight, no release mechanism.'

'You're an intelligent man,' Applejack said. 'You know there is only one . . . answer. You have known from the start.'

'Yes,' Miller said. 'I guess I have.'

Murphy was the duty guard. As the pick-up approached the fence Miller had hoped it would be someone else, someone he didn't know. But it was Murphy, whom he did know, and liked, a big cheerful Irishman, already coming out of his guard hut, torch in hand, as the pick-up stopped.

'Who's that?' The beam of the torch flicked over him.

'Gee, it's you, Mr Miller. Didn't expect you, not Saturday night.'

'Hi, Murph.'

'You're flying tonight?' Murphy was unlocking the gate in the wire fence.

'Just got some gear here,' Miller said. Why did it have to be *Murphy*?

He watched as the gates were opened, fastened back. Murphy was in his forties, once a boy skater who'd tried out for the Montreal Canadiens years back (and failed) and had talked about it ever since. He was chatting briskly, 'Hey, you know what my youngest did with the money you gave him? Little hockey stick. Perfect little thing. Not cut down like he had before. That was real good of you, Mr Miller. Boy, he sure was thrilled with – '

Powerless, Miller watched it happen: the gun hand coming up, the shot and Murphy going down. Six orphans, he thought savagely. Omelettes and eggs. And Churchill in the morning.

'We take him with us,' Applejack said. 'Help me lift him.'

They laid Murphy's body in the back of the pick-up and drove towards the distinctive high-wing silhouettes of the big Consolidated flying-boats, with the detector rings gleaming in the moonlight. The metal ladder was in position, where it had been left, and Miller climbed it, unclipped the fuselage door, hinged it up and put the stay in place. A glance at his watch showed nearly thirty minutes since he'd left the restaurant. They'd be wondering, maybe getting anxious.

Applejack had a little rope sling already prepared, and together they manhandled the packing case up the ladder and into the Canso's belly. Then Murphy. Miller thought about the family at home, waiting, the kids who'd never know. *Jesus!*

Abruptly Applejack spoke from the tarmac below. 'Come down here.'

'What?'

'There is something else. Come down here.'

Puzzled, Miller descended the ladder. He glanced pointedly at his watch.

'Stand to attention.'

'Are you crazy?'

Applejack took a small square object from his pocket, a box of some sort. The headlamps of the pick-up glinted dully on something inside as the lid was opened.

'To attention.'

Recognition set Miller's heart hammering. Almost involuntarily, his heels came together and his hands dropped to his sides, stiffening.

Applejack took a step forward, lifting the object from the box: a black and white ribbon from which hung a cross. An Iron Cross. A cross like his father's, like his son's. He said, 'Why?'

'By special order from Reichsmarschall Hermann Goering,' Applejack said formally. He spread the ribbon with his fingers and passed it over Miller's bent head. 'The Reich respects brave men. Three generations of one family. The Reichsmarschall himself believes it is a unique and historic record. Your father will, of course, be informed of your action and this decoration. He will surely be very proud.' He held out his hand. 'My congratulations, Herr Zoll. Now please climb aboard.' Applejack moved to the truck and switched off the lights.

Miller climbed the ladder in a daze. The Iron Cross – now at *his* throat! As Applejack came up the ladder for the last time, Miller's fingers were on the small metal cross. He said, 'And you?'

Applejack shook his head. 'I am a civilian.'

Miller lowered the door and clipped the clasps into place, then turned on the overhead light. The thought came to him that he was in his coffin now, and had just fastened down the lid. The Iron Cross was almost a posthumous award. 'Applejack?'

184

'What is it?'

'I don't even remember your real name.'

Heels clicked. 'Von Galen.' A little bow.

Miller pointed to the tunnel leading through from the belly of the plane towards the cockpit. 'Engineer's position half way,' he said. 'On the right.' He watched Von Galen move forward on hands and knees, awkward in the confined space, then stand. Only his legs were visible now.

He put out the light and crawled forward, through the familiar tunnel between the wheel housings into the well behind the pilots' seats, then hoisted himself up into the left-hand seat, and began.

He'd done it all a thousand times and the actions were almost, if never quite, mechanical. Miller was too good a flier, too experienced, too aware of pitfall and hazard, to do what the idiots do and neglect checks. In his instructing days, like flying teachers the world over, he'd laboured and belaboured it. 'Listen,' he'd say, 'there's a zillion ways to get dead in an airplane. Weather can kill you, engines can kill you, goddam ground *will* kill you if you don't approach it right. So you approach the airplane the way you approach the ground, right? You make sure everything's done by the book before you even *think* about ignition.'

He'd always preached it. Always done it. But tonight it wasn't possible, not all of it. The Canso had been checked and gassed-up and was ready to roll, and he'd gone over it earlier, at five o'clock. But five o'clock was four hours ago and things can happen in four hours, even to an airplane at rest.

No time now, though; certainly not for externals. He could imagine Alec looking at his watch, wondering. And it was a still night: Alec might even hear the engines start. Probably would.

And then? No doubt about it – Alec would move.

Operating instructions flowed through his mind. 'One

185

pilot will read the appropriate check list and will not proceed beyond an item until he has received the correct reply from the other pilot, who is doing the checking.'

He knew it by heart. And the list ran steadily in his head as his eyes flicked about the cockpit: thirty-three preliminary checks, before starting engines, beginning with log-book aboard and taking in switches, battery voltages, carb heat, prop setting, throttles, bilges, trim tabs. His hands moved easily, confidently, and fast. Altimeters set, oil checked, gyros caged, shut-off valves open, fuel drains closed.

It would have to do. Props clear? He looked left and right. Okay. Start-up, right engine first. Fuel booster pumps on; okay, energize. The props turning, he counted nine blades before ignition, checking meanwhile on the hydraulic lock. Okay, engage. Ignition switch *on*.

The right engine rasped, then roared. Then the left. Mixture auto rich.

Pressures. Yes, okay. Fuel booster pumps off. He took them up to 1000 rpm and ran rapidly through the next important checks, some now wildly unnecessary, performed out of habit. Temperatures and pressures were all normal, generators on.

Quick engine test, running the Cyclones up to 1500 rpm, running the pitch control through one cycle, checking magnetos. The numbers clicked through his head as his eyes ranged over the illuminated gauges.

He dropped the revs and put on his headset. 'All okay back there?'

'I think so.'

Full travel on controls? He moved the stick and looked around, watched the control surfaces move.

It was time to go.

He ran up the engines, watching the gauges, waiting for the magic figures. The Cyclones were almost deafening, the airframe vibrating vigorously. Boost approaching forty-eight inches, revs rising towards two-seven-hundred.

Ready.

Brakes off.

Roll. Turn on to the runway. Run up again.

The familiar shove in the back as she accelerated. He'd always loved that feeling and he loved it now as the Canso began to tear down the runway, eating at distance. He watched for the markers, felt the stick coming alive.

Unstick speed. And she lifted.

Now climb power: thirty-five of boost, revs down three-fifty.

Canso One was in the Ontario sky, turning to swing out over the lake.

Ross glanced at his watch yet again, frowning. Where in hell was Ernie? Looking up, he met Dot's eyes and another apologetic shrug. Caught between anger and loyalty, she said, 'I just can't imagine where he's gone.'

'No. It's half an – ' Ross stopped, hand lifted for silence. 'That's an engine starting up! Hear it?'

Head cocked, she listened. 'I hear it, yes.'

'Shh.' He was concentrating. 'There goes two. You heard the start-up?'

'Sure. But not – not the Canso, can't be.' Dot's eyes were wide. 'It can't be!'

Ross listened to the faraway sound. 'Twin Cyclones. It's a Canso.'

'But not Ernie.' Her eyes pleaded with him.

'Who else?' Ross was rising, taking out his wallet, summoning the waiter. And he was angry.

'But, Alec, he said he was coming back. With the present. He wouldn't do *this*!'

'He said he had a surprise,' Ross said grimly. 'Maybe this is it. Damn fool!' He was counting out banknotes, handing them to the waiter.

'But Ernie *wouldn't*,' she protested, near to tears.

Ross gentled his voice. 'He's done it before, Dot. You know that. Come on.'

187

'Where are we going?'

'The airfield.' He hurried her out, talking as they went. 'You know he does this, Dot. Always has. But this time it's a Government airplane with secret devices aboard.' His hand was on her arm, hurrying her to his car. They could hear the engines, quite loudly now.

Still she protested. 'You know with Ernie, when he does this crazy thing, it's always aerobatics. Something he has to – '

'Get in.' Ross swung the door to, and slipped into the driving seat.

'It's *aerobatics*,' Dot said again, 'to get whatever it is out of his system. And it's not an aerobatic plane.'

'It certainly isn't.'

'So it can't be Ernie!'

'I hope you're right.' Ross had the car moving now, turning out of the parking area on to the highway. 'But I don't think it can be anybody else.'

She sat, slumped unhappily, a handkerchief in her hand, defeated not by his argument but by her own knowledge, knowing who it must be.

Ross drove fast and in silence through the dark outskirts, out towards the airfield. Then abruptly he said, 'You had a fight today?'

She nodded miserably. 'You think that's why he – '

'Could it be? Want to tell me what it was about?'

'Nothing. It wasn't really a fight. It was just – oh hell!'

'Go on.'

'He's been acting strange for days.'

'What do you mean?'

'I – don't know, really. Acting funny.'

'No use, Dot. Pinpoint it. Acting funny, how?'

She was silent for a moment, then lifted a hand helplessly. 'Oh, how can you say? Little things.'

'Like what? Hey look!' Something dark and low roared over the road in front of them, gone in a second, masked

188

by the roadside trees. 'He's taken off. Dot, you can't even fly the thing singlehanded! What in hell's he up to?'

She said miserably, 'Who with?'

'Think, Dot.'

'Oh God. Well, *little* things, like I said. I don't know. Just, he's spent more time in his room. Gone out a couple of times without saying where. But, Alec, he does those things all the time!'

'The row you had?'

'Nothing. Not really.' Tears were being suppressed, but he could hear them in her voice. 'I said he hadn't talked to me properly for days and he said don't nag me. It was one of those. Everybody has *those*.'

Ross didn't, thank God, but he remembered all too well. He said, 'Nothing else?'

'No, Alec. Really.'

He turned off on to the approach. Two hundred yards between the trees and they were in the airfield car park and Ross was turning the Chev, swinging her round so his headlights searched the perimeter. The place was empty.

Dot said hopefully, 'If his car's not here – '

But Ross had seen something. 'The gates are open.' He drove towards them, honking the horn. The guard cabin light was on. Ross braked sharply beside it and got out. The cabin was empty.

He heard Dot's heels on the tarmac behind him and said unnecessarily, 'The guard's not here.'

'He's with Ernie, you mean?'

The thought hadn't struck him, but he couldn't imagine it. 'I doubt it.'

'Then who is?'

'I don't know, Dot. Somebody.'

'Oh, Alec! I don't understand.'

Ross took her by the shoulders, holding her away, shaking her gently. 'Dot, it doesn't help.'

She blinked. 'No. I – '

'There's a radio in the other airplane. Get in the car.

189

Let's see if – ' He gunned the Chev forward as the doors slammed, tore across to the other plane and got out, leaving her to follow. By the time she'd reached the bottom of the ladder he had the hatch open and on its stay and was climbing in, moving forward through the tunnel. He thought fleetingly that the spartan inside of a Canso was no place for fancy dresses and high heels.

Okay. Time to try. The frequency was their own, allocated to the project. He switched to transmit: 'Canso Ring Two calling Canso Ring One. Come in, please.'

Then to receive. And silence.

He tried again. 'Ring Two calling Canso Ring One. Are you receiving? Over.'

Dot, breathless in the well behind him, said, 'Is he answering?'

Ross shook his head and tried again.

No response.

He kept trying, his mind racing as the words came out, fingers moving mechanically. Ernie might not hear: ground to air between aircraft was always problematical. And Ernie'd been gone ten or twelve minutes now; he'd be twenty-five miles away.

Going where? One thing was certain, Ross thought. Ernie was heading for ruin, wherever he was going, unless he could be got back on the ground quickly. Bucketing around the sky for fun in somebody's stressed and borrowed biplane was one thing; unauthorized flights in expensive research airplanes were another.

'Ring Two to Ring One. Come *in*, please!'

And nothing.

Damn it, he'd never understood Ernie. Liked him, yes. Admired his flying, yes. But understood him? Ernie was deep and self-contained and there was more under the surface than on top.

He tried once more. Still no answer. And Ernie going farther away with every second. Precious little chance of ground-to-air contacts now, anyway. He'd have to report it, and once he did so, Ernie was finished.

There was movement beside him: Dot climbing into the right-hand seat. Pity it wasn't a co-pilot. He could chance it, then: go up and give the radio a chance; give Ernie a chance too. One last, very final chance. But alone it wasn't possible, not in the Canso. Then he glanced across at her, realization hitting him. Dot *could* fly. Even had twin-engine rating.

He slipped off the headphones. 'Dot, have you flown in the Canso?'

She looked at him quickly, then her eyes moved away. It was forbidden. He'd forbidden it himself. Joy-rides for wives, friends, and pretty girls were part of the aviation world and always had been, but this project was secret and he'd run it tightly.

'Have you, Dot?'

Her eyes came back. She hesitated, then gave a little nod.

'Flown it?'

She nodded again.

'How much?'

'I don't know, Alec. Three hours, maybe four. Bits and pieces. Oh, please, it was just – we're in enough trouble!'

He looked at her, remembering. Dot's flying had mostly been before her marriage, and when Ernie had an airplane of his own. 'How many hours have you logged?'

'Two-six-fifty.' And she could strip an engine; he knew, he'd seen her.

'What is it, Alec?' Then he saw realization dawn slowly in her eyes. 'I *can*, Alec.'

'Can you? Can you *really*?' This could put his own career at stake.

'I did flight engineer a couple of hours. It's not much different on the Canso. I picked it up.'

He hesitated, then called once more on the radio, praying for a response, but there was only the crackling

191

silence. He let it run twenty seconds, making up his mind. 'Get up there!'

A quick strained smile showed her gratitude, and then she was gone, into the tunnel, up to the flight engineer's position. Ross waited.

'In position, Alec.'

'Okay, let's begin.' He took a deep breath, hating this gamble he was taking. Any more delay and Ernie could well be out of range. Inadequate starting checks. He hated that, too.

But he began the familiar sequence. Log-book. External locks. External locks? Christ, the hatch was open!

He banged his knee painfully on his way back to unhook the ladder and load it, then close the hatch. More haste, less bloody speed, he thought savagely. Back in his seat, he began the checks again, missing many, taking far too much for granted.

On Saturday night, August 8th, 1941, two highly experienced pilots, neither of whom had previously committed that particular idiocy, ran big flying-boats down the runway at Kingston, Ontario, with check lists not completed, and roared off into the night sky.

ELEVEN

Alone in the left-hand seat of Canso Ring One, Miller took in the steady gauges. She was at cruise, twenty-seven inches of boost, two thousand and fifty revs. He'd closed the cowl gill flaps. The mixture was lean, the fuel booster pumps off. The Thousand Islands, scattered in the entrance to the St Lawrence River where it funnelled off Lake Ontario, were behind him now.

He relaxed and lit a cigarette, and gave a little grunt of amusement at the thought that they might be bad for you. There were two packs in his pocket, and he wondered how many he'd smoke as the night wore on. And which would be his last.

The headphones were on the hook beside his head. Nice to fly without them. Like the old days. He'd enjoyed flying best then: with cockpit open and no controllers and the sky free to wander in, and do a little climb and turn, or roll off a half-loop if the airplane could do it and if he felt like it, as he often did. No more of that, though. Canso couldn't do it. Valhalla, he thought. Applejack's Valhalla. No, whatever was at the end, he didn't *want* Valhalla. All the warriors in history shoved in together, just one big brawl throughout eternity. No, thanks. Maybe a nice little cloud, fully-stressed of course and a high-class engine, one of those Merlins they had in Spitfires would do, and a great blue sky that went on forever. Why shouldn't Heaven be like that? One thing for sure, he'd find out soon enough.

He was mildly surprised how cool he felt about it, how easy the acceptance was. Maybe it happened to every-body, when they actually knew, when they were going to

193

die and there was nothing to be done about it. He looked at his watch. Then at the airways map on his knee pad, and the route calculations. He was half an hour airborne, flying low, under a thousand. Thirteen hours elapsed, that was the schedule, allowing for the time zone changes. All of them. Including the half-hour over to Newfoundland. He'd almost missed that. Who'd ever heard of a half-hour time zone change? Well, the Canadians always said the Newfoundlanders – Newfies, they called them – were crazy.

On schedule. If this was his last flight, that's how it would be: on schedule. Perfect to the minute. A shade short of twelve hundred miles, he'd figured, and he was going to come in bang on the button.

On the edge of his mind the faint muttering of the headphones registered, and he ignored it. Applejack – what was his name again? Von what? Yeah, Von Galen – well *he* had solid instructions: don't call me unless it matters. And if you have to, whistle into the mike. Orders, captain to crew. He'd hear the whistle. Anything else could be ignored. He wasn't accepting instructions from any controllers, not tonight. And not again, ever, he thought. No more turn left, twenty degrees, yes, sir, hold it, yes, sir, thank you, sir. Nothing like that.

Nothing. Not after . . . he checked his watch again. There wouldn't be a moon tomorrow. Not for him.

All the same, the headphones drew him. Somebody calling. What frequency was he on, anyway? He looked at the numbers. Their own. Orange channel, allocated to the project and everybody else keep off.

So Alec *was* in the air!

And somebody was with him. Had to be. Who? If he'd rustled up a flight engineer, he'd been damn fast. But Alec *was* damn fast. Not the mechanical man, exactly, but slick, efficient, *right*. Always right. Right even when he was wrong, which wasn't often; the way Scotsmen are, Miller thought, from narrow experience of Scots. Not that

Alec was a Scot, not really. He'd been born there, but had come to America as a kid, grown up here, been educated here, flown here all his life.

So who was with him? Interesting to know.

But not to ask. No communication. Alec didn't know where he was, and wasn't going to find out. But listening might give a clue. Half-reluctantly, half-intrigued, Miller reached for the headphones.

'Come in, Canso Ring One, Canso Ring Two calling.' Repeated. Proper procedure from Alec. He listened as the call came again, found in perplexity that he was smiling to himself. Baffled, Alec? New experience for you. Call it part of life's rich pattern, and add it to all the others.

There'd certainly been plenty. In the late 'twenties and early 'thirties, flying was all experiences: landings in rough fields, lack of instrumentation, weather still a bunch of random mysteries nobody understood enough to give good forecasts. Miller was good, and knew it; Ross just a little better, and Miller knew that, too. Lacked the edge of daring, perhaps, but Ross didn't need it and had had nothing to prove. No charges of cowardice in Alec's background. The only thing you could charge him with was over-seriousness, application.

But there'd been moments, even for Alec. The one near Denver, for instance, where all the intelligence and application couldn't get him out.

How many years back? Miller could recall it as though it were this morning. Some valve part missing for a wellhead in Oklahoma and the nearest one in Long Beach or some place and Alec sent to fetch it. Light aircraft, single engine, no radio and over the Rockies. In March. Could it be done? Certainly it could be done. Heads shaken all round, but Alec's not among them. Plain, sober, unshakable confidence among the freckles as Alec picked his route, or so they told Miller later; he was in the air at the time and heard about it only on his return.

195

Alec had gone by then. And gone missing the next day, and there was a search that wasn't doing any good. Alec had phoned in, the night before, to let the oil kings know all was going well so far. Then taken off.

'Where did he phone from?' Miller had asked. Blank looks. Nobody'd thought to ask and Alec hadn't said.

'He didn't say?'

'Nope.'

Miller had known then, known at once. Alec would have given that information in all normal circumstances. But at the time there had been an abnormal circumstance in Alec Ross's life, in the sprightly form of a dark-haired young lady who lived in a place called Pueblo, fifty miles south of Denver, and there was a chance Alec had made a quiet detour. Miller had reasoned; if you're going to stop over, you might as well enjoy it. What the hell, gas was cheap.

So Miller played detective, and got the long-distance call checked back. The operator remembered. It had come from some place in Colorado that sounded like New Mexico. One moment and she'd check.

'Pueblo?' Miller asked, and now she didn't have to check. So the search area was changed, and Miller flew half across the country to join in, and Alec wasn't found, not hide nor hair, because there was snow blowing thick in the mountains so that flying was difficult and searching impossible. Alec had taken off in fair weather that turned foul an hour later. By now everybody was saying not a chance, not in this weather, not if he'd crashed. Miller had studied the maps and taken off, making a guess at Alec's proposed route. He flew for an hour, and again snow started blowing, coming down from the north-west as it had on Alec. Same problem, lucky in a way, except that it was damned dangerous; so he'd done what he guessed Alec would have done, and headed south to avoid flying into the snow.

It had been a gigantic fluke, of course, but he'd found

him. The weather cleared abruptly and half an hour later he saw the word 'Help' stamped out in deep, shadowed footprints on a snow-slope. Another pass brought a small figure out waving. Miller'd gone as low as he dared and known at once that a landing was impossible, and also that Alec was at least thirty miles from anywhere, in snow he couldn't walk out of: deep-drifted in the valleys and icy in the mountains.

So he'd taken another look, flying over three more times, waggling his wings for reassurance, then skating away with plenty to think about. The ground had looked like an Alpine meadow, and he guessed Alec had tried to make a landing. It was short, too: no more than two hundred yards on a fifteen-degree tilt, ending in a precipice. No place for any airplane.

He wasn't even thinking about airplanes. His calculations were about mountain rescue, dog teams maybe, or ponies. And climbers. On the ground he learned four things: first, that no dog teams existed; secondly, that mountain rescue teams weren't available; third, that there was a warning of further blizzards. The fourth was that a local flying enthusiast named Kenny had built a copy of a German Feiseler design, reputed to be able to land on a nickel and take off from a dime. But home-made. And hand-built. It was there on the airfield; looked like a grasshopper.

Hurriedly Miller sought Kenny out and explained. Could the Feiseler get in and out on a two-hundred-yard slope? Kenny went white. He could fly a little, sure, but he liked building, not fancy flying.

'Will you let *me*?' Miller asked.

Kenny looked at him dumbly.

'Will you?'

He could read Kenny's mind. God alone knew how many hours and how much money had gone into the plane, and here was this maniac going to wreck it in the mountains; no insurance, no nothing.

197

Miller said, 'It's that, or he'll die.'

Kenny conceded. With enormous reluctance.

So now he needed skis. Less difficult: the Feiseler copy was light as they come and it was ski-plane time of year. Suitable ones were found and swiftly adapted by willing engineers and Miller did a couple of quick familiarization circuits, then set off to race a blizzard he could already see approaching.

It gained on him, too, and the winds running ahead of it toyed with the little plane like a ping-pong ball. By the time he reached the snow slope Miller reckoned he had fifteen minutes in hand. If that.

Landing was the first problem. He couldn't land down the slope; if he tried to land across, either he'd turn over or he'd hit what looked like snow-covered rocks to one side.

Which left up, and the wind was wrong, but it was all there was.

He made one dummy-run and found his heart in his mouth. A landing with the nose pointing fifteen degrees up. Not exactly recommended, but no choice either: go in like that, or Alec was likely to die of exposure. Yes, and go in like that and maybe there'd be two of them. In the end he half-stalled the little plane in – and came down on the soft snow so gently he scarcely knew he'd touched.

Then Alec floundering towards him, healthy-looking as hell, apples in his rosy cheeks, and cramming himself into the narrow fuselage behind the seat, and saying he'd paced the distance off, just in case, and it was one-nine-two yards, and what on earth is *this* you're flying? And come on, let's get out of here, huh? And move it or the skis will freeze down and we'll all be stuck here.

And after that a quick rocky run over the snow on max revs and boost and stick back as you run over the edge into the fringe of the blizzard. Loud cheers all round and a very hasty run home with the overloaded little plane

198

sagging and bouncing all over a sky that Miller couldn't even see.

Now, alone in the left-hand seat of the Canso, in the still night, with the river silver below, Miller reflected that if death was close, it had been closer, and he listened with something approaching amusement to Ross's repeated, and now fainter, calls.

I found you, Alec, he thought. Betcha can't find me! And took off the headset.

Accordingly, Miller didn't know and didn't guess, either, that Ross's transmissions had already stopped. If Ernie wasn't answering, Ross told himself, it was for one of two reasons. Either he didn't hear, or he didn't intend to answer. Defective radio was possible, but unlikely: there were two in the Cansos and they couldn't both have gone. He didn't *want* to answer.

Why? Well, because he didn't want anyone to know where he was, or where he was headed, including Ross. So how to find out? Fool, he thought, and tuned the radio to Montreal control and started listening. Somebody was going to notice a pair of loose planes and start asking questions. There was military radar about.

But Montreal? That assumed east. Miller could be headed west or south. North, no; north was nowhere. Three directions, two radios. He switched to intercom and said, 'Dot.'

'Yes?'

'Okay up there?'

'Like clockwork.'

'Leave it, Dot. Come down here.'

She was beside him in a moment. Co-pilot in a silk dress, he thought. 'Tune the radio to Rochester.' He told her two frequencies. 'Then to Toronto. Keep switching backward and forward.'

'Sure.'

Ross said, 'I'm on Montreal. If anyone asks questions about unidentified aircraft, tell me.'

She nodded. 'Clever.'

'Obvious,' Ross said. 'I should have thought of it before.'

He flew and listened, she just listened, tuning and retuning. Neither spoke; both knew this was the only chance of finding an Ernie who didn't want to be found.

Another part of Ross's mind was confronting a different problem. Height. The Canso gave optimum performance at five seven hundred feet and he was climbing towards it, on a heading for Montreal, with the feeling that he'd need what speed he could get. But the climb was losing time, and might be in the wrong direction. Ernie's failure to answer meant he was seeking to slip away unobserved, or as near to it as possible. To do that, he'd stay low. So while Ross made height, Miller would make distance.

No way of compromising, though. He switched to intercom and said to Dot, 'Christ, he must have said *something*!'

She shook her head. 'I'm trying to think, Alec.'

He said, 'The last three days. Go over them in detail in your mind.'

Dot nodded, listening.

The minutes dragged by. Routine communications between aircraft and Montreal control. A DC3 in from Boston, two Hudsons leaving for the long ferry flight over the Atlantic to Britain. No Ernie.

The controller's voice was steady, low and precise: weather, pressure, wind speed, then sharpening suddenly. 'Unidentified aircraft entering Dorval control area, identify yourself.'

Tensely Ross waited, heard the instruction repeated. No reply. The controller's voice took on concern: warning to all aircraft to be on lookout for an unidentified aircraft, approximate position, approximate height, swift instructions on new heights and courses for avoidance, the repeated demand for identification.

Was that Ernie? There were always clowns in the sky, and Ernie wouldn't be such a fool as to wander into busy airspace without . . .

'Unidentified aircraft now heading north,' the controller was warning, retailing course, speed and height to other planes in the Dorval area. The height was lower now, under a thousand, dropping to avoid the radar scan, swinging away into open spaces. Yes, but the clowns would do that, too: go into hiding to avoid retribution. *Was it Ernie?*

No way of knowing, but the information was all Ross had.

'Any traffic, Dot?'

She shook her head.

'Dorval's got an unidentified. Could be him.' Ross wasn't quite at five seven hundred yet, but he dropped the nose and set her on max continuous.

'What'll happen?' she asked.

He shook his head. 'They may send an aircraft up to take a look, but he's heading north, flying low. Not easy to find out there.'

Fringe of Montreal control area, swinging north. Ross checked his map. Ernie nearly forty minutes ahead. He changed course, across the angle, hoping to pick up time and distance.

If it *was* Ernie.

'Listen to Montreal, Dot. Forget Rochester. I doubt he'd cross the border. I'll try him again.'

He switched to Orange channel. 'Canso Ring Two calling Canso Ring One. Come in, Ring One.'

The signal wasn't strong, but Miller heard it pretty clearly, and was more than a little surprised to hear it at all. The Canso radios were operated deliberately on low-power as a defence against listeners and he'd expected Ross's transmissions to get fainter and vanish. The fact that they hadn't meant either that reception was specially good tonight, which it might or might not be; or that Ross had picked the right direction. Somehow.

How? He'd swung north short of the control area, before the radar could get him and was probably too low for it anyway. Had some pilot seen him and reported to Montreal control? Was that why Alec had stopped talking – because he'd been listening to Dorval? It figured – it was the way Alec thought.

He'd been worried about Alec from the start; unreasoningly, maybe, because there wasn't a thing Alec could do. No way he could guess, either. No way Alec could discover where he was going, or why. And even if he could guess, nothing he could do to stop him, even if he found him. The Cansos were unarmed. Of course, if Alec did have an inkling, he'd yell blue murder, whistle up fighter aircraft, but that was a long way beyond the bounds of possibility. Applejack had wanted to disable Ring Two, had even suggested blowing it up before they left, but Miller had talked him out of it. If you really wanted pursuit, fighters on your tail, the whole *works*, that was the way to ensure it. Far better disappearing into the wide black yonder and letting Alec flounder around looking and not finding.

Still it was smart of Alec to be even this near to getting it right. Smart and characteristic. Had it been Dorval? – the radar reaching farther than he'd thought? Interesting to check. Miller tuned the radio, listened and stayed listening. Dorval was way off now, down to the southeast, but the controller's voice came in clearly. It occurred to Miller that Ross, too, was on an unauthorized flight: had to be, because Ross was on missionary work, saving souls, his in particular. He grinned to himself, then chopped off the grin because what Alec was doing would do Alec no good at all. Alec was in charge of the project, the flying end, anyway, and what he ought to have done, and immediately at that, was to report the disappearance

202

of Canso Ring One and get a search going. And clearly he hadn't.

Bad luck, Alec. Sorry, Alec.

What will you do?

Miller thought about it. Alec could make his own flight legitimate: call up Dorval and announce his presence. Dorval knew the Cansos, the long research project, mysterious but familiar, so all Alec had to say was that Canso Ring Two was requesting passage through and they'd give it. What he *couldn't* do was start asking questions about unidentified flying-boats, because if he did the whole thing came out into the open: missing aircraft with secret equipment aboard, universal panic, and no hope of saving the soul of E. Miller, long-time partner and friend.

Yes, Alec was a gentleman. There were rules and regulations Alec wouldn't bend, and lots of them. No bending on air safety, on flying standards or anything else, not where it had to do with airplanes. But the kind of man who'd make allowances, go out of his way to help, ignore the small private transgression so long as it didn't get in the way of the important things. Like the Pueblo detour. Ross had been deeply cut up about that, really hurt; not because he'd detoured to see a girl, but because other people had had to pick up the tab. He'd thanked Ernie, and apologized to him, and given him the gold watch that was on his wrist now, and given another to Kenny. More important, and right in character, he'd refused to claim insurance on his lost plane, even though he'd likely have got it, because the fault was his. The refusal cost him his independence for three long years.

Things seemed reassuringly quiet at Dorval; the controller's voice had been silent for several minutes. Miller clicked the radio back to Orange channel, and got Ross's voice at once, anxious-sounding, a little dispirited, but still putting out the call.

He clicked to intercom and spoke to Von Galen. 'Ross is in the air, looking.'

'Will he find us?'

'No,' Miller said. 'Not a chance.'

Von Galen was cold. There was a heater duct that was supposed to warm the small upright space in which he stood, but the thin stream of warm air from it seemed to be sucked instantly away in the draught that played around his body. It was like standing in a telephone-box in a winter wind with the door open. He stamped his feet on the metal floor from time to time to promote circulation, and would have swung his arms round his body for the same purpose if there had been room.

He was also a little worried. Miller had assured him that the careful route would carry the plane clear, that though the man Ross *might* try to follow, he would be unable to do so, or to take any action if he did. But they had been in the air an hour and a half now, and Ross clearly had not been shaken off entirely.

Nor was the flight as he'd imagined it. Though he was a pilot, his experience had begun in gliders on bright days, and continued in trainers plus a few hours on bombers and he was unaccustomed to the strain of long-distance night flying, the monotony, the loneliness. He told himself that he was on his way to a glorious death for his Führer and his country, but that wasn't how it felt in this icy metal enclosure. There were no trumpets, battle cries, comradeship; just long hours of solitude and tedium until the moment of . . .

He buzzed Miller on the intercom.

'What is it?'

'You're sure? About the man Ross?'

'I'm sure. Stop worrying.'

He looked at the instruments. All steady. There had been nothing to do since just after take-off and there would be nothing more for hours, apart from fuel-tank switching, unless there was some kind of emergency.

Curious, he thought, to be so helpless. He was the instigator, the organizer, the persuader, the planner, of a great enterprise that might change history. He'd done it virtually alone, pushing it through with his own will, setting the spark to a flash of fire that would destroy Winston Churchill himself and, if he was lucky and his calculations had been right, even Roosevelt, too.

In his mind, Von Galen tried to picture the moment. A great battleship, the aircraft approaching, diving, undeviating, exploding on her decks in a huge blast of heat and fire and destruction. The thought of all that heat brought a wry twist to his mouth.

'Montreal control, Montreal control. Unidentif – ' The voice stopped. A pause. Then again, 'Dorval controller. Unidentified aircraft entering Montreal airspace from the west.' But doubt in every syllable.

Ross swore. He could only be the faintest blip, but the radar's reach seemed longer than usual. New equipment maybe.

'Identify yourself.' Still doubt, the controller unsure.

Ross tipped the Canso, turning sharply northward, praying that he would now slip away from them. The controller tried once more, voice discernibly flatter this time: he was trying but not expecting.

Like Miller before him, Ross failed to respond. He wanted to. A lifetime's habit demanded that he should, but he resisted, and pushed the Canso into a shallow dive that served the double purpose of increasing his distance from the scanner and decreasing its chance of picking him up again.

But Ross's worry was deepening. He himself was slipping further into trouble with the passing minutes. First the flight itself, unauthorized, no flight plan filed; bad enough. Now a second unforgivable act: failing to answer when directed to by a major airspace controller. The fact that the Dorval control was unsure an intruder *was* in its airspace was unimportant; the requirements of notification and response lay upon the pilot.

With self-reproach came self-doubt; Ross was anything but sure that Miller was up ahead, and had only Dorval's challenge to rely on. Miller could have gone anywhere; there was no real reason to suppose that he was heading east. But it remained the only chance, if a lessening one. Tracking Miller into Dorval region was one thing; where was he going from *there*?

For the first time in his life, thoroughly baffled by his own actions, Ross found himself simply going on, without any real reason. It wasn't his habit, it wasn't his way, and the chances of finding Miller were slight; there was nothing ahead but a little hope and a lot of sky – yes, and Miller *maybe*. But something – Dot, was it? Or friendship, or even anger? – something drew him east, feeling foolish, heavily aware that the Canso on full tanks had enormous duration. Given strong favourable winds it could even reach Ireland, or a thousand places in the United States, or –

'Damn it, Dot,' he said angrily. 'Where could he be going? Give me a place!'

But she couldn't – only a sad little shake of the head. How can it be so? he wondered. She lived with him, spent days and nights with him and yet – nothing. No idea. Her husband, her *birthday*, damn it, and nothing he'd said or done had led her to expect that he was about to steal an aircraft and set out on some crazy flight to God knows where. Marriage, he thought. A meeting of minds . . . Yet Ernie was fond of Dot, very much so.

He said, on impulse, 'Seems he won't answer me – *if* he can hear. You try.'

'What about the other stations?'

'It no longer matters. Unless we're with him now, we've lost him. We've come too far.'

She forgot procedure, or ignored it. 'Ernie, it's Dot. Come in, *please* come in.' Her voice was cracking.

They waited. No response.

Ross watched her. She'd been distraught at the start, then pulled herself together in the impersonal atmosphere flying demanded, but her control was slipping with the knowledge that if Ernie could hear he was deliberately ignoring her.

'Ernie, *please*. Talk to me. Tell me if you're all right. That's all I want to know. *Please*, Ernie!'

It's not all *I* want to know, Ross thought. I want to know where, and I want to know why. He had a new thought to contend with; had been blinded to it till now. From the moment when, sitting in the restaurant, he'd heard the Canso's engine start, he'd assumed – they'd *both* assumed – that Ernie Miller was off on one of his occasional, and compulsive, breaks: the aerobatic flights that got something out of his system. Over the years it had been a pattern, some tension building up in Ernie that could only be discharged that way. They'd both known it, and made the assumption that this was just a repeat of a familiar event. But it wasn't; couldn't be. Ernie's jaunts were always solo, always aerobatic; it happened when he needed to be alone and fling himself round the sky.

But he wasn't alone now. And if that *was* Ernie up ahead somewhere, he wasn't playing poker with the laws of aerodynamics; this was direction flying. Therefore purposeful. Not impulsive: planned.

Where to? Where after Montreal? North, into deserted Quebec? North-east, along the St Lawrewnce? Due east, over Maine? No, not that. Border-crossing would bring hunters up in fighter planes to breathe down his neck.

'Dot.'

She stopped speaking and looked at him.

'A place, Dot. Any place he's mentioned. Think!'

'But he hasn't, Alec. I'd know – '

'However – well, however unlikely. If he sang "Deep in the Heart of Texas" in his bath, tell me!'

'But he *didn't*.'

'Okay, keep trying.' There was nothing else to do, and quite soon there'd be nothing at all. Without some clue somewhere, they were simply entering a void. The probability that the two aircraft were on divergent courses was strong. He smoked infrequently, but he wanted to smoke now and fished cigarettes and matches out of the seat pocket and offered one to Dot. Then the match.

She inhaled, turned to him suddenly, and said, 'Alec.'

'Yes.'

'Argentina?' She said it hesitantly, as a question, on a rising inflection.

'Argentina?' he said. 'What about it?'

'He wrote it, Alec. He wrote that word.'

'Argentina?'

'On this pad. He's got a phone on his desk, an extension, you know, and I'd gone in there to get some paper to write a grocery list and the phone rang. He was in the bathroom, and I answered and I saw it on the pad.'

'Argentina?' Ross said the word again. 'You're sure?'

'That's what it said. Just written across the pad.'

'Just that – Argentina? Nothing else?'

'No. Just – oh, there was a drawing, I think, a rough drawing.'

'Of what?'

'Well – South America. That shape, you know. At least, that's what I think it was – the shape of South America.'

'The shape of South America,' Ross said. 'For God's sake, why? What was it – places or just the outline?'

'Well, the shape. That's all it was. He flew there, you know, Alec, years back.'

Ross knew. 'He can't fly there now,' he said. 'Canso has long range, but not *that* long.' Phone call, he thought. 'Who was on the phone?'

'Nobody. The Phantom Burglar.' Dot produced a small, tinny, embarrassed laugh. 'Leastways, that's what I called him.'

'Phantom Burglar?'

She said, 'It happened a few times, two or three, anyway. Phone rang and there was nobody there. Whoever it was just hung up.'

It happened, Ross knew. The crook phoned to see if anyone was home. If not, break in. If somebody answers, hang up.

But at Ernie's home, recently? He doubted they had much worth stealing.

'Did it happen to Ernie, too? Or just you?' He watched her face, the effort to remember.

'Just to me, I think. I don't remember Ernie – '

'Has he had any calls?'

'Lately? Quite a lot.'

'Who?'

'You, usually. Most nights. Set stopwatch by you, Alec. But not many apart from that.'

'But some?'

'Well, sure.'

'Who?'

'Gee, I don't know.'

'And he didn't say?'

'Well, no. He doesn't, not Ernie.'

'Didn't come in and say who called him?'

'I told you, Alec. He doesn't *do* that.'

'Who does he know around Kingston?'

She thought about it. 'Not many people, I guess. You, the people on the project.'

'Do they call him, the others?'

'Well, maybe. How'd I know? He doesn't say.'

'Dot, try to think. When the burglar called and hung up, was there ever a call immediately afterwards?'

'I'm not sure. I – yes, there was. Once.'

'Tell me.'

209

'It was nothing, Alec. Just – I answered and he hung up and I told Ernie it was the burglar and then it rang again and Ernie said he'd get it.'

'And he spoke to somebody?'

'I guess so.'

'Who?'

She sat thinking. 'Well, it must have been you, Alec. He took the call in the hall, then when he'd finished I think he said – yes, he did, he said he'd work to do for a while.'

'For me?'

'Well, gee I *think* so.'

'Did he say so?'

'I suppose I assumed . . .'

'When was it?'

'You mean what time?'

'If you can remember. And what day?'

'Well, it was only a day or two ago. Maybe Wednesday. Around nine, as usual.'

Had he called Miller on Wednesday? Ross tried to remember and couldn't. Dot was right that he called often, three or four nights a week. But Wednesday? What had he done Wednesday? Damn it – *Wednesday*! What? He made his mind backtrack.

Wednesday was the day he'd written the report for Martingale. Spent the whole evening on it. Had he called Ernie? Yes, he had! Time? Must have been early. He'd worked five hours, uninterrupted, finished at midnight. So he'd called Ernie earlier, around seven.

He said, 'It wasn't me, Dot. Listen, the thing with Argentina, when was that?'

'Day before yesterday, I think. Maybe the day before that.'

He said, more sharply than he intended, 'Think, for God's sake!'

She looked at him, hurt by his tone. 'I'm *really* trying, Alec, really.'

'You were making a list. When was that?'

'Thursday,' she said promptly. 'That's my market day.'

'So it was the day after the call. The day *after* he said he'd work to do?'

'Must have been. Alec, he couldn't be going to Argentina, could he? Why would he go *there*?'

He shook his head, trying hard to think. Somebody telephones. The Phantom Burglar who probably wasn't a burglar. Hangs up when Dot Miller answers. Waits. Calls again. Then Ernie has work to do, at his desk. Three days later, Ernie steals a plane and vanishes.

Jesus Christ! Ross thought.

So who was with Ernie? The Phantom Burglar? And why were they bound for Argentina of all places, and by way of the bloody St Lawrence river, too? It was absolutely crazy. But then, it was no crazier than stealing the Canso, making an unauthorized long-distance flight, walking out on the birthday party and on Dot. It was *all* crazy.

Argentina. At least look at it. Don't try to understand why, he told himself, just work out how. The Canso's maximum range was around four thousand miles, which wouldn't take her anywhere near Argentina. So? He'd have to refuel. Where? Nowhere without the proper flight documents and a lot of questions. Bermuda was the obvious place, though. Cansos in the Catalina form were ferried to Europe through Bermuda; there was a base there, and fuel supplies. But Ernie couldn't just fly the damn thing in like a car to a garage and say fill her up. Or could he? The thing to remember was that this trip was *organized*. So maybe there *were* papers. And from Bermuda he might make it in one hop to some place like Recife in Brazil. And from there . . .

But Jesus, the *time* it would take! The Canso was no high-speed fighter belting out four hundred miles an hour; an average one-seventy was more like it, and who knew what the winds were!

Searching his mind for half-remembered distances,

Ross estimated the flight from Kingston via the St Lawrence and Bermuda to Argentina at between thirty-six and forty hours in the air. For God's sake! – it was just about impossible, even if Ernie had another experienced pilot with him; the fatigue would be enormous.

But hold it. The Canso was a flying-boat, after all. It didn't *need* runways, didn't *need* equipped bases. It didn't need anything short of a stretch of relatively calm water and a lot of gas, not unless there was some kind of emergency; it could refuel from a boat, just about hole up in a creek.

The Canso really *could* be going anywhere. Even Argentina!

Grimly he brought her round, clearing the Montreal control area now. If Argentina really was Ernie's destination, the route could be forecast; if not with accuracy, still with reasonable confidence. Given that Ernie wouldn't want to enter United States airspace – and he wouldn't – then he'd follow a course up the river till he was east of the state of Maine, then either turn south over New Brunswick, or wait a while and swing south over the Gulf of St Lawrence. It lengthened the flight, to do it that way, and meant he'd be over water the whole way.

But nobody, including Ross, would find him.

Miller had spent nearly an hour tuned to Dorval; but after that first hesitant inquiry there had been nothing more. Alec, if it was Alec, had followed Miller's own tactic and gone away low to the north to fly round the surveillance. And Miller felt as though Alec were still there, somewhere behind: guessing, probably, that Miller was following the river. Miller wondered how he had guessed, but in a way it wasn't difficult to understand. The river was the flier's friend: highway, landmarks, no navigation needed.

Or maybe Alec had actually given up? Two and a half hours' searching with no result; two and a half hours chasing something that maybe wasn't even there? Discouraging. Easy, though, to find out. Miller switched to Orange channel.

And heard nothing. Good. The silence extended. One minute. Two. Then a voice, a light voice, a woman's . . . *It was Dot*! Hell, Alec had *Dot* with him!

She was faint and there was distortion, but through it all he heard her distress. 'Ernie. Just *answer*, Ernie. *Please*!' Repeated. Then silence. Then again.

You bastard, Alec! he thought.

But he ought to have guessed. For Alec to get off the ground as fast as he had, he'd needed somebody at once, and Dot had been there.

'. . . please, Ernie.'

He'd never wanted to hurt Dot, but it was the omelette and the eggs again. And it had seemed to him that the only way was also the best way. He couldn't have explained to her. Dot wasn't the kind who'd listen and understand. Who would, with a thing like this? And Dot was American and proud of it and would undoubtedly have tried to stop him one way or another.

He'd hoped she'd have only twelve hours of wondering, maybe not even worry too much, because she knew his need to fly. Then the answer and she'd know. Tough, sure: there was no way it would be easy for her. When it happened, he'd have been killed in combat. Fighting on the wrong side, from her standpoint, but fighting. Some kind of an answer for her.

But Alec Ross was putting her through the mincer; trying to tail him, using Dot to load the pressure on him, forcing her through a night of strain. Oh, the bastard – even if he didn't know it.

'Please talk to me, Ernie. If you hear me, answer, Ernie – '

He switched off, checked his route. Quebec coming up next, northern detour again. Then rejoin the river thirty miles beyond Orleans Island. ETA at Mont Joli at 3.10

a.m. local, six hours' elapsed flying time. Mmm. Then he'd disappear. A little more than three hours to go, and the odds that Alec would keep coming along the river, make the same detour round Quebec City.

Would he, though? Six hours chasing a phantom. It would be a strain on anybody's determination, even Alec's. God, he thought, I must be crazy. Alec's under my skin. *Nobody* was going to go on for six hours, not even him. He'd have to get discouraged eventually, turn round and go home. Of course he would.

Yes, but Dot wouldn't. Dot might be placid and easygoing, but she had a very powerful streak of female never-let-go. He thought: take her home, Alec. Turn the damn Canso around and take her home. Tomorrow's when she'll need your help, not tonight. Don't put her through any more. He switched on again, hoping they'd gone.

'Ernie, won't you answer, *please* . . .'

He wished he could reach out, hold her, soothe her. Dot was a damn good woman, always had been. It wasn't easy being a flier's wife, especially with the kind of flying Miller had done. Okay, maybe, for the airline captains' wives, with good regular pay and neat schedules and plenty of free time. But the flying *he'd* done, any kind of ship to any place anybody asked, with the constant wondering about the next job – well, it demanded a lot of strength. He knew Dot was often worried, and was grateful she'd never let it show. Sometimes, arriving home, he'd seen how drawn she looked and known she'd been sitting there listening to reports of storms and blizzards. But she never said a word. Just before they were married he'd laid it all out for her: the insecurity, the dangers, the separations. And all she'd done was say, 'Ernie, my dad was a flier. I know all about it. I know what I'm doing.'

He'd traded on it, too, more than he should. Times he should have called her, and had not; times he'd left her shorter of money than was strictly necessary; times, above all, when the mood had taken him and he'd flown wildly, recklessly and wholly selfishly, without a thought of her. Through all of that, she'd made nice homes in cramped apartments, looked after him and his things, endlessly thoughtful.

And now . . .

'Ernie?'

What a *shit* he was! It was as though all the worry in all the years had come out this one night and was concentrated in her voice. He felt tears forming, one beginning to run down his cheek, and the unbidden thought gathering in his mind: would it matter? If he spoke, just once, what difference would it make?

What would he say? Not: don't worry. He couldn't say that; couldn't say he'd be back. Well, he could, but it wouldn't be true, and he felt a sudden, urgent compulsion to be honest with Dot. To tell her the truth. Not all of it, he couldn't do that; but enough so she wouldn't spend the rest of her life trying to solve a riddle. He could say goodbye. Yes, he could do that. And he could say it wasn't any fault of hers, and there was no question *that* was true. He could say go back home, don't try to follow because you won't find me. He could tell her he loved her, because that was true too.

And she'd say, 'In that case, why the hell are you going, Ernie?' He could just picture her saying it: her posture, leaning forward a little, indignant but soft-voiced, like she'd be if the butcher tried to short-change her, but a hundred times more feeling in it. The picture almost brought a smile, but the tugging muscles of sadness at the corners of his mouth made a grimace of it.

If he spoke, what would the consequences be? Alec would know he was up ahead, sure. But he wouldn't know where. He'd no d/f aboard and the sub-detector equipment wouldn't help. All Alec would know was that Ernie was ahead of him. Then, after Mont Joli even that wouldn't be true.

'*Please*, Ernie!' The poor kid was reduced now to that one phrase, repeated over and over.

He forced his mind back to Alec. What could Alec deduce? *He'd know Miller wasn't coming back!* That's what Alec would know. And knowing it, Alec would act, that was certain. Alec out to try to save his skin for him was one thing. Right now Alec had no idea he wasn't coming back. He'd be asking himself what in hell Miller was up to, but he'd believe he was coming back. The moment Alec *knew*, he'd sound all the alarms, yell for the cops. He'd have to; there was no other way for him.

Damn! Dot, I'm sorry. He wished he'd at least left her a letter, but that had been impossible; she might have found it too soon and canned the whole thing. Not if he'd posted it, though. That's what he should have done: written a letter and posted it. But he hadn't, and now he could not. Couldn't even speak to her, though her voice was in his ear, pleading. She'd never pleaded with him, never once.

His mind wrestled with it. Was there a way? One transmission that wouldn't give him away. If he said, '*I love you, Dot, remember that*'? No. Not, remember that. Tell her you love her. Tell Alec to take her home. Emphatic. Then switch off and maintain silence from there. To the end.

How would Alec respond to that? Sound the alarm, or follow the suggestion? Miller thought about it. Alec wouldn't do either, not straight off. He'd want more information, so he'd come right on demanding it, at least for a while. One cheep from Miller would be all that was needed to keep him coming; without it Alec might call it off before too long, turn around, go home.

Or send out an emergency squawk! He *might* do that. In which case, it made sense to keep Alec following. Well, didn't it? As long as they were following, the alarm was unlikely. It was almost a safety precaution to lead Alec on, wasn't it?

Sure it was! If Alec thought Ernie might come back there'd be no alarm. If he was careful what he said, it could be done.

But what about Applejack? If *he* had the smallest notion Miller was transmitting, he'd be down here screaming murder. Furthermore he had a gun. But he wouldn't know, would he? The flight engineer was on intercom only: the set wasn't rigged so he could hear the radio.

He went over it again in his mind. It seemed to hold water. Ernie Miller's hand moved to the mike switch, then hesitated.

TWELVE

Ross was tuned to Quebec, waiting and hoping for something from ground control to indicate unidentified aircraft in or approaching the area. He wasn't hopeful; it seemed to him that Ernie had skirted Montreal to the north, and would do the same at Quebec. But the doubts that inserted themselves in the front of his mind were relentlessly suppressed. He believed – made himself believe – that Miller was up ahead, even though there was no evidence beyond the unanswered challenge from Montreal. His doubts kept telling him Miller might be anywhere, and were compelling. Miller really could be on any course, heading anywhere. The odds that Ross had chosen correctly were long: a straight three hundred and sixty to one: any heading on the compass. In terms of probability the odds were far less, of course: north lay the empty land; west the prairies, the mountains, ultimately the Pacific; to the south lay the vastness of the United States. East? That was faith – plus the challenge at Montreal, and the absurdity of Argentina.

Quebec, as Saturday night shaded into Sunday, was predictably quiet. In his mind's eye Ross imagined the controller, feet up, coffee in hand, talking about the baseball or the movies, glancing at the clock, counting the hours till the change of shift.

Out of the corner of his eye he could see Dot, body hunched forward, talking with a kind of steady desperation: the few words endlessly repeated, hope dimming. Ross had always liked Dot, and he felt a deep pity for her now, with the shine of moisture on her cheek, urgency lining her face. She was attractive, but hardly glamorous

218

or exciting. She'd always been easy for him to talk to, always been a good listener, always friendly and sympathetic. She'd been born, more or less, into flying; raised to the sound of engines and the reek of dope, but that was the only thing about her that was in any way unusual. Dot Miller was like a million others, a good wife, wrapped up in her husband, living her life for and through him. And now Ernie was somewhere in the dark limbo of the night and she was plainly terrified she'd lost him.

Better give her something to do. He switched to intercom and said, 'Time to trim the tanks, Dot.'

She looked at him, knowing it wasn't, not yet.

He made himself smile. 'Off you go. Captain's orders.'

She nodded, climbed out of the seat and disappeared back into the crawl-space. Eyes on the fuel gauges, he waited till she said, 'In position.' Then gave her instructions. When she returned, the tears were gone, but she asked at once, 'Do I keep on trying?'

'Yes. Keep on.'

Miller should be close now to Quebec airspace, but Control remained silent. Below, the great river gleamed gun-metal; above, the stars were bright in a sky decorated with puffballs of cumulus; all around lay the empty night. Ross's eyes moved in instinctive patterns over the instruments; feet and hands made similarly instinctive adjustments to rudder and stick as the Canso roared on, alone in space. But for Miller, he'd have enjoyed this flight. Perhaps it was approaching middle age that made him take such pleasure in competence. Nowadays he rarely felt the urge to fly as he'd flown years before, revelling in the free excitements of the sky.

Squawk! Ross came instantly alert: an RCAF transport on the airlane between Quebec and Montreal was indignant. The lane had been crossed beneath him by 'some damn fool joker with no navigation lights'.

Ross listened. Control demanded to know position, height, aircraft type, heading.

Figures were given, but the RCAF man couldn't be sure of any type.

Quebec was rightly angry. 'Warning to all flights Quebec vicinity. Unidentified aircraft had just crossed beneath airlane . . .' Then the warning repeated. Then the demand: 'Identify yourself.'

Ross swung north a little, listening and interpreting, faith now reinforced. The plane seen by the RCAF transport would be Ernie's, but Quebec hadn't picked him up. He'd crossed the lane on a north-easterly course, flying low. So Ross seemed to be right: Ernie *was* rounding Quebec and would then return to the river. Fine: it gave Ross the chance to catch up a little distance.

'Quebec control. Canso Ring Two. Code G. Requesting permission to enter . . .' He sensed that Dot had turned to look at him.

'Okay Ring Two. Permission granted. Maintain lookout for unidentified aircraft our vicinity . . .'

He thanked Quebec control and signed off. At once Dot was on intercom. 'What is it, Alec?'

'He's up ahead, I think,' Ross said. 'Flying low. Aircraft spotted him heading north-east. Spotted a plane, anyway. Must be him. We fly straight while he's on the arc, so we catch up on him a little.'

They flew on, over the water, past the docks and the river heights. He could even pick out some of the lighted buildings from long familiarity: the Citadel, and there the Château Frontenac Hotel. Dot was sitting very still now, under orders not to transmit while they crossed the Quebec area. Orange channel was in a freak range, selected precisely because it was unlikely to be stumbled upon, but the world was full of people turning dials, and it was important not to let it be known that aboard Canso Ring Two, on its legitimate crossing, was a woman anxiously and colloquially calling up some other ship which clearly wasn't answering. Minutes later, with the city receding, Ring Two was approaching the western tip of Orleans Island, a thirty-mile sausage of land set in the widening St Lawrence. Beyond the island, Ross hoped, Miller would rejoin the river, this time not so far ahead. As he flew, Ross's eyes scanned the sky to the north, praying that coincidence would come clambering into the picture, that he'd actually get a sight of Miller's aircraft as their courses converged. It wasn't likely; it was barely even possible, and it didn't happen. A quarter-hour later, with Orleans Island out of sight behind them, the sky remained obstinately empty.

'Okay, Dot. Start calling.'

Miller, tuned to Orange channel, still had not transmitted. For an hour he had wanted to. The rationale had held good. The wish had turned almost into an imperative, but something had stayed his hand when he reached for the switch, and after that there had been no incoming signal. Had it happened? he asked himself over and over again, as the silence from Canso Ring Two lengthened. Had Alec and Dot turned back? It seemed unlikely they'd done so without a word. They'd surely have signed off . . .

But there'd been nothing. He checked his navigation. A little town lay due south, a thin scattering of lights on the dark earth. That would be Ste-Anne-de-Beaupré. Fine: the river approaching; an all-but-deserted highway all the way to Mont Joli. All clear ahead, then. Hazard, maybe, at Mont Joli, but after that no real obstacle. And Alec and Dot gone. Gone for good, he thought. Now he wouldn't ever hear her voice again.

Suddenly there was a lump in Miller's throat, equally suddenly a loud signal in his ear: Dot's voice! Mechanically he turned the volume down, feeling a kind of confusion: half relief that Ring Two was there, half apprehension at what might happen.

'Are you there, Ernie? Can you hear? Ernie, please answer!'

Much closer now, no doubt about it. Must have transited direct through Quebec. A signal as strong as that came from not too far away. Miller's head turned to look at the sky behind, but there was scarcely any rear visibility from the pilot's seat.

'Please, Ernie!'

The lump was thick in his throat. The grief in her voice almost unbearable. Miller's gloved fingers flicked the switch to transmit, and he said 'Dot,' but the word stuck and distorted and he had to clear his throat before it would emerge.

'It's okay, Dot,' he said.

She shouted, 'Ernie!'

Ross, startled, turned to stare at her. She was smiling at him, her face lit with relief. He switched to Orange channel to listen.

'Ernie, are you all right?'

A pause, then: 'I'm fine.'

The words poured from her. 'What are you *doing*, Ernie? Where are you *going*? Ernie, why didn't you *answer*! I've been calling for . . . oh *Ernie*.'

Ross didn't interrupt. They had contact. Given contact, it might be possible to talk Ernie out of this thing, but it was important to maintain the link, and it was Dot's entreaties that Ernie had answered.

A pause, then Ernie spoke, flat-voiced, *very* flat-voiced. 'Now listen to me. Don't try to follow, you understand.'

Garble. In her anxiety to speak, she'd pressed for transmit too late.

Ernie again. 'Listen to me. I repeat, don't try to follow. This isn't the first time, you know that, Dot. The sooner you leave me alone, the sooner it's over. I repeat, don't try to follow.'

'Ernie, we have to, don't you see?'

Ross cut in sharply. 'Listen to me, Ernie. You've got to

get back on the ground or you're finished. Repeat *finished*, Ernie. Turn now, return to Kingston, and we'll try to work out some story. It's Sunday. We can work out some authorization, make up a framework to cover it. But *you must turn back now*! Over.'

He waited, 'Negative. I repeat, do not follow. Over and out.'

'*Ernie*!' Dot was shattered.

Ross said, 'Ernie, you have to make that turn *now*! That's an order.' It had to be said, but he was conscious how feeble he sounded.

No response.

Angry now, Ross said, 'Why, Ernie, why in *hell*!'

No response.

He controlled himself, returned to something closer to formality. 'I have to report, Canso Ring One. Ground must be informed. I have to give necessary information. Repeat, ground will now be informed.'

She turned to him. 'Alec, do we have to?'

He didn't answer. As his hand reached towards the radio, Dot said frantically, 'Ernie, I love you. If you love me – *please*!'

Ross's hand remained still. He'd give it a few moments more.

A full half-minute went by, then Ernie's voice, emotion in its gruffness. 'I love you, Dot. Sure I do. But don't try to follow. Out.'

That's final, Ross thought. He radioed: 'Canso Ring Two making passage on Code G, repeat Code G, following Canso Ring One, requesting clearance at height two zero over St Lawrence river. This is Captain Ross, commanding. Repeat Code G . . .'

From the moment Ross had threatened to call the ground, Miller had known he'd go ahead. Alec didn't make idle threats. Quickly he switched frequencies and listened. Code G belonged to the project, to the Cansos alone, and all controllers had notification of its priority. The priority angered them sometimes.

Tensely Miller heard the exchange, then relaxed as he realized what it meant. Alec was protecting him still. Taking one hell of a chance, too. He was in very deep now, had committed damn near as many offences as Miller, and was compounding them by putting his own command imprimatur on the flight of both aircraft. Once Alec broke silence, it should have been to report the runaway.

But he hadn't. What he'd done was to put them both temporarily in the clear. It meant that whatever communication was passed to stations along the St Lawrence, Miller now had no cause for concern. Alec would come back to him now, no doubt about it; he had to, because his own head was on the executioner's block and the only way to get it off was to talk Miller down.

He clicked back to Orange channel. A moment later Ross's voice sounded in his earphones. 'Did you hear, Ernie?'

Miller didn't reply. No more communication, he thought. I've said all there is to say.

'I've gone right down the line for you,' Ross said. 'I'm in as deep as you are now. I've saved your goddam bacon, near as I can. Now it's your turn to save mine. Get the hell back to Kingston!'

Miller thought bleakly: I'm pulling them all down. This would finish Alec; Dot was in a hell of a state . . .

And back on the air, too. For the next half-hour her voice was in his ear, pleading, cajoling, asking; endlessly insistent. What he ought to do was turn her off. It would be so easy, a movement of the knob on the radio set, but a movement he felt powerless to make: he couldn't switch Dot off – it was somehow like killing her, to reach out and switch her off, just like that. Then she'd just be talking helplessly and hopelessly. No, he couldn't do that.

As the minutes passed, Miller's resolution waned. His

hand kept wandering to the transmit/receive switch, and coming away again. He wondered whether in some uncanny female way she knew he was going to his death. Women had this – this intuition they talked about.

Finally he did it, the movement made almost unconsciously. He said, 'Tell Ross to take you home, Dot. This is doing no good.'

Hearing his voice put eagerness into hers. She was back at once, wanting to know why, demanding that *he* turn around.

He transmitted again. 'Wish I could say why, Dot,' trying to be oblique, 'but I can't. Go home.'

'Ernie, listen to me. Please, listen – ' and then she broke off, but her fingers must have stayed pressing on transmit and Miller heard her say, 'Alec, what's that? *Alec!*'

Her voice disappeared on the click of the switch.

Miller blinked. There had been real alarm in her voice. Something wrong? He waited, wondering, then said, 'Come in, Dot, come in.'

No response.

'Come in, Dot.' Now it was his turn, he thought savagely.

'Come *in*, Dot!'

Nothing in his headphones but a faint crackle of static. Until . . . faintly, the sound dying: 'Smoke, Ernie, it's – '

Fire? Was that last word 'fire'?

'Repeat, please. Did you say fire aboard?'

No response.

'Your signal unclear, I say again your signal unclear. Did you say fire? Come in, please!'

Nothing.

Miller's brain raced. If she'd said 'fire' . . . And she *had* said smoke, he'd heard that, no doubt about it. Smoke, fire, airplanes. *Christ!*

He tried again, drew no answer. A trick? Could it be that? – could it be Alec putting out a panic message,

225

trying to turn him in that way because he wouldn't turn for anything else?

He kept calling, with increasing anxiety. What the hell to do? If Alec's airplane was on fire, he had to do *something*, couldn't just fly on. No – he couldn't do that. It was his fault, his . . .

His boot hitting the rudder bar, hands moving on the stick, he swung the big flying-boat round in the nearest thing she could do to a tight turn. Signal strength had been very high; Canso Ring Two couldn't be far away. Ring Two was following, therefore almost certainly over the river. Miller straightened her, hauled back on the stick and gave her boost and revs for a faster climb as he began to fly back along the northern bank of the St Lawrence, grabbing for height, as his eyes stared through the side window, searching the river's gleaming surface for movement.

But the movement came beside him. He turned his head quickly, to see Applejack scrambling into the right-hand seat. Crazy, but he'd forgotten about Applejack!

Von Galen was yelling at him. 'What the hell are you doing?'

Miller pointed to the headphones, and watched them go on Applejack's head.

'What are you doing?'

Miller said, 'Going back. Aircraft in trouble behind.' He stared out of the window, not looking at Applejack; not caring about him either; his mind full of thoughts of Alec and Dot in a burning plane.

'No!' Applejack was shouting. 'You must turn again, get back on course!'

Miller ignored him, mentally counting. Ten minutes converging meant sixty miles, and they hadn't been that far behind, not with the signal strength –

'Turn!'

Miller shook his head.

* * *

226

Von Galen's hand moved towards the automatic pistol in his pocket. Then stopped. He stared in incredulity at the bulky figure, resolutely turned away from him, gazing out of the window. He said, 'What aircraft?' was again ignored, and thought angrily: how did Miller *know* there was an aircraft in trouble? He'd been told to ignore the radio, neither to transmit nor receive.

'What aircraft? How do you know?'

Miller's hand moved to the mike; he heard him say, 'I got the call.'

'But –'

'We have the time,' Miller said. 'Don't get worried. There's a plane in trouble. I'm looking for it. Keep quiet, huh?'

But Von Galen didn't, couldn't, keep quiet. They were on probably the most vital mission of the whole war, and this idiot was turning back to look for some aircraft in trouble. He said, 'I order you. Get back on course.'

Miller didn't even turn his head. 'Don't order me, sonny. And keep *quiet*!'

As Von Galen sat fuming at his own helplessness, abruptly realization came; Miller had thought from the beginning that the other man, this Ross, might follow. Yes, and he'd also been quite sure he'd lose him easily.

'Ross. That's who it is?'

A nod.

'Ignore him. We cannot *afford* this nonsense.'

Miller's finger on the switch, his voice saying, 'He's got my wife aboard. There's a fire.'

'Miller, this flight *must* go on!'

'Not till I'm sure. One way or the other.'

Miller, aware of the pistol Von Galen possessed, knew it presented no threat. Von Galen was a pilot, so he said, but he sure couldn't fly this ship where it had to go, not in a zillion years. He might hold her in the sky, no great difficulty in that, but he'd never find the route, navigate her across land and water to Newfoundland. He could forget the gun, forget Von Galen too, until he could be sure Ring Two wasn't about to fly into the ground.

Four minutes now. They must be getting near. But he could see nothing moving: neither a black shape over the water, nor the glow of a burning aircraft in the sky. Miller's eyes hunted the southward arc of his vision. How far behind had Ring Two been?

Something seemed to move, half behind the metal window-framing. He moved his head, trying to pick it up again. Yes, there! He watched it, saw the tiny red pinprick of the port wingtip light. It was a plane. Was it the Canso? On another bootful of rudder, Miller flung his aircraft round, still climbing. Already the other aircraft was dead abeam. Also it was holding course, straight up the middle of the river. Keeping it in sight, he continued his turn, watching the altimeter. Nearly four thousand now, and the plane below him flying low, only a couple of hundred feet above the water. It *must* be Ross; nobody else would be flying like that.

He turned on to course behind the low, scudding shape of the other aircraft, and put Ring One into a shallow dive, gaining speed, gaining distance, waiting for the moment when the silhouette would tell him with certainty what aircraft he was now following. Almost mechanically, his mind estimated distances. Four miles, three . . . soon, now. Two miles. She was high-winged, he could see that. Slowly the details came into shape: wings, the upward curve towards the tail, the twin engines, wing-mounted, close to the fuselage.

'It is?' Von Galen demanded.

Miller nodded, concentrating.

'There's no fire!'

So Ross *had* been playing tricks, Miller thought. Damn Ross! The Canso was flying straight and level, no smoke, no gleam of fire. He heard himself exhale as his anger at

Ross mixed and warmed with relief that Dot and Ross were at least safe.

She'd said 'fire', though. And sounded afraid. Smoke. Fire. Fear. *Was* it a trick? Dot was certainly no actress.

'Canso Ring One calling. Are you okay? Come in, Ring Two.'

There was silence as the Canso forged steadily on. They must be all right, Miller reasoned. If there'd been a fire of any severity, Ross would have put the flying-boat down on the water. But concern still nagged.

'There's nothing wrong, nothing at all,' Von Galen said angrily. 'They're trying to trick you!'

'Maybe.' Miller watched a moment longer.

'We must get away,' Von Galen urged.

Miller's teeth gnawed at his lip. Though his mind told him the Canso was in no danger, and that if there'd been a fire, it was out now, his emotions demanded certainty. Above the skimming flying-boat he saw the vast puffballs of gathering cumulus. That was one way, not too chancy.

'I have you in sight, Canso Ring Two. I do not see fire. Are you okay? Come in, please!'

There had been a spurt of smoke, a smell of burning and not much more. Ross guessed it was a loose wire or a smashed valve, a short circuit, insulation material singed. He had used the portable extinguisher and now there was no trace even of heat, let alone fire. But the radios seemed to be out, both of them.

Switching from one frequency to another, he got nothing, not even static. Receiving on Orange channel he heard a dim hum, but that was all; there wasn't even the click as the transmit button engaged. He'd have to turn back soon. With no radio there was no possibility of further contact with Ernie; furthermore he was now a danger to airborne traffic.

But there remained the chance that Dot's final words had reached Miller: that the knowledge of fire aboard

Ring Two would bring him back. Miller would know they were near, would guess their course. He'd come back now.

Ross held straight. Miller was ahead: if he came back, it would be over the river, or beside it, and if Miller came in sight, Ross intended to simulate distress, sideslip the Canso to an awkward landing, in the hope of tempting Miller down. He could see no other way.

A nudge. Dot's hand on his arm. 'Alec!' She pointed to his discarded headphones. 'It's Ernie!'

He slipped them on quickly, heard Miller's voice, faint but clear: 'Come in, please.' So on Orange channel he could still receive!

'. . . repeat, I have you in sight.'

Ross and Dot Miller looked at each other, the same question in both minds. He tried to transmit, but the thing was dead. He could receive, but only on Orange channel.

Miller's voice said again, 'I see no fire. Can you transmit?'

Where *was* Miller? Ross's eyes ranged the sky ahead anxiously, though he knew Ring One would not be there; Ernie would now be above and behind, in the watcher's place.

'Can you receive me?' Miller was asking. 'If you receive me, waggle your wings.'

Ross hesitated, trying to work it out. Ernie had turned back, because the thought of fire had impelled him. But now what? And if Ernie'd been watching, he'd know Ring Two was flying straight, steady and low: not an aeroplane in distress. So the sideslip to a bad landing was out.

He waggled his wings.

'Okay, Alec. I see you. Two questions. First, can you transmit. If not, waggle your wings.'

He's not coming close, Ross thought, just standing off and observing. He'd have expected Miller to fly alongside, make a visual inspection, but Miller wasn't going to do that, because Miller didn't want to be seen.

230

So Miller's flight wasn't over.

Still, he had to answer. Once more he waggled the Canso's wings.

'What's the fire situation? If it's out, waggle your wings.'

Ross turned to Dot, knowing now. Once Miller was sure of their safety, he'd leave them. He said, 'Get up to the observation bubble. See if you can spot him!' He held the plane steady as she left the seat and scrambled through the crawl-space.

'Repeat, Ring Two, if the fire is out, waggle your wings.'

Dot's voice on the intercom. Mercifully *that* still functioned: 'Can't see him at all.'

'Stay there,' Ross said curtly, 'and *try!*'

Once more Canso Ring Two went into the slow rocking motion that tilted first one wingtip, then the other.

Ross knew what was coming now, and it came at once. 'So long, Alec,' Miller said. 'Go home and take Dot with you.'

'What do you see?'

'Nothing.' She sounded on the edge of tears.

'Above,' Ross said tightly. 'Christ, he *must* be near! Above and behind. *Find him!*'

'I can't . . . can't see a thing. Not a – *yes*, Alec! Out to the left, maybe a thousand feet above. Oh God, he's swinging away!'

Frantically Ross swung the nose round, heading for the north bank, staring up towards the area of sky where Miller's plane might appear. That cloud. Hell, Miller must be making for that cloudbank! He saw Miller then, watched him for perhaps two minutes, as Ring One rose towards the hanging whiteness at the base of the vapour ball, then vanished into it.

Ross neither saw the third aircraft nor heard the exchange that took place. But Miller had seen it: an RCAF fighter, perhaps on some kind of night training, that slid in behind Ross and required him, in youthful and officious tones, to identify himself. Miller watched, amused. No way Alec could reply; what would the kid do? The signal was repeated. Ross flew on.

'I must ask you to follow me,' the kid radioed snappily. 'You will take up station – '

Miller intervened. 'Listen, sonny,' he said, borrowing Ross's designation, 'This is Canso Ring Two on Code G operation. Repeat, Code G. And if you don't know what Code G is, find out, huh? Then go back and jerk some more sodas!'

He was smiling a little as he headed into cloud. It was all clear now: they were safe – and there was nothing more he could do.

He turned to Von Galen. 'So let's go get Churchill.'

Blind, in cloud, flying on instruments, Ross knew the hopelessness of it. There'd be no more sighting of Canso Ring One; with the radio gone, there could be no further communication, unless Ernie chose to use his radio, and there had been an unmistakable finality to Ernie's last, 'So long.' Yet he was damned if he'd give up now. Ernie was going *somewhere*. He wasn't pottering round the sky; he wasn't flying for fun. There was a destination and there was a purpose, and though he could not for the moment imagine what either of them might be, some logical termite digging around inside his head told him it ought to be possible to reason it out. He'd already thrown his career out of the window. Up to this moment he'd been telling himself it could all be squared off when he got back to Kingston. But it couldn't, and he knew it. There were too many hours on the machine, too much fuel used, too many infractions. No possibility, now, of trying to explain it away as some kind of test or training. The words on paper at Montreal and Quebec would come back down the line to condemn him. Even if he told the exact truth: that his subordinate had taken off for some

232

unknown and crazy reason and that he'd had no alternative but to attempt to follow, it just didn't hold good.

He should have found a phone the moment he knew Ernie had gone: found a phone and yelled alert, handed the job to the RCAF and let Ernie take what he surely deserved. But he hadn't. He'd been a fool from the start and the foolishness had multiplied until there was no escape now for either of them.

Ernie's fault, damn him. Ernie'd done it, Ernie had flown on, letting him go in deeper, ruining both of them.

But why?

Where could the answer lie? He knew Ernie. Dot knew Ernie. Nobody on earth knew him better. He called her back to the right-hand seat. It was a contest now. So far he'd been defeated all along. But not finally, oh no. Not finally. Not yet.

She opened her bag, took out a handkerchief, and mopped at her eyes. She looked shrunken, ten years older, despairing.

Ross said, 'He's still going along the river. Has to be. He may be one side or the other, but that's his direction. We've three hours to Mont Joli, and we're going to use them to think!'

THIRTEEN

Paper. He needed paper, and his briefcase wasn't here. No need for it when he'd gone out to dinner. God, to dinner . . . Well, he'd burned so many damn boats, he might as well burn another. He reached for the sacred log, ripped out two pages and held them out to her. 'We're going to list everything we know about Ernie. Everything.'

'I don't even have a pencil.'

Ross had. He gave it to her.

'What are we looking for?'

'Anything that doesn't square up.'

'In his whole life? Alec, that's – '

He said, 'We've time, Dot. Get it all down on paper, where we can see it. I don't even know where he was born, for God's sake!'

'Asunción, Paraguay,' she said. 'It's on the wedding papers. His father was American, a small-time trader.'

'Mother?'

'American too, I guess. I don't know. Not even her name. He never mentioned it.'

'Write that down,' Ross said. 'Mother's name unknown. Where'd he go to school?'

In twenty minutes they had a biography of sorts. 'Quite a few blanks,' Ross observed.

'Not after he came to the United States,' Dot said, automatically defensive where Ernie was concerned. 'We know most of it after, let's see, yes – after 1928.'

'When I met him.'

'Some ways you know him better than me, Alec. I've only known him since 'thirty-three.'

'How did you meet?'

'You know how.'

'Tell me again.'

'My dad had a little hangar in Kansas, place called Pratt. Repairs, maintenance, gas. Ernie came in with a big tear in the wing fabric and I fixed it. He was kind of surprised, me being a woman.'

'How long before you were married?'

'A year.'

'Write it down.'

They went over the years of flying, the adventures, the business failures, lengthening the little dossier. How many times had Ernie gone off on his aerobatic solos? What were the reasons, if any? Eventually Ross asked quietly, 'Would you say he's honest?'

'Ernie. Oh sure, he's honest.'

'Money? Girls?'

'Money, sure. Girls, well, I wouldn't know about girls.'

'What do you mean?'

'Alec, I just don't know. He's been away plenty. Maybe he's had chances. He never told me.'

'And did you ever suspect?'

'No.' She said it with convincing firmness.

Ross's mind was back in the past, on his trip to see the girl in Pueblo, and on other similar jaunts through the years. He was trying to remember whether Ernie had ever . . . but he couldn't think of an instance.

'Did you, Alec?' she asked evenly. 'Did you suspect?'

'No,' he said. 'I never did.' His mind dwelt on it a little longer.

'You're sure?'

'It's tempting, Dot. That's what bothers me. Plenty of pilots have gone off on unauthorized trips to see their girls. It would be an easy explanation for this. But I can't see Ernie doing it.'

'Good,' she said. 'I'm glad we can cross that off.'

He went back to honesty. 'Look, this trip's illegal, it's

235

dangerous too, the way he's flying it, dangerous to him and everybody else in the sky. In that sense it's dishonest.'

She said, 'Why did you pick him, Alec, for the project?'

'He's a damn good pilot. Toughness, reliability, stamina.'

'You think he's dishonest?'

'Well, no. If I'd thought that – '

'Me too. Only I didn't just give him a job. I *married* the guy.'

'Okay, but we know he's been concealing something. He's been planning this thing, and somebody else is in on it. Maybe it's your Phantom Burglar, maybe it isn't. But somebody. And he did it without you guessing anything was going on. Phone calls, work at his desk, planning a route, even planning to walk out on the party and not come back. I'm not being brutal, Dot, but give me a word for that.'

Tightly she said, 'Deception.'

'That's right. I'm sorry, but it's right. Now, have there been other deceptions?'

Her hand lifted from her lap and fell back in a little gesture of defeat. 'How'd I *know*? If he's been deceptive, it's worked, that's all.'

'Is he secretive?'

'I don't think so. No, I wouldn't say – '

'In little things. Money, maybe – do you know about his money?'

'Just that we don't have much.'

'But not how much?'

She said, 'Gee, sometimes, maybe. I don't know. It's not important.'

'His desk?'

'What about it?'

'Does he keep it locked?'

'Not that I know. Alec, I never go *near* it, except once in a while if the phone rings.'

'Mail. Who opens the mail?'

'He opens his. I open mine.'

'Together?'

'What's that mean?'

'Does he open it when you're there?'

'Well, sure.'

'Always?'

'Maybe not. Accounts, things like that, he'll take to his desk. Not look at them for a week, sometimes.'

'And when he's away? What happens then – do you open his mail in case there's something important?'

'No.'

'Why not?'

'I don't believe in it, Alec. It's called privacy.'

He sighed.

She said, 'This mail thing, Alec. It doesn't matter. It truly doesn't.'

'He never gets unexplained letters?'

'Not that I know. Look, what happens most days is he gets out of bed and makes me coffee. Picks up the mail and brings it in with the coffee.'

'So he *could* – '

'Sure he could. If you want to think that way. I just happen to think he doesn't.'

'But the phone calls. With those he – '

'Okay, so it was fixed by phone, Alec. We already know that.'

'No. We suspect. We know nothing. But we have to suspect everything. Look, Dot, he's not doing this for nothing, and he's not just playing about. He's embarked on something that's damned important, to him anyway, and to us because he's involved us. With a thing like this, there has to be a clue somewhere. Look, go over that list. Everything. If there's something funny, tell me. Anything.'

She shook her head. 'Gee, I really don't know. Like what?'

'Call it discords. Wrong notes. If anything didn't sound right. However small.'

'Music? He's not interested in that, Alec.'

'I don't mean music. By discords, I mean – '

'I understand what you mean. Little things. You remember the wedding?'

'I was there.'

'In church. Me, Ernie, you and Chuck Stetter.'

'Yes.'

'It was Ernie who wanted it in church, not me. That the kind of thing you mean?'

'Not exactly,' Ross said. 'Plenty of people – '

'He's never been to church since. Me, I'd have been happy with a Justice of the Peace, but Ernie wanted a Lutheran Church, and that's where it was. He even chose the hymns. You remember?'

'Not the details, no.'

'Just the few of us in that big church. Organ-playing, though. The works. And he chose the strangest hymn.'

'No, Dot, I don't think – '

'You asked, Alec. I'm going to tell you. We had the Wedding March and "O Perfect Love" and – this is the funny thing, we had "Glorious things of Thee are spoken".'

'So?'

'Well, it's kind of a weird hymn at a wedding.'

'Why?'

'It just *is*, Alec.'

'Okay. Anything else?'

'You did ask me.'

'Think, Dot. Anything more? Did you fight about things?'

'Not really. Well, just little fights, the way people do.'

'You weren't exactly cooing last night.'

'No.'

'Why not?'

'It was nothing.'

'Tell me.'

'Oh, I told you. I was angry he hadn't bought a present and I needled him a little. That's all. I thought he'd forgotten and gave him a little hell.'

'That's it?'

'That's it.'

'He had a lot on his mind,' Ross said. 'But he didn't forget. He used the present as an excuse to leave.'

'We've been over that. Look, Alec, it's real hard. I can't *think* of any discords. Try it on yourself, you'll see how hard it is. Did *you* ever fight?'

'Yes,' he said, remembering. 'We did, once.'

'What about?'

'It was just a brawl. Bunch of us in a bar, must have been 1933, just after Prohibition ended. We got to arguing politics. I recall Ernie said Roosevelt was a Communist. We were all a little drunk.'

She said, 'He's not the only one who thought *that*. Plenty still do. You fought with Ernie?'

'Bar-room brawl, that's what it was.'

'Nothing since?'

'No.'

She said, 'He doesn't talk politics.'

'No, he doesn't.'

'He doesn't think we should go into the war, though. I know that.'

'We'll be in,' Ross said. 'Dot, go back to that paper. The one with Argentina on it. And the map.'

'What about it?'

'Describe it again.'

'It was just a sheet on a scrap pad; little eight-by-five pad, you know the kind.'

'But was there anything else?'

'I don't think so.'

'Picture it in your mind. Better still, try to draw it.'

She chewed on the pencil for a moment, then wrote, and handed him the paper.

'Like that? The word written diagonally. The drawing –'
He turned the paper in his hand, trying to find something,
anything. 'Handwriting? Not printed capitals?'

'No, handwriting. I'm pretty sure. I don't draw South
America too well.'

'And that's all?'

'I think so.'

'Be sure, Dot. Try to see the paper in your mind.'

She said, 'Maybe there were numbers.' She reached
across and pointed with the pencil. 'Yes, some numbers,
I think. Right there.'

'What were they? How many?'

'Like a phone number, maybe. Would it be four? Yes,
four, I think.'

'Try to think what they were, Dot. It could be
important!'

'I'm *trying*. Let me think.' Her eyes closed tight. 'Give
me the paper.' When he passed it over, she said, 'Here.
About like this. Could it be eleven something? Oh God,
I don't know!'

'Write it.'

She put in two ones and two question marks. 'I can't
remember. I'm not even sure of the ones.'

Ross stared at the paper, trying to make sense of it.
Argentina. South America, of which Argentina was part.
A four-digit number, perhaps beginning with two ones. It
made no sense. 'There was nothing else, you're absolutely
sure?'

'That's all there was.'

'There's no connection. Argentina and South America,
sure, they're connected. But the number? It's six thousand miles flying down there, seven even, given the route
he's on. So why two ones? It can't be distance. Too
precise for altitude. Time? Eleven something. He'd gone
by then. Did it look like a time notation, Dot?'

'It's not that clear, Alec. All I have is an impression.
It's not a photograph.'

240

'When he writes down a time, twenty-four-hour clock, does he put the period in, after the hour figure? You know – does he write twenty-three period fifty-nine, or just twenty-three fifty-nine?'

'You'd know better than me, Alec.'

'That's true.' He tried to remember, and couldn't. But Miller had flown Ring Two. It would be in the aircraft log. He got it out from the pocket beneath the seat. 'He puts the period in.'

'Crosses his sevens, too,' Dot said. 'I always wondered why he did that.'

'Some people do. Europeans. Not the British, but the others. South Americans too, so it seems. Taught in school. Habit stays.'

She said softly, 'We've nothing, Alec, have we? *Nothing*!' For a long time now she'd been in control of herself, diverted from despair by the need to think. As he watched, the despair returned to her face.

'No,' Ross said. 'Not much.' Orange channel hummed in one headphone but the hum was all there'd been for two hours now. Ernie had meant that 'So long' of his. He wouldn't speak again.

On Canso Ring One, Miller had spent the last hour giving free flying lessons. Shortly after he'd headed into cloud, Von Galen had said, 'Teach me to fly the Canso.'

No prizes for guessing why, Miller thought. Teach me to fly so that I can kill you if you do anything stupid. Make yourself vulnerable.

'I don't think so.'

'Why not?'

'You got an instrument rating?' They were flying at five thousand seven hundred, in and out of steadily thickening cloud.

'No.'

'That's why.' Miller pointed through the wet windows.

'It's not as easy as it looks, pal. Not even for a bright, intelligent New German.'

'You're not criticizing the New Germany?'

'I've never seen it.'

'Then don't. But it's a pity you won't see it. Germany is a great nation now, the greatest of all, the greatest nation on earth. Proud, strong, victorious! Thanks to the –'

'People,' Miller said. 'The army, the general staff. The *Luftwaffe*. People like my son.'

'Thanks to the Führer.'

'Yeah.' Needling Von Galen amused him. It was childish and irrational. They were going to die together, a few hours from now, Von Galen for his Führer, Miller for – what? Not for the New Germany. Not for Volk, Vaterland, Führer. Well, not for Volk and Führer, not when it was put like that. For Fatherland, yes. For an oath perhaps, that he'd taken long ago; it pulled at him still, pulled him hard: an oath not to be broken. But no, he thought, it wasn't really even that. More than anything, it was shame: twenty years and more of living with proof of cowardice, twenty years' knowledge that his own father wouldn't speak his name, that his own sister had written to him only three times, had written only out of duty and in total contempt. Face it, he thought, *that's* the reason!

Beside him, Von Galen changed tack. 'What is the time now?'

Miller glanced at his watch. Then at his schedule. 'I'm estimating Mont Joli at three-ten local. There's a time zone change.'

'Two and a half hours.'

'That's right.'

'So it's midnight.'

'Yeah.'

'And it is the day we die together. If I'm right. If the ships are there.'

'They better be.' Today, Miller thought. The day I die.

He swallowed and looked down at his body. In a few hours it would be – what? Cinders, pieces of meat blown far and wide? That was the reality, but it was difficult to imagine, even to believe.

'So the condemned man,' Von Galen said, 'should be granted the last request. It is traditional.'

'And yours is to fly this ship?'

'Yes.'

'Don't take no for an answer do you?'

'If I had, Herr Zoll, we would not be here now.'

Miller looked at him sardonically. 'I know what you're thinking, pal.'

'Do you?'

'Sure. You've got a gun. You're thinking that if I chicken out you can shoot me and do the job yourself. Why should I go along?'

'Why? Because it is your duty. You forget I know about you. You "chickened out" – what an expression! – once before.'

'I was a kid then,' Miller said. 'Just a kid.'

'Is the child not father to the man?'

'Don't worry. I won't chicken out now.'

'I'd prefer to believe that. Indeed, I do believe it. But it is *my* duty to establish every necessary precaution. So – you will teach me to fly this aircraft.'

Miller shrugged, and thought: Why the hell not? A few hours to live: why worry about it? But the pilot in him remained dominant. 'Not here,' he said. 'And not in cloud. Once we're lower, over the sea, when we have daylight, I'll think about it.'

'I insist.'

'Insist away, pal.'

Von Galen argued for an hour and at last Miller relented. 'Okay, we'll go down, try and get under the clouds.' He made the descent a slow one, Ross still in the back of his mind. Having lost Ross, he had no wish to see him again. Ross could still land Ring Two someplace and

243

set up a squawk and, though it was unlikely in the wide spaces into which they were headed, Ring One might still be spotted, even intercepted.

Unlikely, but the chance existed.

He began the lesson one and a half hours short of Mont Joli, with two thousand feet showing on the altimeter. Cloud cover was thickening all the time now, up to somewhere around seven-tenths. Beneath it there wasn't a lot of light, but enough, and the darkling silver of the river gave him easy orientation. Von Galen turned out to be a reasonable pupil: not brilliant by a long way, but he had a mechanical competence, though hands and feet were too heavy and too correct; he could fly, but had no natural feel. Miller showed him how to trim her, turn and bank, apply boost, feather the props. Then he began on the engine start-up sequence.

'Not necessary,' Von Galen said.

'You're learning to fly,' Miller replied. 'Do it right. Anyway, it passes the time.'

An hour short of Mont Joli, he rose abruptly from his seat.

'Where are you going?'

'To take a look back. Maybe take a leak, too. You want to check me out?'

'You're leaving me here?'

'Sure. Fly her.'

From the observation bubble he scanned the sky behind with care. There was no sign of Ross's lights. If the lights were on, he thought. Ross might, probably *would*, be flying blacked-out now, especially if by some chance he'd managed to stay close.

But there was no sign.

He used the chemical toilet. Last time for that, too? Or once more, when the time got closer and pressure on the bladder began? Back in the pilot's seat, he ran his eye over the instruments and found Von Galen had at least held her straight and level.

244

'Okay. I have control.'

'What now?'

'We go low. Real low.' He took the Canso steadily down as he talked. 'There's a military airport at Mont Joli. I don't know if they have radar, couldn't find out easily, but it's more than likely. So what we do – we go right down to water level, ten, twelve feet, no more. And we stay on the north side of the river six miles clear of the military base to keep the sound out of their goddamned ears. Once we're past, we're okay. But we have to get by Mont Joli first.'

'I understand.'

'Yep. But just so it's completely clear, I'm giving you orders. Don't let your hands anywhere near the controls, right? Don't get absent-minded and think you're still flying. Sit still and let me concentrate!'

Slowly he brought the Canso down towards the water, levelling out at a hundred feet, then beginning carefully to inch her lower. The sensations were familiar but, as always, disconcerting: at height an aircraft feels as though it is suspended in space, and there is scarcely any sensation of movement. Low, it was like being on a racetrack, with the water flashing below the Canso in a blur of speed. Just once he flicked a glance at Von Galen and noted with a certain satisfaction that he was white-faced, pressed back in his seat, hands gripping the seat arms tightly.

No need to look at the schedule now. Miller had learned this bit by heart.

Dot said, 'Is there any water? I'm thirsty.'

'Should be.'

'Want some?'

Ross shook his head. He was thinking about Mont Joli, whether to go down there and put out the alarm. It was what he ought to do. But what would happen if he did – what aircraft did they have there, and what chance would they have of locating Ernie? There was no visibility to

245

speak of; it was the middle of the night, and once Ernie was clear of Mont Joli, he'd be out in the great wide spaces around the Gaspé Peninsula. The RCAF boys would have no more chance than he had. Less, even.

Not that he had much. From Mont Joli the whole damned world funnelled wide, the river, the sea, the gulf – everything. So far he'd stayed with Ernie; of that he was relatively sure. But only because Ernie'd stayed with the highway. Soon, though . . .

Dot came back. 'I've been thinking. What do you do with a stolen airplane? I mean, it's got serial numbers, it's military. How do you get spares? In Argentina, I mean?'

I didn't even consider it, Ross thought in irritation. 'Not easy,' he said.

'Anyway, who'd want it? Does Argentina have an air force? Look, Alec, he's going there with the Canso and all this stuff you have aboard. They want it, is that why he's going? Because they're paying him? Alec, I just don't see it.'

He didn't, either. The Canso was one of the Consolidated PBY series, not even a new design; they'd been flying since the mid-'thirties. He tried to think, casting his mind back over the thousands of aviation magazines he must have read, hoping to recollect something about sales to foreign countries. The British had them, he knew that. And there'd been a couple used on scientific expeditions. Maybe there were some in Australia, too. Yes, that was likely. But South America?

He said, 'There's a whole series of PBYs. Getting spares, you have to designate – '

She interrupted him. 'So it doesn't fly long before somebody knows where the ship is, right? Soon as there's an order, with the serial number, Consolidated take one look, and say, "Hey, that's the one that was stolen by Miller, at Kingston!" So no spares. Is that *right*, Alec?'

'You know it is!'

'So the Canso's useless after a while. Quite a short

while. Why do they want it, Alec? Do they want what's aboard?'

'The sub-detection equipment? Why would they? They're not in the war.'

'Tell me about Argentina, Alec.'

'Christ, I know nothing about it. South American country. Big. Takes up most of the south of the continent. Beef producer. Pampas, gauchos. Capital's Buenos Aires. That's it.'

'Neutral?'

'Yes. All South America's neutral.'

'So what do they want with sub-detection equipment?'

'America's neutral,' Ross pointed out. 'And we're developing the damn thing.'

'Yes, but it's different.'

'I know.' I also know, he thought, that we're approaching Mont Joli, and it's decision time. If I go blinding ahead, they're going to pick me up and maybe scramble somebody to inspect. Even though his clearance signal *had* gone down the line. They'd radio, they'd get no answer, so they'd very *likely* come up to inspect, even require him to land. Then there'd be long explanations and lost time. But if he flew by, what then? He'd still be chasing Ernie into the wide blue yonder, but with even less idea where to go.

Dot said suddenly, 'Alec!'

Something in her voice made him turn. 'What?'

'Who'd want the anti-submarine detector?'

He frowned.

'Face it, Alec. Who'd want it?'

Germany? He said, 'That's crazy, Dot! You can't see Ernie – '

She said, 'Give me one other explanation.'

'Hold it!' He tried to grapple with the elements spinning in his mind: Ernie taking it to the Germans – *why*? No, he'd never – And what about Mont Joli? Go in there and say, 'It looks as though Ernie Miller's delivering secret equipment to the Germans!' 'What makes you think so, Captain Ross?' 'Well, it's all I can think of, I mean there's no other explanation.' 'Tell us about him. He ever done this before?' 'Well, yes, but . . .' They'd be alarmed, yes. Stolen aircraft always alarmed everybody. But believe him? Well, they might, but they'd take convincing, and by then Ernie would be long gone.

If only he could radio!

What if he didn't go into Mont Joli? What then? If they stayed in the air, the odds against finding Ernie were already long and would soon be millions to one. But even then, they were better odds than Mont Joli had. If Ring Two gave up now, Ernie was clear and away. As long as they were in the air, there was a chance, however faint, that something could happen to put them closer to him. He made his decision, and pushed the stick forward.

'What are you doing?'

'I'm going to try to slip past Mont Joli,' Ross said. 'It may be what Ernie's doing. Probably is. It's also the last logical place we might get near him, so for Christ's sake keep your eyes open!'

He levelled her off at a hundred feet, and inched lower, coming close to the northern shore.

Miller had spotted the mouth of the Saguenay river minutes earlier, and the few lights of Tadoussac scattered on the dark shore. Les Escoumins next, then Sault-au-Mouton.

Careful now!

The southern shore lay due east of him here, but the southern shore was what it was. He said to Von Galen: 'See any mountains over there?'

Von Galen looked. 'No.'

'Watch for them.' The mountains were around Bic, and once he'd got them located . . .

'There are lights.'

Miller nodded. That would be Rimouski.

'Yes, I see mountains!'

'Let me look.' Hell of a thing at this height, to look away, but he risked a glance. Dim dark shapes along the horizon, with the lights up ahead. Okay, fifteen miles from Bic to Rimouski, a little more to Mont Joli.

The water tore past beneath them. Miller estimated he must be six or seven miles out. Just a few minutes more. He lifted his watch in front of his face, counting. From past Mont Joli, he could make the turn. Twenty-five miles. Eight and a half minutes. Christ, he was low; once or twice he had fancied he'd heard the water kissing the hull, but maybe it was nerves or imagination. Not a thing to think about, though, and if he touched hard at this speed he'd cartwheel; flying-boat or no flying-boat. Shaped hull or not, you don't touch water at a hundred and seventy-five miles an hour!

His hands were sweating on the wheel too; gripping too damned tightly, he thought. He tried to relax as the minutes ground by.

'See the boat?' Von Galen yelled.

Oh God, he hadn't! It seemed to leap at them as Miller hauled back on the stick, praying, and skimmed just over it. Did I give them the kind of fright they gave me? *Concentrate.*

They must be due east of Mont Joli now. Had he shown up on their screens? That hop over the fishing-boat had taken him up to sixty, even seventy feet; it could have happened. Still, the river was widening with every mile. He gave it five more minutes, then began a slow, wide, eastward curve: he wanted a point between Mont Joli and Matane, and must judge it perfectly, or there'd be a bright flash on the hillside and it would all be over. Nor was it easy. The climb must begin at exactly the right moment. Too soon and Mont Joli would spot them, if they hadn't done so already; too late and he'd hit the hill.

Miller corrected course again. Some time in the next few minutes, Mr Applejack, you're going to be looking for clean pants. Yeah, me too, maybe. Should he warn him? To hell with it, let him enjoy the new experience. There weren't too many to come.

Now another course alteration: flying straight lines, heading in towards the coast, the water still racing by beneath, and the rising ground, just barely visible, tearing towards them.

He held it as late as he dared, increasing revs and boost now, then hauled back on the controls. Twelve hundred feet, that was the height of the hill.

Christ!

He watched the land rear as the Canso grabbed for height . . .

FOURTEEN

Ross stared anxiously ahead. He'd brought Ring Two down so low it was almost skimming the river surface. At this height the chance of spotting Miller in Ring One was infinitesimal. If he'd gone high the chance would have increased, but Mont Joli would have had him.

'If you see the smallest movement, Dot, *tell me!*'

God, but this was dangerous! He hurled the Canso along the river, mind clear of everything but the need for concentration. Mont Joli over there. Had they seen anything? Ironic if they knew where Ernie was. How soon before he dared lift the ship? Twenty-five or thirty miles – and by then Ernie could have turned anywhere. The fact that Ernie had followed the river so far didn't mean he'd continue to follow it. Far from it.

But he might. That was the notion Ross clung to. As long as Ernie stayed with the river, Canso Ring Two had an outside chance of staying with Ernie.

'Watch out – a boat!' Dot said sharply.

But he'd seen it in time to steer away. All the same, there'd be some heavy cursing down there at a plane so near and so low. In French. *Merde!* And worse.

The sky clear. A hundred and eighty degrees in the horizontal plane, ninety in the vertical, and nothing moving in any of it. Not the smallest trace, not the faintest glimmer. They were well past Mont Joli now; a few more miles and he could lift her, get a better view. *And* lose distance as he climbed.

'Come in, Ernie!' He tried to will Miller to speak, the words repeating over and over in his brain, trying to reach

251

out over the water, penetrate a mind that had already signed off.

And still only the hum in his ear.

Beside him, Dot Miller sat rigid in her seat. Experienced flier though she was, this hurtling passage over water in the dark at extremely low level was wildly frightening. There was no margin: a small miscalculation, a patch of particularly cold water affecting the air above it, a slip of a hand, an engine faltering: any of them could drop the Canso suddenly and she knew that to hit water at speed was like hitting concrete. Her fingers dug into the padding on the arms of her seat as she tried to put her fear aside and search for a sight of Ernie's plane, but her gaze kept lowering to the onrushing water below. A breeze, a wave, that was all it would take. Through her headphones she could hear Ross humming softly to himself. His face was almost fierce with concentration, yet his body seemed relaxed; he leaned back in his seat, hands and feet poised on the controls, under heavy strain, yet in clear physical balance. And humming all the time. She wondered why he did it. Alec often hummed as he flew. No different, really, from humming as the housework got done. People hummed; it was something they did.

So was daydreaming, my God! She could have missed Ernie, letting her mind drift like that. She almost glared through the windshield, hunting the sky for him. Ernie, where *are* you?

Ross's hand lifted briefly. A few lights away to their right. 'Matane,' he said, and hauled back on the stick. 'I'm going up to five thousand. For God's sake keep looking. If we don't see him now . . .' The sentence remained unfinished.

'What time is it?'

He calculated. 'Three-thirty-two local time.'

Six hours, she thought, since Ernie'd taken off. Nearly seven since she'd last seen him, rising from the table. Oh God, why had he done it? And why choose her birthday?

He'd *used* her birthday. Not that birthdays mattered so much, not now, as more and more of them lay behind. All the same, why? If he had to go, why choose her birthday?

Something clicked in her mind. He'd chosen it because he had to. He wouldn't otherwise, not Ernie. So the date was important.

'Alec.'

'Go ahead.'

'He *had* to go. Last night, I mean. If he hadn't, he'd have picked another day.'

Sentimentality, Ross thought.

Dot said, 'What's so significant about today? Yesterday was the ninth of August. What could be important about August tenth?'

Ross shook his head. 'Nothing that I know.' And added, 'I reckon we could have lost him, Dot. For good, now.'

She nodded. She felt tears welling in her eyes and tried to control them. Keep looking, she *had* to keep looking.

'Germany,' Ross said. 'What made you think about Germany?'

'Gee, I don't know. It came into my head. There's no other reason.'

'It doesn't make any sense.'

'No,' Dot said, and added, hating herself, 'but maybe we'd better look at it. What could he get out of a thing like that? Money?'

'He could, I suppose.'

'But he'd be finished – with me, with America – '

'And with flying,' Ross said.

She nodded. To Ross that would be the greater loss, she thought. Would Ernie think like that?

'Even in Argentina?' she asked.

He thought about it. 'I don't know. It's cowboy country down there. Maybe word wouldn't reach, or he's got things fixed.'

'Is Argentina pro-German?'

'I think it may be. Yes, I think so.'

She said, 'So he takes the Canso down there and it gets handed over to the Germans. Does that make any kind of sense?'

'Maybe it does. Show them what they'll be up against.'
She could sense that he was resisting even the idea.

'Alec, we've *got* to think about this! You said he'd have to refuel at least once. That means he's arranged for it. If he's doing it for the Germans, maybe he's arranged it with them.'

'For Christ's sake, Dot, why'd he do that? Ernie's an American.'

She felt her heart thud. That thing he'd been humming. That tune – it was the hymn. 'Alec!'

'Mm?'

'Sing, "Glorious things of Thee are spoken".'

'What?'

'Sing it!'

'Why?'

'Sing it, Alec. You've been humming it. Now sing it.'

She saw his head turn to her, saw him frown. He said, 'It's coincidence.'

'Is it? It's *Deutschland über Alles* with different words!'
Her stomach leaden, as though the bottom of it was sinking away, but her mind racing.

'Dot, that's crazy!'

'Where's that list we made – now, Alec, what have we got here? No, listen. He's born in Asunción, Paraguay. *Not* in the United States. He insists on that hymn, which just *happens* also to be the German national anthem, at our wedding. And it's not, believe me, it's *not* a wedding hymn. Then – yes, look! Okay, it's a little thing, but it was you looking for little things: he puts a cross stroke on his sevens, right? And he called Roosevelt a Communist.'

She knew she was staring at him, waiting for his reaction. She said, 'It hangs together, Alec.'

'Not really. They're suppositions. That's not evidence, Dot.'

'Evidence?' she said. 'It's evidence all right. It's not much, but it all points the same way. You know he speaks German?'

'Ernie? I never heard him.'

'I did. In Chicago one time we met some folks in a hotel. They were German. Ernie talked to them. He said he learned it when he was a kid, in Paraguay.'

'Maybe he did.'

'Oh, sure. Alec, I'm his *wife*! I'm the one should be saying it's not possible and I don't believe it. Now I think I *do* believe it. Stop resisting. He's stolen a hundred thousand dollars' worth of plane, with secret stuff aboard. He's flown off, and it looks like he's not coming back. Alec, for God's sake! You don't want to believe it and neither do I, but what if he's pro-German, taking that plane somewhere? We happen to think it's Argentina, but it needn't be. Maybe he's got some kind of date with a ship – '

'An Argentine ship?'

'Any kind of a ship. He puts the Canso down on the water and they strip the equipment out. What's so impossible about that?'

'Nothing,' Ross said.

'Right. So have you anything else that fits what we know?'

'No.'

He's accepted it, she thought. 'Okay, Alec. It's your baby. But what the hell,' Dot demanded, 'do we do now?'

He sat for long moments with a face like stone. Then he said, 'We have a little calculating to do.'

'You calculate,' she said. 'Me, I have to cry.' Her world was crashing and she felt a terrible need to tumble with it into some kind of void. Ernie not just a thief, but a traitor. Ernie – her own *husband*!

* * *

Miller was watching the altimeter and the approaching hill, eyes flicking from one to the other. If he'd left it too late there was nothing he could do now. In a couple of minutes the Canso would be either floating over the hilltop, then dropping down towards the Matapedia Valley on the other side, or it would be burning nicely on the slope. Get to the valley and they were clear away; miss, and . . .

The hilltop made a black line across his vision. There were no features to be seen, no colours, no rocks, no shapes, just blackness against the lighter dark of the sky, and a single star bright in a gap in the clouds.

He found himself grinning, jaw clenched, but grinning all the same, taking a chance for one final time and revelling in it. He said, 'Enjoying your flight, sir?'

Von Galen plainly wasn't. An arm had risen involuntarily to protect his face, and his eyes were wide as he stared at the hillside.

'Passenger needs clean underwear, miss,' Miller said over his shoulder to an imaginary stewardess. The hill seemed to loom at them, and it really wasn't impossible the crash would be here and now, instead of a few hours hence.

'Come on, baby. You have a date with a very important man,' he told the straining, vibrating Canso as she roared for height, with her engines at full throttle and the whole structure vibrating. 'Come on, come *on*!'

And she came on beautifully and abruptly they were over the crest; he felt a sudden impulse to radio Alec and invite him to come and watch what happened next. Alec, if he'd continued along the river, would still be able to hear, still be in range. He flattened the impulse and as the ground fell away on the far side of the hill, Miller put the Canso's nose down and headed her down into the Matapedia Valley.

Next point of reference: Campbellton, New Brunswick.

Estimated time of arrival: he looked at his schedule: four-fifty. Three-fifty on his watch. Time zone change. Add an hour, but do it at Campbellton, forty minutes ahead.

'Listen, Applejack.' He turned to inspect the pale face that looked at him from the right-hand seat.

'It was reckless,' Von Galen said harshly.

'But necessary.' Miller grinned at him. 'And now we're all clear ahead. As long as the airplane holds together, we've got no problems till the last one. Hey, did you remember to get a flask of coffee?'

Calculate. Ross had spoken the word, demanding it of himself. But what was there to calculate? He'd no way of verifying the distance to South America; all he could do was guess, and he'd done that already. Anything else? Europe, how about that? The Canso had a range of four thousand: it might reach Europe. The hop from St John's to Ireland was eighteen hundred. A thousand plus from Kingston to St John's. Ireland to Germany? Ross had no idea: six, seven, eight hundred miles – including a passage over Britain, where the air defence was scientific and bloody efficient. Still, add up the numbers. A thousand, plus eighteen hundred, plus eight hundred. Two thousand eight, three thousand six. Add in a couple of hundred more.

It was on, just; but it could be done! Ernie'd be drifting in at the end, on almost empty tanks right at the limit of his range, and exhausted, too, but Europe was possible. Occupied France, maybe. Or perhaps he could shorten it: great circle route to the Norwegian coast, something like that. Ernie'd had the advantage, the opportunity to work it all out. The numbers would be clear in Ernie's mind; he himself could make only wild guesses. Ross had never piloted across the Atlantic, but he'd listened to people who had, and knew there were frequently highly favourable winds; headwinds on a west-east crossing were unusual. That was in Ernie's favour, too.

But still he could see no reason. Ernie was American; his life was in America; his whole style was American. Ernie was an independent cuss in a thoroughly American sense. So how could he have the loyalty to Germany that an action like this demanded? There'd been no trace of it. Ernie had been like plenty of others; a freelance pilot, skilful and determined; give him a job to do, and he did it. He worked hard and flew responsibly. Well, most of the time. Those occasional aerobatics had never seemed more important than the late-night drunkenness with which many fliers unwound. Throughout the months of the project, Ernie had been an exemplary pilot, giving it everything he'd got. Was that so he could steal the Canso and its equipment at the end? It couldn't be; they weren't at the end, yet; further refinement was still necessary. The anti-sub-detection equipment worked, but was not yet at optimum performance, so why hadn't Ernie waited, stolen it when all the bugs had finally been ironed out? Now, if he was taking it to the Germans, he was taking something incomplete, with bugs still in it. New equipment was due in from Martingale the following week, incorporating further modifications, so why hadn't he waited for that?

Dot *must* be right about the date. If it was the equipment the Germans wanted, it would have made more sense to wait. So it might be something else, an entirely different imperative.

So: not the Canso, not the equipment. Cut those out, and what was left? A mission tied to a date. And the date was August tenth. Sunday, August tenth, nineteen forty-one.

Where? What? Why?

They sat a mere couple of feet apart: two battled minds focusing on one man, examining him from inevitably different viewpoints. Ross knew Miller as one of his own kind: a professional pilot wedded to the air, whose thought processes were essentially similar to his own. For

Dot Miller he was something else, infinitely more subtle: the man whose life she shared. To Ross he was conditioned by training and requirement, therefore of largely predictable response. To Dot he was a creature of some complexity. Ross thought of Miller in terms of logical process, Dot in terms of emotional reaction, and she was looking now for something in the life they had shared, anything that could have pitchforked Ernie into an event as grave and as incomprehensible as this.

She'd loved Ernie more than he loved her. From the beginning she'd always known that. Ernie had two powerful emotional ties in his life, as most men seemed to. Job and wife, and often, as with Ernie, the job's hold seemed the stronger. She'd never tried to fight it, always understanding the hold the air had upon him. But the second place she had in his life had always been a strong one. Ernie always came home, was always glad to come home, happy to remain there until the next trip. He'd always treated her well and been considerate, not like some of the pilots she knew who treated their homes like hotels and their wives like waitresses.

She'd wondered sometimes if there were other women, but never seriously. Last night, when he'd taken off, that had been the first thought to surface in her mind. But she had not really believed it and did not even think about it now. Her mother had once told her that men were interested in things and women were interested in people and she'd better get used to the idea, because that was what life was like. She'd been right, too. Ernie wasn't much interested in people. He had a few friends, but not many: the kind of backslapping relationships pilots always seemed to have, bumping into each other at airfields, then flying off again, not seeing each other for months at a time. In Ernie's life, she'd been the people and the airplanes had been the things, and there wasn't much else. He wasn't interested in sport or politics or cars or fishing and camping. He'd have liked to have children, so he said, and so would she, but children hadn't come along.

Ernie had a few ideas, sure, but they were mainly concerned with flying. Such reading as he did was aviation magazines and pilots' memoirs. He'd always loved talking about flying, and appreciated having a wife who could understand, follow what he'd said, and knew enough to discuss it with him. She'd always loved it when he'd got out the maps and some of his models and retraced a famous flight or a dog-fight, explaining to her why men were drawn to an adventure, and how they conquered or lost.

She wondered if that was what had drawn him to the Germans. He'd theorized a lot about the *blitzkrieg*, frankly admiring the German dedication to supremacy in the air, the dive-bomber that prepared the way for everything else. In her mind's eye she could see him now, see the enthusiasm in the broad lines of his face as he said, 'This war's all about airplanes, and only the Germans understand it. America doesn't. The British only half.'

How long ago was that? Only a few weeks.

She'd said, 'What about those British fighter pilots? And their Navy? That was why Hitler didn't invade.'

'Wait,' he'd said. 'You'll see. Those ships are vulnerable from the air. Everything is. It's just a matter of the right plane in the right place at the right time. A couple of guys in a bomber could send a thousand in a battleship clear to the bottom. You can't get a battleship into London. It's a heck of a job to land an army. But planes can do it easy. Any day, any time. With planes you can think big, Dot!'

He wasn't really warlike, though. His enthusiasm was for flying; he loved the idea of possibilities that went on expanding forever, faster, higher, better. That was Ernie, with his practical life and his practical dreams. He was practical in everything he did. With that thought, she

260

found a phrase had crept back into her mind. *The right plane in the right place at the right time.* Ernie, the very *practical* man, in the right plane, at the right time.

The right time for what?

With planes you can think big.

Suddenly urgent, she said, 'Something big, Alec!'

'What?'

'Something really big. I've been thinking about it. It'll be something like that. Something only a plane can do. But big!'

'I don't see –'

She cut him off. 'I know it. Don't ask me how, but I do. He's not just stealing a plane, he's not giving this equipment to the Germans or anybody else.'

'But we worked out –'

Again she cut him off. 'We *didn't*, Alec. We made some guesses, and they're wrong. They're not what he'd *do*!'

Ross looked at her, seeing the intensity, the conviction in her face.

'I just know it!'

He thought: Wives always do. They think they know their husbands. Then the man goes off and does something, and they say: I don't understand, he's not like that! Then he thought: Don't be too cynical. She could be right.

'Big,' he said doubtfully.

She said, 'If it's Germany. If it's the war . . . Alec, what *is* going on? I don't read the papers, you do. Is there something one plane could do – one man in one plane?'

'Hell, I don't know. There can't be, though. Not here. Dot, the war's in Europe, it's three thousand miles away! He might get to Europe, but that's all. He couldn't do anything there. He hasn't got bombs, he couldn't attack.'

'No.' She paused. 'Alec, that figure, the one he wrote. Eleven something. Suppose, just suppose, it's miles. Or

261

maybe it's a time and for once he didn't put the period in. Just work it out. Both ways. Distance and time.'

He said, 'Navigator's table is back there. Go ahead.'

'Me?'

'Why not?'

She switched on the table light, got out the charts and the instrument case, looked at the chart legends. She placed the point of the compass on the chart at Kingston, Ontario, and drew in a circle at a range of eleven hundred miles. Then another at twelve. Somewhere between those two . . .

The first line passed through the far north of Quebec, ran through Labrador, over the Gulf of St Lawrence where it narrowed towards Belle Isle Strait, then down through Newfoundland to arc out over the Atlantic, until it met the eastern coastline of the United States far to the south.

She followed the track of the second line: the same thing, a hundred miles further on. The land between the lines consisted of uninhabited territory, almost all of it. Northern Quebec was empty, Labrador likewise. Newfoundland was remote, a few towns, but mainly empty, too. Then the vast arc of the Atlantic.

Dot Miller stared at the map. She felt achingly near to something that was just beyond her comprehension. Ernie must have measured distances on an identical chart. Where-to-where, though? Kingston to *somewhere*.

Somewhere. Not nowhere. A place. But then, it needn't be a place, not if it were a rendezvous at sea.

Okay, try it with time.

'Alec, where will we be at eleven, if we keep going?'

'Eleven what? Local time, Kingston time?'

She'd forgotten the time zones. They'd be out of Eastern Standard into – what? Into Atlantic time.

'Local,' she said.

'In a straight line?'

'Yes.'

'Labrador. Dot, he's not going into Labrador!'

'Where else?' She felt that in some way Alec had become negative. The Alec Ross who'd taken off in pursuit, who'd divined Ernie's route, who'd broken all the rules, wasn't there any more; he'd been replaced by a sceptic, unwilling to entertain new thoughts.

'Depends on the course we take. Way out beyond Cape Breton, out over the water. We could be over Newfoundland. Down through New Brunswick we could hit Bar Harbour, Maine, even Boston from the look of things.'

Time and distance roughly the same, Dot thought, and no indication of which the figure referred to. It had to be somewhere important to the war, though, and she wasn't sure if any of those places mattered. Boston was a big city, of course, but – oh hell, if he'd been going to Boston, it was like the man said, he wouldn't be going this way. *This* way led to Labrador, to Newfoundland, to Nova Scotia and to the ocean. She settled herself in the seat. She wasn't going to move until she knew. She didn't believe Ernie could hide a thing like this from her. Not all of it. Somewhere she'd find something . . .

Miller looked at his watch, then rubbed his eyes and shook his head a little. The movement caught Von Galen's eye.

'Course and speed are correct?' Von Galen asked.

'On the button. Just coming up on Campbellton. ETA at four-fifty and that's when we're going to hit it. So then we turn –'

'You're tired,' Von Galen said. It was close to an accusation.

'Don't worry – I'm not going to fall asleep.'

'Give me the times for the remainder of the trip.'

'Well, let's see.' Miller consulted his schedule. 'I estimate three hours five minutes from Campbellton to Sydney, Nova Scotia, arrival Sydney at seven-forty-five local time, though we don't go over, we bypass to the north. In a few minutes we cut over from the Matapedia Valley and fly down the river over a little town called Dalhousie, then out over Chaleur Bay. From then on we're over water all the way.'

'And you are tired?'

'A little. It's not important. You?'

'Also.' To Miller's surprise, he added, 'I am also a little bored.'

'Yeah? Me, in a way, I'm enjoying this trip. Won't be making any more, might as well enjoy this one.'

'You have things to interest you. I have not.'

'No? Well, I can find you something. Let's get the fuel tanks in balance.'

'Now?'

'Why not? Keep everything trimmed, that's my way. Up you go.'

Miller fussed, watching the gauges, getting it exactly right. There was no point, of course: the Canso could get there without moving any more gas around, but, hell, it gave him satisfaction, and it kept Applejack busy. At Campbellton he swung east.

When Von Galen resumed his seat, Miller said, 'Be daylight soon. More to see.'

'The last look.'

'Yeah.'

'It's very strange,' Von Galen said, 'to think . . .'

'Maybe it's better not to think.'

'No. This is a conscious thing we are doing. We are aware. It is strange, all the same, to be . . . so calm. We should be excited, exhilarated, full of glory!'

'That's flying,' Miller said. 'Long hours of boredom, they say, punctuated by moments of sheer terror. You have one of those coming up.'

'How will you feel?'

'I have no idea,' Miller said. It was true, the thing was too big to imagine.

'You have experience. I have not. Do you remember how you felt – before?'

'Delicately put,' Miller said. 'I remember very well. They came at me and I panicked. I tried to get away and I got away. I was very young, completely inexperienced then, and overwhelmed. Still worried it'll happen again?'

'Of course.'

'Yeah. Well, it won't.'

'And if it does,' Von Galen said coolly, 'I shall know what to do. As you know.'

'Just tell me,' Miller said, 'what makes you so damn sure *you* won't crack?'

'You think I will?'

'I don't know. I did once. You might.'

'No.'

'I'm glad to know it.'

'It would disgrace the Führer.'

'Yeah. There's one other thing,' Miller said. 'All this, it's on the basis that everything's there the other end. Churchill, Roosevelt, all kinds of people, all kinds of ships. Suppose they're not?'

'They will be there.'

'And if they're not?'

'We discussed that.'

'Not really. You're so sure.'

'Yes, I am. But I suppose you would land somewhere. You have malfunctioning instruments and concussion. You can remember nothing, not the flight, nor the reason.'

'It won't wash.'

'It won't have to,' Von Galen said, 'because they're there. And we are going to a glorious death for Germany and the Führer!'

'Yeah,' said Miller. He looked again at his watch and stifled a yawn. He, too, was a little bored, and shouldn't be; it was bad piloting. He found himself looking forward to dawn: not long now, and it would be good to come out

265

of the night into daylight. For a while. Before he went
into the night again.

Ross was trying to think of something big, but his brain
seemed tired. That was one of the traps of the time before
dawn: things seemed to shut down inside his head. You
could still do things, still act and react, but somewhere
after midnight doors seemed to close, and they opened
again only with light. For far more than an hour he flew
automatically. His eyes roved the gauges, his hands and
feet reacted in a series of reflexes to the changing circumstances of the air around him, compensating for the small
lift, the drop into a pocket, without conscious thought
involved.

He was effectively in neutral at this moment, and he
knew it. Even the course he was flying was neutral. To
right and left the banks of the river receded as he flew
further into the widening funnel mouth of the St Lawrence, and he was taking the Canso along midway
between them, then turning over Anticosti Island, making
no decisions, trying to think constructively, but not suc-
ceeding. He watched the light come, dim and grey at first,
then brightening. His face felt stiff, his body lethargic. He
made himself think.

Something big? The Germans were still driving into
Russia; U-Boats seemed to be winning in the Atlantic –
he knew plenty about that and the figures were frightening. The detector might help a little there. Maybe Ernie
was taking it to the Germans, even though Dot said he
wasn't, out of some female instinct or another. What else?
There was Lend-Lease, war materials pouring over to
Britain: planes, ships, tanks. What was it FDR had said:
the Arsenal of Democracy. Well, it was a mighty big
arsenal.

He ought to remember more. Damn it, he'd listened to
the news on the radio last night, after he'd showered and

while he changed to go out to dinner. Dinner with Ernie, his old pal Ernie.

Forget that. What had been in the news? Details of the German advance. A lot of those. Places with Russian names he didn't know. And the Japanese were being awkward in the Pacific, a lot of unpleasant noises there. Tokyo intransigent, the commentator had said, Ross recalled the phrase. Couldn't recall, though, what they were being intransigent about.

There'd been something, too, about FDR. What – yes, that's right: he'd left Washington and they all wondered where he'd gone. Fishing, probably. FDR was an old fox. Hold it, though . . . Ross sat up suddenly. He tried to focus his memory. There'd been speculation about where FDR was and some thought that he might be meeting Churchill, and if he recalled it right, Berlin radio had said so, said it didn't matter, wouldn't affect the course of the war.

Something big?

It couldn't be that – could it?

The right plane in the right place at the right time.

Desperately he tried to draw further details from his memory: anything about when or where. But that was the mystery; nobody knew. It was just guesswork, Roosevelt was at sea in his yacht, that was the basis of the speculation. Where was it they'd said? New England, was it?

'Dot,' he said, 'if you're really looking for something big . . .'

FIFTEEN

Still nothing on the chart rang any kind of bell and she'd searched it until her eyes ached. But she remained obstinately convinced there was something if only she could spot it, could comprehend what was important, could comprehend *why* it was important. The trouble was it was a chart, not a map, and the area was unfamiliar to her. It showed air routes, but not too many places. The pencil lines of previous flights criss-crossed it here and there, but all those marks were back in the Great Lakes country; there were none of significance out here because the chart hadn't been used out here.

But there were a couple of tiny amendments, added in red ink to bring the chart up to date. One gave a revised frequency and the date of amendment, another the letters USA, also with a date. Last year's date. She was unsure of its meaning and it was not Ernie's writing anyway. But she glared at it, trying to understand.

Ross's voice said in her ear, 'If you're looking for something big . . .'

'Tell me.'

'Something on the radio news last night. Roosevelt may be meeting Churchill.'

She blinked. '*May* be? What's that mean?'

'FDR's disappeared from view. The radio said he – '

'You mean *now*?'

'That's the theory. But it's all speculation.'

'Where?'

'That's the thing. Nobody knows where he is.'

She said harshly, 'Nobody knows where Ernie Miller is, either!' Then closed her eyes tightly, struggling to find sense somewhere in all the chaos. But she couldn't. When she opened them, the chart came into focus, but her mind was elsewhere, on two men in places unknown. One the President of the United States: the other a pilot in a stolen plane, a pilot with hitherto unsuspected German connections; her own husband.

USA: the United States. Her eyes took in the notation again.

'Alec, where could Roosevelt meet Churchill?'

'Any place in the world. Except – '

'Except Argentina,' she said.

'That's right.'

She returned to the co-pilot's seat, the chart in her hand. 'What's that mean, Alec?'

He glanced at it. 'United States base.'

'Isn't Newfoundland part of Canada?' she asked. 'Do we have bases – '

'It's a British colony, I think. The British handed over a few places in exchange for – ' His voice died away. 'Holy *God*, why didn't I think of that! That place – you know what its name is?'

Dot Miller shook her head.

'It's called Argentia.' He spelled it for her. 'Only the letter "n" missing. Put the "n" in and you've got Argentina! We *know* where he's going, Dot!'

Her first response was apologetic, shock forcing it from her, the words idiotic in her ears even as she spoke. 'I never heard of it. It looked like Argentina.'

'Don't worry about it. We have it now. Measure off the distance.'

She went back to the navigator's table, used dividers and checked three times. 'It's way short of eleven hundred,' she reported.

'Maybe you misread.'

'I think it was two ones. I'm almost sure.'

'Then Ernie misread.'

'No, he didn't.'

Dot was right, Ross thought. Ernie wouldn't misread or miscalculate. Ernie'd go over the figures very carefully indeed, and get it right to the yard. When she was back in the seat, Ross had thought of the answer. 'He's flying another route.'

'Why?'

'Several possibilities; most of them involve staying clear of pursuit. Hold the chart for me. Now look, he knew we were behind him. He also knew there's an important RCAF station at Mont Joli, and he had to get by there without being picked up, and there was always the chance he wouldn't, because some stray plane might see him and report. He'd be challenged, intercepted, couldn't risk that. So he'd plan to slip away first chance he could.'

'Where would he go?'

Ross said thoughtfully, 'I wonder if he knew. Yes, probably he did. There's a trick route the bootleggers used, running booze into Maine. Right there. You fly over the hill and drop down into the valley.' Ross's finger traced the path. 'The smugglers turned over New Brunswick into Maine. Ernie'd go this way.'

'It adds distance.'

'Yes, it does. Around a hundred miles or a little more.'

'Eleven hundred plus.'

'That's right! And from here he's – yes, by the time it's light he's over water, all the way.'

Silence now between them as the questions rose in their tired minds. If Ernie Miller was going to Argentia – and it was still *if*; impossible to be certain despite all the calculations, all the beliefs, all the instincts – *if* he was going, what was his purpose? Was Roosevelt really there? Was Churchill?

Ross was trying to drag more of that broadcast out of his memory; he'd only half-listened, his attention at the time on cleaning his shoes and tying his tie, and the words which had been unimportant then were vital now.

Dot said, 'How would he know, Alec? How would Ernie know?'

'That news broadcast. They quoted German radio.'

'But they didn't say where they'd meet?'

'Hell, no.' He struggled to recall it. 'German radio said FDR was going to meet Churchill. That's all. It was part of a story they had. The big question was where FDR had gone.'

'I don't see it, Alec, I really don't. Look, Ernie hears the broadcast – no, come to think of it he didn't, because we didn't have the radio on! So okay he hears something somewhere and he steals the Canso and sets off for Argentia. That's crazy.'

Ross picked the hole at once. 'Where did German radio get it?'

She blinked. 'I don't follow –'

'I mean *they* had a source. If Ernie's going there, he must have heard it from the *same* source.'

'What kind of a source? Alec, a thing like that, it would be kept real close, top secret. Wouldn't it?'

'But the Germans say they know.'

'Then we're right. Oh God, I didn't want to be right! But if the Germans told Ernie, then he's . . . he really *is*, Alec. He's flying for them!'

Ross nodded grimly. 'We have to do something now.' He swung the Canso into a turn.

'Do what?'

'Go back to Mont Joli. We've no radio, they have. We lay it all out for them, they pass the word along. It's all we can do.'

'Turn *back*?'

'We have to.'

'Where are we?'

'Here.' Below, just to the south, was the eastern end of Anticosti Island.

She looked at the chart, trying to estimate.

'We're close on midway, Alec!'

'Can't be!' Mentally he cursed the time that had slipped by.

'But we *are*. Winds?'

'Tail wind.'

'Then we have to go on. Bring her round again, Alec. You must.'

He obeyed, feeling diminished, out of control. 'Dot, get me a wet cloth.'

She went back to the drinking-water tank, soaked her tiny handkerchief and brought it to him. He scrubbed it hard over his neck, forehead, eyes and wrists. 'Now check the distance to Argentia and to North Sydney, Nova Scotia.'

Back at the table she used the dividers again, calculating twice to be sure.

'Four hundred to Argentia, two-eighty to North Sydney.'

Ross said, 'We ought to go there.'

'Why?'

'There's a flying-boat base. They can radio ahead.'

'It's forty minutes' difference, Alec, that's all. Have we that much in hand?'

No knowing, Ross thought. Ernie had started out with fifty or sixty miles advantage, then lost it. But he himself had lost time too, flying anything but a direct route to Argentia: hoping he was following Ernie up the imagined highway. There was two and a half hours' flying time to Argentia now, near enough. He checked his watch. Over Anticosti Island the time zone had changed. It was seven-forty-five now, Atlantic Standard time.

He said, 'Argentia around ten-fifteen.'

'I wonder,' he heard her say, 'what time Ernie's planned to arrive?'

Miller was looking at his watch too, going over the schedule again in his mind, making an almost identical calculation. Cape Breton's highlands were coming up, so North Sydney lay fifty miles or so to the south.

Von Galen watched him check. 'Well?'

'We're a little ahead of schedule. Tail winds pushing us along.'

'You must slow down.'

'Is that so?'

'We cannot afford to be early.'

'Relax,' Miller said. 'It's done.'

'Good. There will be only one chance, remember that. No turning, no second run.'

'I know it. Listen, you didn't tell me just how you worked this thing, how it started out.'

'It took a long time.'

'I'll bet.'

'If you wish to hear . . .'

'I do.'

Miller knew the essence of it, but the detail surprised him. Von Galen wasn't a guy he'd choose to spend a lot of time with, but whatever else he might be, he was unusually intelligent and determined. The acuteness of the observations, the ingenuity of the forecasting, were breathtaking.

Listening, his mind went back twenty-three years, to the granting of his commission, to the day Unterleutnant Ernst Zoll swore on oath that his life was to be dedicated henceforth to the greater honour and glory of the Fatherland and to the destruction of the enemy. Almost a quarter of a century, and it was still the same enemy: still the same British, who'd come at him that clear morning and flown away leaving his youthful dreams of heroism to lie destroyed under a pall of disgrace.

There was a special kind of justice, too, in the Sunday part of it. Miller distrusted politicians, and always had. There'd been a congressman once, up for re-election, who'd shaken Miller the voter's hand and said more or less straight out that a vote for him was a vote for God!

Ringing sincerity and the eyes of a pawnshop keeper. Church twice every Sunday and his snout as deep in the trough as he could push it.

Was Churchill a religious man? Was Roosevelt? He doubted it. But Applejack had them weighed up; he'd calculated their imperatives as he'd calculated everything else: the one time they'd be sure to be together, and out in the open.

'Brilliant,' he said.

Von Galen said, 'A true privilege. Think of the soldier who dies for a yard of ground, or worse, dies retreating. Then think of our destiny!'

Destiny. Valhalla. Applejack was a great one for the big words.

Two hours to go.

On Canso Ring Two another mystery had been cleared up. Two remained. Dot, folding the big chart in limited space, had turned it sideways, and realized that the rough shape Ernie had drawn, and which she'd thought was a map of South America, could as easily be a bad sketch of Newfoundland. One lay east-west and the other north-south, but Ernie'd never been able to draw and there was enough resemblance to confuse.

The other mysteries were not, however, easy of solution. What would Ernie do when he got to Argentia? And Dot kept asking herself the significance of Sunday. But that didn't seem important. What Ernie intended was, on the other hand, of enormous importance.

Ross, wide awake, sentient and ashamed of himself, said, 'Let's go over it again, Dot. We have a scenario here. Churchill and Roosevelt meeting at Argentia. The Germans know it, but nobody else does. Nobody except Ernie and whoever's with him. But *he* does know. So he takes the Canso, and he flies it to Argentia. What in hell he's going to do when he gets there, I can't imagine. It's not a bomber, it's a flying radio laboratory. No bomb bay, no bomb racks, no bombs, not even machine-guns. But there's a plan, there has to be! This whole thing has been reasoned out. Ernie left on a schedule, so he'll fly on a schedule and arrive at a specific time, because that's what the plan requires. Why? He's going to be there right about the time we are. Ten-fifteen. What's he going to do, for God's sake?'

She shook her head. 'Could *they* be flying in, Churchill and Roosevelt?'

'Yes, of course they could. He shoots them down, does he? He's got no guns, and the Canso's not a fighter plane. There are three things he can do, and none of them makes any sense. He can fly around, he can fly past, or he can land.'

'Who's with him?' Dot asked. 'That could be important.' She sounded suddenly hopeful. 'It could be like that, Alec. He's taking someone to meet them, maybe!'

Ross considered it. 'No.'

'Why not?' She was clinging to it. 'Somebody going along secretly. Somebody who's been called to attend.'

'Like Mackenzie King!' As soon as he'd spoken he regretted the heavy irony. Dot's face fell; she'd found a moment of hope and he'd stamped on it.

They crossed the coast, deeply worried, somewhere south of Corner Brook with the Canso on an east-south-east heading. Two hundred and twenty-five miles to go: one and a quarter hours to find an answer. Ross began to study the chart. Argentia lay well inside a huge inlet called Placentia Bay, and the long Burin Peninsula extending sixty miles to the south-west sheltered the bay from westerly winds. If Miller had flown down the Mata-pedia Valley and headed out via North Sydney, over the ocean, he'd come in from a little south of west. Sure, he'd do that; he'd have to. Given that Miller was behaving like a thief in the night, he'd stay low, out over the water, as long as he could, and then either hop over the long peninsula, or fly round the tip of it, direct into Placentia Bay.

One or the other.

When Ross reached Argentia, he'd tell them about the direction. Yes, but tell them precisely what? Tell them an unarmed flying-boat was heading their way, purpose unknown? He knew no more than that, therefore he could tell them no more. If all the suppositions were true, and if Churchill and Roosevelt *were* down there, action would certainly be taken, and in a hurry. He felt dazed with the ifs and buts. It remained guesswork. Probably when they reached Placentia Bay it would be empty except for a few flying-boats. Churchill and Roosevelt had the whole wide world to go at; they could be anywhere. Why there?

But if they *were* . . .

It occurred to Ross suddenly that their presence would mean inevitably the presence of other things, including heavy defences.

'Dot, listen. Argentia will be ready. They'll know about the German broadcast.'

'I hadn't thought – '

'What's more,' he said, 'anywhere Winston Churchill goes will be guarded like Fort Knox and then some. Roosevelt likewise. There'll be flying-boats at Argentia, and they'll be armed because they do Atlantic patrol work. Maybe ships, too – warships, with anti-aircraft armament. We should have gone into North Sydney!'

'Why? I don't see why. We can land – '

'They won't let us *near*, Dot! We can't just let down and sound the alarm. They won't let us do it. We've no radio. If there's an air patrol we can't reply to a challenge. Air defence will take us for an intruder. They've no alternative. If we just keep coming, they'll shoot first and wonder about it a long time later.'

Dot's eyes were wide. 'But, Alec, they'll recognize the Canso. It's not a German plane.'

'It's a missing plane, don't you see! One of two missing planes. Back at Kingston they'll have put out an alert.'

'But you did signal, Alec. Before the radio burned out.'

'Hours ago. Nothing since then. Look, Dot, you know what happens. Kingston reports two aircraft missing. Then they hear about my report. We're last heard of heading straight up the St Lawrence. They ask Mont Joli. Mont Joli has nothing. So we're missing. They'll be searching; they'll have put the word out. Kingston *knows* this flight's unauthorized! Christ, if we were just going into a field somewhere that would be one thing, but at Argentia? No. At Argentia they would know what the Germans said. Some loose plane flying in – it will have to be stopped!'

'You really mean there's nothing we can do. *Nothing!* We just – '

'If we'd time we could make for Gander, try and get a call through from there. But we haven't. That's Rames Island we just passed. Gander's an hour and more away.'

Ross dug at his tired eyes with finger and thumb. It was all still *ifs*. They didn't *know* Churchill and Roosevelt were in Argentia. If they weren't, the whole trip had been rainbow-chasing. He said, 'We've got to find out if they're there, and the only way is go and look.'

'But they'd shoot us down. You said so.'

'Give me the chart. Let's have a good look at the place.'

Fifty miles to the south, Canso Ring One was in cloud. Miller and Von Galen were silent now in their seats, each alone with the knowledge that they had entered the last hour of their lives. Very soon it would be time to drop down through the overcast, down to sea level and begin the long run in.

Miller had wondered how he'd feel. Now he knew: hands and feet felt cold and there was a sensation as though a large cold rock filled his chest and stomach. Yet he felt still and steady, curiously unexcited, surprisingly unafraid, though his heart was thumping. There was a job to be done, and he made a single demand of himself: that it be done well. Seventeen thousand two hundred and twenty-eight hours of flying lay behind; this was one more, and the final one, but the same discipline applied. He was conscious of the meaning of each movement of the second hand of his watch, but it was a peripheral awareness; the centre of his mind was securely locked on the mechanical requirements of the flight.

Now. A push forward with his hands, the nose tilted down, and Miller looked watchfully through the water-dotted glass, waiting to sight the sea. The last tendrils of hanging vapour vanished as the altimeter registered two thousand eight hundred feet – barometric pressure uncertain, so height uncertain, too; he didn't like it, but it wasn't important. Ahead a strip of land lay on the horizon.

'Miquelons,' Miller said. 'French islands.'

'If they're French, then they are *ours*.' Von Galen's face was drawn, Miller saw, but the eyes glittered.

He didn't reply, feeling no urge now to talk, to exchange banalities, to listen to high-flown phrases about a Führer of whom he knew little and cared nothing. He wanted only to fly this mission as it should be flown, and finally show to his father and his sister that their long contempt was baseless. He wondered if his father was still alive, decided he must be, unless death had come in recent months, a proud old man, approaching eighty, his pride scarred by his son, restored by his grandson.

Miller chased the thought out of his mind as the Canso came down to under a hundred feet, turning a little north to pass the tip of Grande Miquelon. A hundred and twenty miles to go. Forty-one minutes.

'Give me the chart.' He folded it, laid it across his knees, rechecked it. Very likely a long straight run to the target, long enough for counter-attack. He said, 'Tell me again.'

'Here.' Van Galen's finger stabbed at the map. 'It is the best anchorage. The best in Newfoundland. This sound within the bay is secure from all wind directions. That is why they're bound to use it.'

And the whole bay to cross to reach it, Miller thought. 'They may be some place else.'

'They must be *there*!' Von Galen insisted.

Must, not will, Miller noticed. 'They better be,' he said.

Slowly the long shape of the Burin Peninsula began to rise out of the sea, a faint, low line at first, growing thicker. There were several hills, Hare Hill the highest; thirteen hundred and twenty-five to hide behind before he burst out to attack. He couldn't distinguish it yet. Not quite. But it was there. And soon . . .

Hare Hill loomed towards Canso Ring Two. Ross, too, had come low. The only way for him to discover whether Placentia Bay was remote and unimportant, or had now turned temporarily into one of the most important and secret places on earth, was to use his eyes. He intended now to approach from behind the sheltering high ground, to climb sharply over the hilltop and then, as rapidly as he could, to scan the waters of the bay. He was worried that Placentia was so big, and dotted with islands, too; some of the islands had high points of nearly a thousand feet that would screen his view.

'If they're there, Dot, there'll be activity,' he said. 'That's what we have to look for. If the bay's empty, it's all for nothing. If it's full of ships . . .'

He left the sentence unfinished. There was nothing to add; if the bay was full of ships, their dilemma remained, and still he could not see what action he could take.

He increased boost, waited, and moved the throttles, then pulled back on the controls, lifting the throbbing Canso into her climb. Glancing to right and left, he could see no ships patrolling off the tip of the peninsula, but he knew that if they were there, the westward turn of the land would screen them. Five hundred, six . . . seven . . . and the land was rising sharply. Eight.

'Look!' Dot cried, pointing.

To his right, between the hills, he saw the long, low shape of a warship: a destroyer, he thought, out on the wide mouth of the bay. One thousand – and the hilltop stark now against a grey sky. Moments to wait . . .

The panorama of the bay was far bigger than he'd imagined: a great sweep of water and islands. His eyes ranged systematically and anxiously over it, starting in the far north, sweeping southward. Ships! Christ, a *hell* of a lot of ships! Almost dead ahead on the other side were at least two big ones, and the water in between held others, some moving, trailing white wakes – forming an unmistakable screen.

He flung the Canso round, returning to shelter on the safe side of the hill, yelling, 'How many did you count?'

'I got to thirteen, Alec. You saw the big ones?'

'I saw.'

'There were planes, too.'

He'd missed them. 'Where?'

'Out towards the sea. Flying-boats. Biplanes. I don't know the type.'

What the hell to do now? Ross tried to work something out. Go back over the hill, perhaps. Maybe drop down on the water fast and taxi across. But the taxi would take forever, even with the Canso up on the step, skimming.

'*Alec!*' It was almost a scream. Dot pointed, her hand shaking.

A plane, low over the water, was coming towards them. He took in the characteristics; high wing, twin engines mounted close together over the fuselage, the gleam of the ring. His stomach sank. It was Ernie: no doubt of it.

Ross kicked at the rudder bar, tipped the Canso round in as tight a turn as it could handle and headed directly for Ring One. Too late for anything else now. Somehow Ernie must be headed off.

* * *

Miller, preternaturally alert, ready for surprise developments, had not been prepared for this one. In the instant of sighting, his jaw dropped in astonishment. Ross *here!* It was imposs – but no, it clearly wasn't impossible: that *was* Canso Ring Two! *And* with Dot aboard, and Ross flying. He watched the plane's shape drifting down the side of the hill, making a quick turn, now heading straight for him. He thought: Get Dot out of there, Alec! They were closing very fast – Listening? – would Alec be still listening, after so many hours? Miller's hand flicked the transmit switch and he shouted, 'Canso Ring Two. Urgent, Alec. Get out of here. Out of the way. You'll get Dot killed! Do you hear me . . .'

Von Galen, too, had by now seen Ross, but he'd seen him a moment later, and it had taken a vital second or two longer to identify the Canso. He was still gaping when Miller's voice suddenly yelled in his headset, shouting the warning.

If Von Galen's first reaction had been slow, his second was not. All along he'd had a deep nagging feeling that Miller would again fail in the crisis, and he *was* failing, all his attention on his wife when nothing but the target could possibly count now. As Von Galen's left hand grabbed at the stick, his right was already dragging the pistol from his pocket. It snagged briefly, but he ripped it clear, brought it round, and fired directly at Miller's head. The shot smashed Miller across the seat, to hang grotesquely in his harness. Von Galen let the pistol fall, then, to get both hands on the controls, seized now with a sudden fierce delight. It was, after all, *his* plan, *his* opportunity to strike the great blow for Germany and the Führer. It was fitting that he, Baldur von Galen, should strike the Führer's enemies down!

They had heard the frantic message clearly; had heard, too, the shot that ended it: the sharp crack that cut off Miller's voice. Miller's hand had been on the transmit button, Ross knew. He saw Ring One stagger briefly, then straighten.

'That was a shot!' Her voice rising wildly.

He could only nod. It had been unmistakable.

'Alec! Ernie's been shot!'

Ross didn't reply.

'Oh *God*, Ernie – !'

Ross swung round in another turn, across Ring One's approaching track. No further word from the Canso, and no question now in his mind that this was in some way an attack. What kind he didn't know and couldn't guess. But the crack of the shot had smashed through all his doubts.

Ring Two had gone by him; the warning pass in front had not diverted the flying-boat a single inch from its course. Ross again flung Ring Two round; boost and throttles. He must catch up and then overtake, get Ring Two interposed between Ring One and the target, force it to slow! The hill was so damn close. Would there be space? He watched the Canso in front begin to lift . . .

Von Galen hauled the handles back into his stomach, hand reaching up for the throttle levers. The close pass of the other plane had shaken him; for a moment he'd thought that Ross was deliberately going to crash into him, as he should have done. Instead Ross had shown weakness; just a warning pass – as if that would divert him! All this man Ross had achieved was to put himself at a disadvantage. Now, glancing left and right, Von Galen could see no sign of the other plane. It must be well behind, and now it would stay there, helpless. He pushed the throttles right forward, then his heart lurched as he felt the momentary sag. Boost *first*, Miller had said. Damn! His hands moved frantically, backing the throttles, bringing in boost, watching the pressure climb; the wait seemed endless.

His stomach was in his mouth. The Canso had lurched awkwardly and for a moment he'd thought it would stall.

But it was under control now, lifting towards the point ahead where the hilltop rose from its ridge. Another glance left and right. Ross still wasn't in sight.

And over that ground, just over the top, lay the two great enemies! If he was right, and he no longer questioned it, the predicted pattern would be under way: two men deeply rooted in naval tradition, attending morning church service at sea.

Together. On deck. In the same ship.

And he'd know which one. The decks would be crowded.

Von Galen's watch showed eleven o'clock – the timing perfect.

Ross, seeing the sudden lurch as Ring One floated up the hillside just ahead, guessed what had happened: the pilot, unfamiliar with the Canso, was looking for speed. Ernie wouldn't have done it. But Ernie wasn't flying the attack now.

What *kind* of attack? Whatever kind, there was no chance of getting away with it. They'd hunt him to hell and gone. The whole thing was suicidal and Ernie must have known it. *Suicidal!* The word burned into his brain. A suicidal attack! No bomb racks, no bombs . . . but it wouldn't matter, *not if the Canso was loaded with explosive!*

He was overhauling now. Ring One had a steeper angle of climb, therefore Ross had the greater forward speed. Was there time to ride forward over Ring One, then drop – flatten it into the hilltop? His eyes measured distance. He'd have to try; there was time for nothing else.

Ross swallowed. In his mind he could now visualize the attack Ring One must intend: the flat-out dash across the bay, the direct crash into one of the ships. Somehow the man flying now must know which ship.

He was closing over Ring One, his nose no more than

fifteen feet above her tailplane as they cleared the tip of Hare Hill.

He said, 'Dot,' and turned his head. She looked back at him out of eyes shiny with tears. He took in the sharp irony of the party dress, the necklet he'd given her glowing gold at her throat.

She said steadily, 'I know.'

'There's no other way.'

She said simply, 'No,' and turned her head away.

Ross looked down. Ring One's nose was invisible beneath; a slice of her wing lay just below his side window.

'Here we go, Dot,' Ross muttered, pushing at the control column, dropping Ring Two suddenly, his body tense for the impact.

But no impact came. Ring One must have dropped, too, and at the same moment. He pushed the nose down harder. Christ, if he didn't get him now . . .

He could see nothing below. His own aircraft was blocking any view of the other machine. He banked sharply, hoping for a sight . . . and felt a sudden, harsh juddering rack the Canso; heard the sharp cracketing from the port engine. He glanced quickly sideways, feeling the whole plane lurching, going out of control.

The port propeller had stopped altogether, its blades bent, and the Canso was rearing to starboard. What in *hell?*

'Alec, look!' Dot was half-standing, craning forward.

He couldn't look; he was too busy wrestling with the controls, striving to hold the Canso straight, to keep his wingtip out of the goddamned trees. Somehow that first, vital pass had damaged him more than it had damaged Ring One. He must try for another . . .

Dot was shaking his arm. He said savagely, 'Not *now!*'

'But you did it, Alec. At least, I think you did.'

He'd got the Canso more or less straight.

'Where?'

She pointed.

Below to his left Canso Ring One was in a long dive towards the water.

Dot said, 'I only got a glance, but I think the prop chopped his rudder and right elevator. That's what – ' She stopped. Clearly the dive was now out of control; Ross could see the ripped tailplane, the frantic waggling of flaps and ailerons achieving nothing. In a moment, Ring One was going in, and going hard . . .

Beside him, softly, Dot spoke Ernie's name.

SIXTEEN

From his look-out post high over the superstructure of the battleship *Prince of Wales*, Leading Seaman Arthur Barnes was shamelessly using his binoculars to watch the scene on deck. Hell's delight, what a gathering of bigwigs it was! They were *all* there, all the great names, assembled on the quarterdeck under the four big guns. He could actually see Churchill, glasses on the tip of his nose, hymn book in hand. No cigar for once; Barnes grinned to himself. And there was Roosevelt, right there beside him, and all the ministers and Chiefs of Staff, British and American: must be enough gold braid to dress *Prince of Wales* overall.

He's always thought Roosevelt was crippled, so it had been a surprise to hear the President was coming aboard for morning service, and Barnes had wondered how he'd do it. A bosun's chair was a funny business if you didn't have control of your limbs, and not very dignified, either, for transporting a bloke like the President of the United States.

But Christ, if Roosevelt didn't have much in the way of legs, he certainly had plenty of guts. Barnes had watched a few minutes earlier as an American destroyer secured alongside the big cruiser *Augusta*, which had brought Roosevelt here. Then the destroyer had moved away and come slowly round *Prince of Wales*'s bow, with the President and a lot of scrambled-egg-covered caps round him on her bridge. She'd inched closer. Obviously somebody had been measuring heights, water-to-deck, because the decks were level. Unusual, that, considering she was a destroyer and *Prince of Wales* a bloody great battleship, but that must be why they'd chosen that particular destroyer.

When she'd secured alongside, a gangway had been thrown across and he'd expected Roosevelt to be carried over, but instead the President had stood up and put his hand on the arm of a young officer – who, to Barnes's sharp eyes looked uncannily like him – and very slowly he'd walked across the gangway. Bloody good job this was a calm harbour – Roosevelt's balance hadn't been too steady, but if you ever saw determination! He'd come over dead upright, step by awkward step, with Churchill and the skipper waiting to greet him with the British Chiefs of Staff.

Then the band had played the anthems, and they'd walked very slowly along the quarterdeck to the rows of chairs set out facing the guns. There Roosevelt had turned, and even that was difficult for him to do. But when he sat down to face the two chaplains, you could see the President was bloody pleased with himself. Pleased as Punch, he looked!

The words of a prayer floated up to Leading Seaman Barnes's high perch. They were praying for the invaded countries, talking about the day of deliverance. Well, if this business here was anything to go by, and America really was coming into the war, that day would come a bit faster.

Barnes heard the Royal Marines' band strike up. Some people thought a band was a bit funny for a church service, but you got used to it. Good tune, too, this one.

O God, our help in ages past . . .

I'm dying for a fag, Barnes thought. And nobody's looking, for once, not with that lot to look at. He fished the packet of Woodbines from inside his tunic, took out the lighter his wife had made in the munitions factory from a cartridge case, closed his hand around it, lit the cigarette and inhaled.

By gum, that was good! Yes, it was a good day all

round, this one. His eyes swung, more idly than a look-out's should, round the horizon, and for a moment he thought he saw a bright flash, just below the hills far over there in the distance, but he wasn't sure, and it didn't come again. Probably a plane shoving out a Verey light for some reason. Long way off, anyway . . .

It was the purest chance that Barnes saw the explosion, and it was seen by no one else in the entire fleet, for the very natural reason that all eyes were on *Prince of Wales*. As the music floated across from Ship Harbour, Argentia Sound, and out over the wide waters of Placentia Bay, no one was looking at Hare Hill.

But one other man was looking and he was not a part of any ship's company. For the thousands afloat, this was an hour of pride and thanksgiving and hope.

For Joseph Patrick O'Hara, standing alone on a clifftop near the appropriately named Patrick's Harbour, it had been a morning of desperate anxiety. He'd found difficulty getting there at all, but had managed it on a borrowed motor-cycle, riding through the night round the coast road from St John's.

Now he did not watch the ships, which he could not see. He stood waiting for an aircraft to appear. He had young eyes, and high quality lenses, and he glimpsed first what looked like two aircraft at the distant hilltop. Then he saw a bright flash in the water at the foot of Hare Hill.

Finally he saw a flying-boat float down to a landing on the water and begin to taxi in the direction of a patrol boat which was already tearing towards it . . .